He lifted her and carried her over to the bed and stripped her naked before tearing off his own clothes, scattering them all over the room in his urgency.

'Walter, let me gather up the clothes—'

'Leave them!' he ordered, then plunged down on top of her, burrowing and snatching, bruising tender skin and the flesh beneath, paying no heed to her gasps of pain.

It was then that she realised that in her new husband's eyes marriage was a taking by the man and a submitting by the woman. As far as he was concerned there was no question of sharing love. He didn't need or ask for her love – only her body.

And he had every right to take that whenever and in whatever manner he chose.

Because to Walter Shaw and men like him that was what marriage meant.

Also by Evelyn Hood

A Matter
of Mischief

EVELYN HOOD

sphere

SPHERE

First published in Great Britain
by William Kimber and Co Ltd in 1988
This edition published by Warner Books in 1998
Reprinted 2000

Reprinted by Time Warner Paperbacks in 2002
Reprinted by Sphere in 2009

A CIP catalogue record for this book
is available from the British Library

ISBN 978-0-7515-1892-1

Papers used by Sphere are natural, renewable and recyclable products,
made from wood grown in sustainable forests and certified in accordance
with the rules of the Forest Stewardship Council.

Mixed Sources
Product group from well-managed
forests and other controlled sources
www.fsc.org Cert no. SGS-COC-004081
© 1996 Forest Stewardship Council

Typeset by Derek Doyle & Associates, Mold, Flintshire
Printed and bound in the UK by CPI Mackays, Chatham ME5 8TD

Sphere
An imprint of
Little, Brown Book Group
100 Victoria Embankment
London EC4Y ODY

An Hachette UK Company
www.hachette.co.uk
www.littlebrown.co.uk

To Claire and Don Guinn

Chapter One

1775

A stone flew past Margaret Knox's cheek as she turned into the narrow lane from the Sneddon.

Another landed in one of the many puddles that made the lane an obstacle course whatever the weather, causing filthy water to splash over her good skirt.

She stopped short, clutching her small daughter's hand so tightly that Christian squeaked a protest. Only yards away two bodies were locked in fierce combat, staggering like an ungainly four-legged monster, rebounding from the slimy wall of one building to lurch across the few feet of space and collide with the slimy wall opposite.

Fights were commonplace in Paisley's slums. As often as not the combatants were clawing, scratching women, as dangerous as any man once they got the blood-lust. But these fighters were mere lads, one in his teens, the other scrawnier and several years younger.

The stones were being hurled by a ragged little girl, her thin face red and puffy with angry tears, her body racked at intervals with bouts of coughing. Although she threw hard her aim was poor. A few people stood at the close-mouths or leaned from windows, watching the struggle with vague interest. Some of the men egged the fighters on, but nobody did a thing to stop them.

Margaret hesitated. Her husband Gavin had warned her often enough to keep out of things that didn't concern her, but that didn't deter her, if she thought she could be of some use to someone.

A fight, though, was a different matter. It was a personal thing, an issue that had to be settled by the people concerned. Besides that, Margaret, on her way to one of the

7

slums at the far end of the lane with some food for an old woman who lived alone, had four-year-old Christian to think of.

'Come home –' She tugged at her daughter's hand. 'We'll come back another time.'

Christian dragged back on the grip that would have whisked her away from the scene, her hazel eyes wide in her round little face.

'Leave him alone!' she screamed raucously as the smaller boy was tripped up and thrown with a teeth-jarring thud to the ground. Another stone sailed dangerously near to Margaret. The girl who had thrown it squatted in the dirt to rummage for more ammunition and, finding a stick, proceeded to beat the older boy about the shoulders whenever she got the chance.

'Christian –'

Even as Margaret spoke the small hand left hers and Christian sped down the lane to where the older boy was pinning his adversary face-down on the ground, holding him with one hand and both knees. His free hand gripped the neckerchief about the other lad's throat and began to twist.

The girl dropped her stick and hurled herself onto his back, pummelling at him with her two fists. He shook her off, and she rolled on the ground in a paroxysm of coughing before getting to her knees, ready to throw herself at him again.

Margaret's heart was in her mouth as she saw her first-born child, her only daughter, advance with determination and pick up the stick that had been dropped. She clutched at it two-handed, waiting her chance to use it.

The thought, 'What's Gavin going to say about this?' flared into Margaret's mind. He could be disapproving enough about her own refusal to conform to his picture of a surgeon's wife. He certainly wouldn't take kindly to the news that his daughter had been allowed to involve herself in a street brawl.

She pushed between two men without ceremony and caught Christian's arm, pulling her aside, almost tripping over a bundle that lay against a house wall. Just then a newcomer, an older girl with long black hair flying about her head, sped past her and rushed towards the warriors.

She pushed the other child back against the wall beside Margaret and thrust a small parcel into her arms before launching herself onto the older boy's back, hands locked about his chest in an attempt to throw him off balance.

The young victim had managed to turn his head sideways so that his features were no longer being ground into the mud. But the neckerchief was still biting into his throat, and the part of his face that Margaret could see was purpling, his visible eye bulging. The breath whistled painfully in his throat.

'Let him go, Walter Shaw!' the girl panted.

'I'll let him go when he begs me to!'

'He can't! You'll kill him!'

He ignored her, giving the scarf another twist, and bringing a horrible choking gurgle from his victim. The younger girl, still clutching the cloth-wrapped bundle that had been pushed into her arms, broke into panic-stricken sobs.

Christian made another bid to hurl herself into the fray, but her mother's hand caught her and held her back.

'Do something –' Margaret appealed to the watchers, but they were too intent on the struggle to want to spoil their own enjoyment.

Little enough happened to brighten their drab lives, and they weren't about to put a stop to a good fight.

The throttled boy's hands scrabbled at the ground, his nails scratching audibly on one of the big stones that had once causeyed the lane, but were now few and far between, mere islands in the mud.

The girl dug her knees into the youth's ribs, releasing her grip round his body so that she could grind the knuckles of her two fists into his ears as hard as she could.

With a yelp of pain he released his victim and spun round like a dog trying to free itself of a stone tied to its tail. The girl was catapulted into the air, landing on a causey-stone that caught her hard between the shoulder blades, forcing the breath from her.

The younger boy, sucking air into his tortured lungs,

tried to push himself upright as Margaret reached his side.

'Leave him be –' she said crisply as the younger girl, sobbing, 'Lachie – oh, Lachie –!' tried to hug him. 'Let him get some air, lassie!'

She set down the basket she had been carrying, steadied the boy as he swayed on his hands and knees, and gently massaged his heaving chest, noting as she did so that every rib could be easily counted beneath his thin torn shirt.

The terrible whistling sound in his throat eased, and his head came up at last. Margaret left the girl to help him to his feet as she turned her attention to the other two.

The boy had managed to pin the winded girl down. She struggled, but he had captured both her wrists in one large strong hand, forcing them to the ground above her head.

He was sitting back on his heels, grinning triumphantly down at her.

'Now, Mistress Islay – beg my pardon nicely.'

'No!' She kicked out at him, but only succeeded in freeing her legs, shamefully bare for lack of decent undergarments, from the folds of her skirt. He cast a swift look at them, and Margaret saw that his eyes were suddenly hot.

'Then I'll claim my forfeit –' he said, and the watching men sniggered as he moved to kneel astride his new victim, and bent to seek out her mouth with his own.

She struggled like a wildcat, twisting and writhing, trying to eel her way out from under him. Caught off guard, he almost lost his balance, clamping his hands about her shoulders in an effort to force her into submission.

Her head whipped round and her teeth found their mark in the soft mound just below his right thumb.

He howled and released her; then, as she clung to his hand like a terrier holding a rat, his other hand caught her a painful blow across the cheekbone and with a muffled cry of pain she let him go and fell back.

Clearly, someone must do something. Margaret looked about for the stick her daughter had been wielding a few minutes earlier, but before she could reach for it a newcomer forged a way through the watching crowd, tossing people to left and right. Then the youth was plucked from the ground by a hand the size of a leg of mutton hanging in the meat market.

It gripped him painfully by the ear. Its owner, a mountain of a woman with a face that looked as though it had been fashioned from dough and had never been finished off in the oven, shook her captive vigorously, and his howls increased.

'Brawlin' in the streets!' Glasgow Annie, unofficial queen of that part of Paisley's slums, spoke with the disgust of one easily able to forget her own brawling when it suited her. 'Brawlin' wi' a slip o' a lass!'

She released him, and he immediately nursed his bitten hand.

'It's bleedin'!' Panic gave a womanly squeak to his voice. 'Look what she's done to me!'

'Look what you near did to our Lachie!' The girl's voice shook with rage. 'He's just a wee laddie – nothing like as old as you are –'

Even in her distress, her voice was light and musical with tones that sang, rather than spoke, of the mountains and glens of the Highlands.

Paisley was used to such voices these days; they belonged to the displaced clansfolk who had been driven in their thousands from their homes in the thirty years since the great battle at Culloden, forced to leave the land of their birth, the ground that had been theirs by natural right for generations, to make way for the sheep and cattle that were bringing new, undreamed-of prosperity to the landowners.

Walter began to spit out a flood of abuse.

'That's enough,' Glasgow Annie ordered. 'One o' these fine days, Walter Shaw, it's me ye'll tangle wi' – no' a wee bairn or a defenceless lass. An' when that day comes –'

She moved in on him and he backed away nervously, blood dripping to the ground from his injured hand.

Rumour had it that years before, when she was a young girl in her native city, the slopes and valleys of Glasgow Annie's body had been a source of infinite pleasure to men. She had earned a fortune by selling her favours. But the fortune had been spent on drink, and the drink had turned sweet curves into unsurpassable mountains, a coquettish smile into a grimace, a saucy nature into a hot, quick temper.

Men of courage had been known to flee in terror from Glasgow Annie's wrath, and Walter was no exception.

'How – how am I to do my work at the looms with this hand now? Tell me that?' he whined self-pityingly. 'She's taken my livelihood from me, the besom!'

'Only yer livelihood?' Glasgow Annie simpered, a terrible sight to behold. 'Come tae Annie, my darlin', an' I'll relieve ye o' yer manhood as weel!'

Walter's face, pale with the shock of finding himself injured, flamed as the watchers gave a roar of delighted laughter.

The boy he had been warring with was still supported by the two girls who had fought so hard to save him. The older girl said something to him in their native Gaelic but he twisted away from her, his face sullen, muttering something in the same tongue.

Scarlet drops showered the girl's tattered dress as Walter's bleeding hand was flourished accusingly in her direction. 'As for you, Mistress Islay McInnes –' he rolled the title sneeringly on his tongue. 'I'll have plenty to tell Mister Todd about you! Give me the pirns I came for and let me out of this place!'

Margaret realised that the bundle she had almost fallen over when she snatched Christian out of danger was a bag of pirns bearing newly-spun yarn for the looms. Walter spotted it and snatched at it, lifting it carelessly, so that the opening hung down.

Islay McInnes cried out in anguished protest as some of the precious reels, the result of hours of labour at a spinning wheel, fell out into the mud.

'I'll tell him on you,' Walter babbled, retreating up the lane backwards, his injured hand pointed accusingly at the girl who had bitten him. 'He'll have the militia on the lot of you!'

Grinning, Glasgow Annie spun round, turning her back on him. With a gesture that might have looked coquettish fifteen years before, she flipped up her skirts and waggled her huge buttocks at Walter, who gave up all pretence at further bluster and ran, washed along the lane and around the corner by a wave of laughter.

Islay turned to the younger boy and girl, her face twisted in quick disgust and her arms spread as though trying to protect them from the coarse Lowlanders they were forced to live among.

'As for you, laddie –' Annie rounded on Lachie as soon as the older boy disappeared. 'I've telt ye afore – if ye must fight the likes of him, ye'll have tae learn tae cheat the way he does.'

His hand was still clasped to his sore throat. Above it his dark Highland eyes sparked anger and defiance at her.

Without a word he turned and marched in through the low door leading to one of the single-roomed houses in the street, his thin little back rigid with humiliation.

Islay, suddenly aware that her skirts were still twisted up around her slim bare legs, hurriedly shook the ragged folds into some semblance of decency.

Then she nodded to Margaret before she and the younger girl went into the house together.

The watchers, their entertainment over, began to drift away. Annie turned her attention to Margaret.

'Good day tae ye, Mistress Knox. Ye'll be on yer way tae see Granny Ferguson?' Her doughy face split into an ingratiating, gap-toothed grin, like a parody of a lady greeting visitors in her parlour.

'What was all that stramash about?'

Annie shrugged, a shrug that set up a corresponding wobble all the way from shoulders to ankles. Christian, fascinated, watched the rippling blouse and skirt.

'Ach, it's the Heilanders. They're too hot-blooded. Thon wee laddie's like a fightin' cock – Walter well knows that it takes only a word tae set the wee laddie goin'.' Annie said casually. Then she peered short-sightedly down over her huge breasts at Christian.

'Yer bairn's growin' fast,' she boomed.

The little girl stood, feet planted firmly in the mud, and looked up at her, head tilted to one side. Then she said thoughtfully, 'So are you. You're awful fat.'

'Christian Knox!' Margaret gasped, scandalised. Annie's face swelled, reddened, then a laugh that started somewhere deep in her massive chest broke forth with a bellow.

'Ach, away, Mistress Knox, I mind the day ye'd have said somethin' o' the same yersel' as a bairn. An' I mind the day,' she added, leering at Christian, 'When I wis as wee and bonny as you are, my pretty henny.'

'You must have eaten up all your porridge,' Christian suggested, and was hustled away by her mother to the accompaniment of another wheezy gobbet of laughter.

It took a lot to embarrass Margaret Knox, but even so her face was burning as she whisked her daughter in through the doorway of the hovel where Granny Ferguson huddled her stiff old bones close to a fire that was so poor it couldn't have offered warmth to a mouse.

As she put the food she had brought into the empty store cupboard, then sat for a while and let the old woman talk, Margaret's thoughts were elsewhere.

'What d'you know of the Highland family down the lane?' she asked suddenly.

Granny Ferguson, alone in the world since her only son, a weaver who had once worked for Margaret's father, had died of a lung disease, enjoyed a good gossip. 'The man's a sojer, somewhere over the water, and the eldest boy with him. The woman worked herself to death, poor soul, trying to keep the bairns. The older girl's a relation of theirs, and she does her best to look after the other two now. A kindly neighbour, she is – she looks in on me now and then, and never comes empty-handed, for all they've little enough themselves.'

Margaret took in the information thoughtfully. Later, when she and Christian were walking back along the lane, she paused outside the Highland family's door and rapped on the faded, gapped planks.

Chapter Two

The three people on the other side of the door stared at each other when they heard the summons. Morag's eyes were round with fear, and Lachie, obviously convinced that his tormentor had come back, began to get up, bristling like a small fighting cock.

Islay pushed him back into his chair. 'Stay where you are! Morag –'

She held out the rag she had been using to soothe the boy's sore throat, and her cousin, who had been spreading the muddy pirns over the table, wiped her hands hurriedly on her skirt then took the cloth and dipped it into the bowl of cold water as Islay opened the door.

The well-dressed woman who had helped Lachie stood outside, her little girl by her side.

'I've come to see if the laddie's recovered.'

Islay hesitated, then stepped back to admit entrance into the room, 'Will you walk in, mistress?' She heard the half-challenging note in her own voice. There weren't many respectable folk in Paisley who would have set foot in Jenny's Wynd, let alone in one of the houses. They were all afraid of catching some terrible illness, or being robbed. But this visitor only hesitated for a fraction of a second before stepping down into the single tiny room. The child followed, taking a firm fistful of her mother's figured silk gown.

Islay gave the caller time to accustom her eyes to the gloom and observe the uneven floor of beaten earth, the small glassless window half-covered by a piece of sacking to keep out wind and rain.

The few furnishings in the room consisted of a table, some stools, a couple of low beds and some shelving that had been roughly nailed together out of odds and ends of wood.

The spinning wheel stood by the fireplace, flanked by a basket of flax on one side and a basket of empty pirns, still awaiting the linen yarn the weavers needed for their work, on the other.

As she saw her Lowland home anew through the visitors' eyes Islay felt deep embarrassment wash over her. Then she lifted her chin high, and consoled herself with the thought that at least the place was as clean and neat as she could make it. It was no shame to her if she and the children were forced to live in conditions that they wouldn't have wished on their hens or pigs back home.

Courtesy demanded that she ask, 'Will you take some refreshment?'

Both Lachie and Morag stared, knowing full well that there was nothing to share, apart from water from the street well and the meagre store of day-old bread that Islay had just brought home, having earned it by scrubbing out the bakery.

She ignored them, her eyes on the visitor who said, mercifully, 'Thank you, but no. We took some tea with Mistress Ferguson.'

To cover her relief Islay took a straw from the hearth and held it to the poor fire; when it blossomed into flame she lit the crusie-lamp on one of the shelves. The flame smoked and flickered; the acrid smell of burning oil caught at the little girl's snub nose almost immediately, making her sneeze.

Lachie sat at the table, head bowed, one hand still caressing his throat gingerly.

'Are you all right, laddie?' the lady asked.

'I'll kill him!' he replied huskily, between gritted teeth.

'Lachie, that's not the way to speak before guests,' Islay reproved him in their own tongue. His dark head came up at once and his eyes blazed at her.

'Speak English! The Gaelic's dead to us now!'

His shame at being vanquished by the older boy then rescued by females made her want to cradle him in her arms and comfort him. He was still a child, when all was said and done – a child who had been forced into ill-fitting adulthood before his time, and tried too hard to carry his responsibilities like a man.

But she couldn't do that. Instead, she joined their visitor, who was examining the muddied pirns on the table.

'Were many wasted?'

'Enough.'

'Sixpence, at least, we've lost,' Morag said drearily, and Islay rounded on her.

'Hush, Morag!'

'He said he'd tell Mister Todd,' Morag went on as though she hadn't heard. 'What if –'

She stopped. She and Islay gazed at each other, so closely locked in their shared fear that the others were forgotten for the moment. What if Mister Todd, the weaver who held the purse-strings, decided that he didn't want the wild, trouble-making Highlanders to spin yarn for his looms any more? How would they survive then?

'Is it Jamie Todd you spin for?' the lady asked. 'I know him well. I'll tell him what –'

'We don't need to ask anyone to fight our battles for us,' Islay told her sharply, then added in a gentler voice. 'I've seen you in Jenny's Wynd before. Your man's Mister Knox, the surgeon, is he not?'

'My father makes folk well again.' The child ventured out from behind her mother's skirts to proffer the news proudly.

Islay swallowed. 'It's my place to tell Mister Todd what happened. I'll go and see him myself, in the morning.'

'But won't you let me –'

Islay's eyes, large with fear and determination, met and held Margaret Knox's.

'It's my place,' she said.

Chapter Three

Gavin Knox had been in Glasgow from mid-morning. Most of the time since he had kissed his wife good-bye and left his home had been spent amid the gore and noise and suffering of an operating room, and he looked tired and drawn when Margaret herself ran to welcome him in from the rain-swept doorstep.

Her heart turned over at first sight of him, as it always did. The practical side of Margaret's nature, the side that dominated her life – indeed, the side that she had thought made up her entire life before she met Gavin – was acutely embarrassed by the way she felt about him.

She was a 28-year-old woman, after all; mother to two children, mistress of her own house, and still, on two days of each week, a teacher to the pauper children in the Town House school-room. But just a glance from Gavin's clear hazel eyes, the touch of his hand, the joy of waking in the mornings and seeing his dark head on the pillow close by hers, made her feel like a girl in one of the romantic stories her lifelong friend Kate Miller enjoyed reading.

It gave her some consolation to know that she was not alone in her foolishness. Gavin, as sensible and level-headed a man as anyone would hope to meet, a surgeon respected the length and breadth of Glasgow as well as in Paisley, was as passionately in love with her as she was with him. Why this should be so, Margaret couldn't think. But it was, nevertheless, and she was oh, so glad of it!

'Father!' Christian, who had scorned their attempts to teach her to say 'Papa', came scudding from the kitchen and across the hall, her joyous voice raised so loudly in greeting that Margaret, afraid that small Daniel would be wakened, shushed her vigorously.

Gavin only had time to take his wife into a swift, light

embrace before the little girl was upon them, tugging at his wide-skirted coat. With a glance that promised Margaret a more appropriate greeting once they were alone he swung his daughter up into his arms and carried her into the parlour while Margaret went to the kitchen to see if Ellen was managing the evening meal without help.

Gavin was sprawled in his favourite chair when she returned to the parlour. His long legs, still booted, stretched across the rug before the fire. He had unbuttoned his waistcoat, and in his hand, its contents glowing like a precious ruby in the firelight, was a glass of his favourite claret.

Christian squatted on the rug by his feet, her voice running on like one of the burns that rushed down from the braes to join the river that flowed through Paisley.

Her grandfather, Duncan Montgomery, had been known to say more than once that Christian had been born with a busy tongue; she had certainly learned to speak early, while her brother, a more solemn child, had only a fraction of the vocabulary she had possessed at his age.

Margaret looked fondly at the little tableau before her, then realised to her horror that Christian was saying, 'Then we went to see Granny Ferguson –'

'It's time for bed, Christian,' she interrupted.

Gavin's eyes were closed; he looked tired. But now his lids lifted and he smiled at his wife. 'And time, I hope, for supper. What do we eat tonight?'

' – and there were all these folk in the lane –' Christian pattered on like the rain that fell steadily outside.

'Beef, and broth made from the bones.'

Gavin yawned mightily. 'Good. I'll swear that the fowl they gave me at the Infirmary had reached its ninetieth year before they took mercy on it and wrung its neck.'

'Then Glasgow Annie picked him up and –'

'Daniel was too tired to wait up for you after all. He's been in his bed this past hour, and asleep almost before the coverlet was over him.'

'I'll look in on him and put on some fresh linen before I eat. I feel as though I've been wearing these clothes for a week, instead of a day.' Reluctantly, Gavin set his glass down and got to his feet.

'Christian, come along to your bed.' Margaret held out her hand to her daughter. By tomorrow, she thought thankfully, Christian's tongue would be chattering about some new adventure and she would have forgotten the incident in the lane by the river.

Gavin had reached the door and opened it when Christian asked, her voice clear and bell-like, 'Why doesn't Glasgow Annie wear anything underneath her skirts?'

Gavin, on his way out of the door, stopped, pivoted on one heel, and fixed his daughter with a look that would have made anyone else quail. 'What did you say?'

Christian never quailed. She didn't know the meaning of fear. 'Why doesn't Glasgow Annie wear anything under her skirts?' she repeated.

Gavin's face flushed a dusky red. He threw a quick, puzzled look at his wife, read guilt in her blue eyes, and fixed his attention on Christian again.

'What makes you think that?' he asked, with deceptive gentleness.

'After the fight, when she'd pulled the big boy away from the other boy – before I even got a chance to hit him with my stick –' said Christian, suddenly recalling a grievance ' – she did this –'

To Margaret's horror she scrambled to her feet, turned her back on her parents, and whisked the skirt of her warm wool dress up in passable imitation of Annie's crude sexual gesture to Walter Shaw.

' – and everyone laughed, and the big boy ran away. And Annie didn't have anything on under her skirt. She's awful big. I told her she must have eaten all her porridge.'

'I think,' her father said, his voice still mild, but with a cutting edge of cold steel beneath it, 'that it's time you were in your bed, my lady.'

*

Supper was a silent affair. As she drew the curtains before sitting down at the table Margaret saw that the rain had gone and the late-summer evening was clear and calm. She took her seat opposite her husband and waited for the domestic storm to break.

Gavin, seemingly lost in thought, ate his way steadily through each course as it was laid before him.

When they went back to the parlour Margaret sat by the fire, her mending in her lap. Gavin paced the floor.

'You've been taking her down to these – these stinking hovels again!' he said at last. 'Down by the river, where it's alive with vermin and filth and disease –'

'It's never done me any harm, and I've been down there often enough in my life.'

'You've been fortunate. My daughter might not be.' His voice was low and intense, as it usually was when he was angry. Gavin rarely shouted. 'I told you before, Margaret, if you must go visiting the folk that live there, then do so alone. God knows I've no control whatsoever over your movements. I recognise and freely admit that. But I will not have my children exposed to danger.'

It was her turn to feel anger. She had been in the wrong, taking Christian with her, knowing that Gavin wouldn't approve. But even so his high-handed attitude incensed her. 'Gavin, you speak as though you birthed the children entirely on your own. They're mine as well as yours – perhaps more so, since I carried them and bore them.'

'All the more reason to cherish them and keep them safe from harm.'

'Christian's as strong as a – a horse!'

'Have you forgotten that we almost lost her to the croup before she completed her first year?'

Could she ever forget that? Margaret recalled, as vividly as though it had happened only a few hours ago, her anguish as she paced the floor with her first-born, watching the flushed little face, listening to the child's choked, gasping breath, something like the sound the young lad in the lane had made that very day as his tormentor drew the neckcloth tighter.

'Christian outgrew the croup! There's not been a thing wrong with her since!'

'If you must visit the slums, you're not to take her with you again. I mean it, Margaret. And if you won't listen to me, then by God,' said Gavin, his eyes bright with anger, 'I'll stop you from going as well, somehow – even if it means locking you into your bed-chamber when I'm not here to watch over you.'

'We can't make poverty and suffering stop happening just by turning our backs on them!'

'I know that,' he said with a contempt that sent a surge of colour to her face. 'I'm reminded of it every day I walk the wards in the infirmaries. I don't spend all my time caring for moneyed folk, you know – only part of it. I don't turn my back, Margaret. I thank the good Lord every day that I can protect my family from poverty and want and the suffering they bring. But I'll not have Christian exposed to it in any manner!'

There was a short, angry silence, then, 'I'm tired,' Gavin said stiffly. 'If you'll excuse me, I'll retire.'

She bowed her head in silent, formal assent, biting back the angry words that wanted to pour out.

Alone, she cleared the table, carried the used platters to the kitchen, and sent Ellen off to her bed, refusing the woman's offer of help. She needed to occupy her hands. That way she could block out the thoughts that seethed in her mind.

But later, as she sat by the parlour fire, with the house silent about her apart from the ticking of the clocks, the needle that was repairing a tear in one of Daniel's garments with swift, assured efficiency slowed and stopped.

Gavin had the right of it; she was sensible enough to admit that. Christian, despite her sturdy independence, wasn't much more than a baby. It was foolish to expose her to unnecessary peril. God knows there were dangers enough for her to navigate as she grew without her mother seeking out more.

But deep down in Margaret lay a fear that her children, born to privileges she herself, a weaver's daughter, had never known, might grow to accept unquestioningly the vast gulf between those with more than enough money and those with none.

Since her marriage she had met many rich people at gatherings and at dinner tables. Most of them displayed such indifference to the misfortunes of their fellow men that it made her skin crawl to be in their company. She couldn't bear the thought of Christian and Daniel growing up to be like those addle-pated, shallow puppets.

The needle went about its work again, then slowed and stopped as she recalled the other side of the coin – the Highland children in their damp, dark little room near the river. Vividly, she saw again the expression on Islay McInnes's face as she stared down at the ruined pirns.

The handsome clock in the hall struck the hour and Margaret gathered up her work and put it aside. It was time she was abed.

Contented snoring could be heard faintly from the rear of the house as she started to mount the stairs. Ellen was sound asleep in the little room off the kitchen. The children were also asleep in the room next to their parents' bedchamber – Christian snug beneath her coverlet, Daniel with arms outflung and hands loosely fisted above his head.

There was no sound from the bed she shared with Gavin. The fringe of light from her candle gave her a glimpse of him, eyes closed, lashes against his cheeks, dark hair tumbled over his forehead.

Margaret stripped her clothes off and put on her night-shift, cool and still smelling pleasantly of the fresh summer's day when it had been stretched over a bush in the back yard to dry.

She took off her lace cap and let her dark brown hair fall about her shoulders so that she could brush it out.

It vexed her that her hair, which had had a curl to it in childhood, had straightened over the years. Daniel had inherited her blue eyes and her straight, silky hair; fortunately, Christian had her father's thick tresses, with a vigorous wave in them.

The brush moved from crown to tip with an even, soothing rhythm. The mirror showed her candle-lit face, cloaked in the fall of long hair, as that of a pale, mysterious stranger.

The sight reminded her of a Hallowe'en party that her aunt Mary MacLeod had once held, and a game they had played that night. Each girl had to sit alone before a mirror, eating an apple and combing her hair. The tale was that she would see her future husband's face reflected in the mirror.

The face Margaret had seen in the glass on that long-ago night had belonged to her childhood friend William Todd, who had crept into the room to speak to her. Gavin had followed hard on William's heels, but she hadn't seen his reflection.

Gavin, however, was the man she had married, and William was dead now, drowned in the rain-swollen River Cart.

She missed him sorely. William had been her closest friend, the only person she had been able to confide in. She wished with all her heart that he had lived, instead of dying so young, and so cruelly.

She shivered, laid the brush down, and turned to blow out the candle. Its light picked out the gold flecks in Gavin's hazel eyes, wide open and studying her.

'How long have you been awake?'

'Long enough.' He pushed the bedclothes back, held out his hand to her. 'Come to bed, Margaret.'

She blew out the candle and walked bare-footed, with the assurance of one in familiar surroundings, across the night-black room to the bed.

Gavin's hand closed about her arm, drew her down beside him. He shifted so that she could nestle in the warm hollow his body had vacated, and gently pulled the covers over her.

'Of all the men you could have bewitched and tormented, Margaret Montgomery,' he whispered, 'why did you have to choose me?'

His body was hard and eager against hers. The quarrel was over. There would be others, no doubt – many others. That was part of marriage as far as Margaret and Gavin were concerned.

But always, there was the forgiving, the coming together again, the loving.

And pray God, Margaret thought as she let herself melt against him and felt the hard planes and angles of his face beneath her palm, may there always be the loving.

Chapter Four

Jamie Todd, normally the sunniest of men, was in an irritable mood. His mother, Kirsty Carmichael, had been summoned to the neighbouring town of Barrhead first thing that morning because of some domestic crisis in the home of Jamie's sister, Kate. Which meant that Jamie and his step-father, Billy Carmichael, had been obliged to make shift for themselves.

Two handless men in the one kitchen, particularly when one of them was old and stiff and clumsy with the rheumatics, and therefore given to dropping things, didn't make a good start to the day.

Furthermore, Kirsty's absence meant that she would not be spinning any yarn for the looms that morning.

At a time when work was scarce, Jamie's reputation was as good as his father's had been. He had eight looms under his care now, four in the High Street shop his father had worked before him and four in the shop he had taken over in Wellmeadow almost two years earlier.

They all worked on linen cloth, and they needed as much yarn as he could obtain for them. Although the Paisley weavers had built up a very good name for themselves a number of looms in the town were lying idle for lack of orders. Jamie worked his looms in partnership with his close friends Duncan and Robert Montgomery – a partnership that stood all three men in good stead. Even so, Jamie found it hard to keep all his looms employed. The fact of the matter was that in buying over the Wellmeadow shop he had taken on more responsibility than he could comfortably handle. But his nature wouldn't let him admit that to anybody, and so he worried over his financial obligations in silence.

Then, of course, there was that dolthead Walter Shaw – at

the door first thing that morning, with a hangdog look in the grey eyes that couldn't quite meet Jamie's, one hand bound in a grimy cloth, and less than the number of pirns he had gone out to collect from the spinsters the day before.

Jamie, his stomach uncomfortable after the makeshift breakfast he and Billy had managed to cook between them, his head buzzing with the list of all that he had to do that day, had boxed the young weaver's ears there and then on the doorstep, before the interested and amused gaze of the passers-by. Then he brusquely ordered the lad back to the loom shop, where he would have to spend the day making himself useful as best he could, fetching and carrying for the others while his own loom stood idle, the web Jamie had managed to contract for it half-finished.

Walter slouched off. Jamie thumped the door shut and stamped along the passage-way to the weaving shop. He had just reached it when the door-knocker made itself heard.

'I'll go,' one of the other men offered.

'Stay where you are. There's no point in bringing all the looms to a standstill. I can see that it's precious little work I'll get done this day!'

He tramped back along the passage and threw the door open, almost lifting it from its hinges in his irritation.

Islay had worked for most of the night in the crusie's flickering light while Lachie and Morag slept curled together in the wall bed. Towards dawn, with enough pirns filled to make up for those spoiled in the mud, she had joined the other two beneath the thin blanket, falling at once into an exhausted sleep haunted by uneasy dreams.

In the morning she carefully dressed herself in the best clothes she had, brushed out her long hair until it shone, and fastened it back beneath a threadbare lacy cap that had once, a long time ago, adorned the head of some well-to-do lady. Then, leaving what remained of the bread to make breakfast for Lachie and Morag, for there wasn't enough for three, she set off for the High Street with reluctant feet.

Her courage almost failed her when she saw that Jamie Todd himself stood at his street door haranguing Walter

Shaw, his rugged face angry beneath the thatch of blazing red hair.

As she watched, the master weaver aimed an open-handed blow at his employee's head, then stepped back and slammed the door shut.

Passing women and children gawped at the spectacle, then laughed. Walter, shoulders slumped in humiliation, turned away, and came face to face with Islay.

He flushed scarlet at the realisation that she had witnessed his humiliation, and glowered at her.

'Come to gloat, have you? Pleased with yourself at taking a man's livelihood from him?'

She glanced down at the bandage on his hand, then back to his face. 'I'm vexed, Walter. I didn't mean –'

'Damned Highlanders! Why did you have to come to Paisley and get under the feet of decent folk?' asked Walter, pushing roughly past her.

Miserably, she watched him go and then, with every muscle in her body poised to flee for her life if necessary, she rapped on the sturdy wooden door.

All too soon footsteps sounded on the stone passageway within, the door opened, and Jamie Todd was looking down at her.

'Aye?'

'Mist – M –' Her lips fluttered, then firmed. The fingers of her free hand twisted in the ragged folds of her skirt. She made a determined effort at the name, and this time it came out clearly. 'Mister T – Todd –'

'Aye, that's my name, lass. Well, state your business, for I've more to do than stand here all day.'

Her lips fluttered again, and were brought under control again. 'It was me that bit Walter.'

'Eh?'

'I b – bit Walter Shaw.' Then, as he said nothing, but continued to stare with bewildered incomprehension, she fisted her two hands before her over the handle of the basket she carried and said in a rush of outgoing breath. 'He was fighting with my kinsman Lachie so I bit him to make him let go. It's my fault he can't work and the pirns fell in the mire and –'

'You bit my weaver?' He seemed to be finding it hard to make sense of the situation.

'Aye. I'm mortally vexed, Mister Todd. It was wrong of me to injure his hand, and him working on the looms. But I had to make him let Lachie go, for he was throttling the laddie.'

'Lachie?'

'My cousin. He's only twelve, but Walter knows Lachie must fight him, being the man of the house, so he –'

'What's your name?'

Her tongue moistened her lips. She was still poised to run. 'Islay, sir. Islay McInnes.'

She held out the basket and Jamie Todd took it and glanced at its contents then back at her, his blue eyes puzzled.

'Where did you get them?'

'I spun them, in place of the ones that got spoiled yes – yesterday.'

'But – lassie, you must have been working all night!'

'I had to make up the number of pirns. Mister Todd, you'll – you'll not take the work away –?'

His jaw set truculently. 'I should, for what you've done to my weaver. But you can tell your mother that I'll overlook it this once. Just this once, mind.'

'My mother's dead –' Islay started to say, but to her horror tears of worry and exhaustion suddenly misted her eyes. Her mother had already been ailing when they were put out of their home. She had died soon afterwards, in the dark draughty corner of a barn.

Not a day went by without Islay recalling that terrible time. The mere thought of her dead mother at a time when her own courage was at a low ebb was too much.

She saw consternation and then embarrassment come into the face of the man who looked down at her. He began to say something, but Islay, beyond words now, turned and stumbled back along the footpath, anxious to get out of his sight before her tears won her over entirely.

It wasn't until much later, when she had sobbed her heart out in a quiet corner, that she realised that she had forgotten to claim payment for the pirns.

Chapter Five

On one side of the entrance passage of the Todds' High Street building was the big room that housed the looms; on the other was a smaller room where Billy Carmichael, Jamie's step-father, had plied his trade as a cobbler before the rheumatics put an end to his work.

Margaret had persuaded Jamie to let her move two small inkle looms in there, to enable some of the women from the Poors' Hospital where she taught to weave ribbons and earn a few coppers.

Before going to talk to him about the three children who lived in Jenny's Wynd she put her head round the door and had a swift word with the women working on the looms. Then she left them and opened the other door.

Weaving shops were always noisy. The babble of voices – for in Paisley, at least, the men gossiped just as much as the women – vied with the steady clack of the big looms. A pair of linnets chirrupped in a cage by the window. The room was large and, as always, it seemed to be lit by Jamie's mop of fiery red hair. He was working away at his loom and unusually silent, but a welcoming grin split his face when he looked up and saw her. Margaret and Jamie had always been close, even although she had refused to marry him years before.

She waited in the passage until he joined her. Then she asked, 'Jamie, d'you have a weaver called Walter Shaw?'

His face darkened. 'Aye, in the Wellmeadow weaving shop. Have you come to lecture me about him too?'

She raised puzzled brows.

'First I'd Walter at the door with a sorry tale about a wounded hand keeping him from his work, and pirns falling in the mud. Then a wee lassie from down by the river came with some nonsense about biting the man – biting him,

as if she was a dog! – and spoiling my pirns into the bargain.'
He shook his head. 'Then, if you please, she gave me pirns
she must have spun during the night, and ran away without
waiting for her money.'

'She's not a wee lassie, she's almost a grown woman. And
you must have said something to fright her if she ran from
you.' Swiftly Margaret gave her account of the scene down
by the river the day before.

'It must have been the younger girl who came to the door,
then, for she was only a child. And I said nothing to fright
her,' Jamie protested.

'You'll let the girl go on spinning yarn for you, won't you?
She's fair desperate for the money. And if you could mebbe
find work for the laddie –'

'But they're Highlanders, Margaret! Highlanders are all
fingers and thumbs when it comes to weaving, you know
that yourself.'

'Mebbe so, but they're decent enough folk, trying to earn
their bread like the rest of us.'

'Why should I go out of my way to help them? Highlanders cause nothing but trouble, and Walter can show you his
bandaged hand to prove it.'

'Yesterday's brawl was no fault of theirs! It was Walter's
doing, I'm sure of that.'

Jamie glowered down at her, but he could never resist
Margaret for long, and they both knew it. 'Aye – well – she
can go on spinning for me, if that'll please you,' he said at
last, reluctantly. 'The good Lord knows I need all the
spinsters I can get to keep the looms going.'

'And d'you think you might find some work for the boy?'

'I'll make no promises. But I'll go along to Jenny's Wynd
myself and have a word with them.'

'You'll find them in a miserable room, the poor souls.'
Then Margaret was struck by an idea. 'Jamie, isn't the
dwelling house above your loom shop in Wellmeadow
empty?'

'I'm planning on using it as a store.'

'Och, it's too good to waste as a store!'

But Jamie had had enough. 'Find somewhere else for
your Highlanders. I must get back to my loom,' he said

crisply. 'I've had too many interruptions today as it is. If you've got the time you might go on up and talk with Billy for a while. The man's lonely without my mother about the place.'

'Is she still at Barrhead?'

'Aye. Both Kate's bairns are down with some fever.'

'What is it?' Margaret asked sharply, and he shrugged.

'Nothing serious, from what I hear.'

'Run back to your loom, then – but think on what I'm asking you. I'll have a word with Billy.'

Margaret eased past him to where a flight of stone steps led up to the dwelling house above. There, she found a more sympathetic listener in Jamie's step-father.

'Jamie's not as hard as he makes out, lassie,' the old man said. 'He's got a lot of responsibility, what with eight looms to see to. And things arenae easy just now.'

'But Jamie's surely not having any trouble finding work. He's said nothing to me about it – or to my father, or I'd surely have heard.'

'He's not the sort who would.' Billy knocked his pipe out against the side of the kitchen fireplace.

'He needs a wife. If only Beth had lived –'

Her voice tailed off, and they were both silent for a moment, thinking of what might have been.

Shortly after he returned from the Army, Jamie had become betrothed to the young woman who worked as companion to Margaret's aunt, Mary MacLeod. But Beth, who wasn't strong, had died during an outbreak of pleurisy that swept through Paisley a few months before the wedding.

'If I could just think of the right person –'

'Now don't go black-footing, Margaret. Jamie wouldnae thank you for finding a wife for him. Better trust to Fate.'

'Mebbe,' Margaret agreed. But privately, she was of the opinion that Fate would be none the worse for a nudge in the right direction.

Chapter Six

Ellen ushered Margaret's young brother, Thomas Montgomery, into the tiny dining room while Margaret and Gavin were still at their evening meal.

The three Montgomery men, Duncan and his sons Robert and Thomas, were all alike; of stocky build and medium height, with dark hair and clear, honest blue eyes.

But whereas Duncan and Robert had strong, square faces, Thomas's was still round, overlaid with the rosy bloom of youth, despite the fact that he was now twenty-five years of age, and a qualified physician.

A bachelor, he still lived under his parents' roof. This, coupled with the fact that he was the youngest of the three Montgomery children, led his family to think of him at all times as 'wee Thomas', a habit that rankled deeply with him.

But there was nothing youthful about his face as he advanced into the room, brusquely refusing Margaret's invitation to share their evening meal.

'I'm not here as a guest. Gavin, I've need of your help.'

Margaret, who had heard that Kirsty had sent for Thomas to go to Barrhead that afternoon, felt a chill creep towards her heart.

'Kate –?' Her voice shook, and Gavin came to her, put his arm about her.

'Kate's well enough, but both the children are down with fever.' He looked at the couple before him, his eyes dark with the news he had to tell. 'It's the pox, Gavin. The serving-girl took it first, and she died two hours back.'

Margaret sensed the sudden tension in Gavin's body. His arm fell from her shoulders. 'I'll come at once,' he said, and went from the room.

Margaret and her brother looked at each other wordlessly. There was nothing to say.

The pox. The two words circled through her head in time to some macabre tune.

The pox. She had seen men, women and children fall victim to it in the Poors' Hospital. Most sufferers died but Margaret knew some who had survived.

There was Jockie Gray, who had been blinded and terribly disfigured by the disease. There was Mirren Tennant, a woman of Margaret's own age, who had been turned into a simpleton and now lived in the Poors' Hospital, roaming the rooms hour upon hour, keening to herself.

Few recovered fully – but some did, Margaret told herself, doubling her hands into fists, digging nails into palms, determined not to give up hope.

When Gavin came back, shrugging into his coat, his bag in one hand, she said, 'I'll come with you.'

Both men shook their heads, and Gavin said sharply, 'You must stay here, Margaret, and see to your own bairns.'

There was no sense in arguing. She knew, looking at their faces, that they had already shut her out, pushed her into the background. All at once they had become strangers to her, medical men with no need or time for anyone else.

She followed them to the front door, watched as they clambered into the carriage that had brought Thomas from Barrhead. When they had gone, rattling off through the gathering dusk, rounding a corner, passing from view, she went slowly back into the house to begin the long wait for Gavin's return.

As she lay alone in the darkness later she thought of the little family in Barrhead. Archie, easy-going and devoted to his wife and children; four-year-old John and three-year-old Alyson; laughing, lovely, red-haired Kate, who was eagerly awaiting the birth of her third child in a few months' time.

Margaret closed her eyes then opened them again hurriedly as pictures of smooth, formerly healthy skin covered with pustules imprinted themselves on the insides of her lids. She sought the comfort of the window's grey shape in the darkness of the room, and watched as it lightened, and dawn came.

*

Carriage wheels rattled to a standstill outside the gate a few hours later, as the birds were pouring out a joyous, full-throated welcome to the new day.

Margaret tossed a shawl about her shoulders and was at the front door by the time Gavin came wearily up the path.

She flew into his arms and he held her tightly, hungrily, burying his mouth in her hair, before holding her back so that he could look down at her.

'How are they?'

His face was haggard. 'The wee lad's gone, but I think Alyson'll recover now. Come inside – I'm in sore need of warmth, and some food.'

The kitchen was quiet and still warm from last night's fire. Its embers glowed dull red in the range and Margaret poked it into life again, refuelling it from the coal scuttle that was filled last thing every night.

Gavin slumped wearily into a chair by the table, staring at the wall, seeing pictures there that she couldn't see. That was just as well, she realised as she set bread and cheese and ale before him.

He ate hungrily, and persuaded her to share the ale with him. She wasn't fond of the liquid's bitter taste, but it helped to ease the painful block of ice that had formed in the very core of her being.

The kettle boiled and she made tea, asking at last, as they both sipped the hot liquid. 'How are Kate and Archie taking it?'

Gavin reached out and put his hand over hers. His fingers were warm; hers, she realised, were very cold. 'If – God forbid – you and I should be faced with such tragedy, Margaret, I pray we'll find the courage they've shown.'

'I should go to Barrhead.'

'Kirsty's there. And you've your own bairns to think of. You can't afford to bring the sickness home to them.'

He left his chair and came to her, holding her close.

'I'd do anything, Margaret – anything! – to find out how to put an end to bairns dying like that, almost before they've had a chance to live,' he said fiercely against her hair.

Then the door opened and Ellen, still tousled from her bed, stood looking at them in sleepy surprise.

*

Five minutes later Margaret sat on her tumbled bed and watched as her husband stripped his soiled clothes off, letting them lie where they fell. He washed quickly in the warm water he had brought from the kitchen, then dressed in clean clothes and tied his dark hair back with a broad ribbon. Gavin had always scorned wigs and powder, though many of his colleagues favoured them.

'Must you go to Glasgow today? You should get some rest.'

'I must. There's work to be done.' He drew her to her feet and kissed her, a hard, possessive kiss. 'I'll come home as soon as I can.'

At the front door he took her hands in his, raised them to his lips.

'Sometimes, Margaret,' he said against her fingers, 'It's only the thought of the three of you, well and happy and safe in this house, that keeps me from giving in to despair.'

Then he went, and she was alone once again.

Chapter Seven

Jamie Todd strode along the Sneddon, carrying in one hand a basket of flax to be spun into yarn for the linen weavers, in the other a bag of empty pirns, the wooden reels that the yarn was spun onto.

Above, the sky was leaden, weeping a thin drizzle of rain to add to the stinking puddles under Jamie's booted feet. His fiery head was the only splash of bright colour in the drab day.

The weather suited his mood. A few hours earlier he had watched his young nephew being hurriedly buried. His mother was still in Barrhead with Kate and the rest of her family.

A stray trickle of rainwater from a wet straw thatch found its way beneath Jamie's collar. He shivered, partly at its icy touch, partly because his thoughts were back in Barrhead with his sister.

It did a man no good to feel so useless in times of adversity. Jamie was used to taking life by the throat and shaking it; nobody could do that where illness and death were concerned.

He turned down Jenny's Wynd and stopped to survey the place, his nose wrinkled with disgust at the smell of soaked, rotting rubbish. Once, over a century before, the tiny houses had no doubt been adequate enough. Now dampness seeped into them from the River Cart, which ran past the bottom end of the lane, adding its own stink to the already over-laden air. Refuse lay piled against damp house walls, filthy water dripped from thatched roofs, windows gaped like empty eye sockets.

It was a wonder that every resident in the place hadn't fallen victim to the pox or one or other of the fevers and lung complaints that abounded in the town.

A few men lounged in a doorway; he asked where the McInnes family lived, and was directed to a house near the far end. The shrunken ill-fitting door was flimsy. Inside, a child was coughing; a harsh, wrenching sound. Jamie lifted his fist and thumped briskly on the door.

For a moment he thought that it was going to give way beneath his hand. No doubt the people inside would think that it was the militia that had come calling, he thought, and followed the commanding thump with a more sedate tap of the knuckles. Nothing happened. He was about to knock again when it opened.

Jamie peered into the dim oblong and saw the under-nourished child who had delivered the pirns and admitted to biting Walter Shaw.

*

Islay drew her breath in sharply as she recognised the caller. Then she stepped back, gripping the edge of the door so tightly that her fingernails almost sank into the soft, rotted wood. 'You'll come in, Mister Todd?'

The man hesitated, as though he would have preferred to stay outside, then stepped through the doorway, ducking his head beneath the lintel.

Then he gave an abrupt exclamation, stumbling and almost falling headlong into the room, because he hadn't realised that the sill of the door was several inches above the inner floor.

Instinctively, Islay caught at his elbow, releasing him as soon as he had recovered his balance.

Morag, sitting on a stool by the fire, coughed again, and Mister Todd stared at her, then at Islay.

'Are you the lassie who bit my weaver?'

'Aye, sir. Islay McInnes.'

'And what age might you be, Islay McInnes?'

'Sixteen years past.'

'Indeed?' There was no mistaking his surprise. 'I took you for –' He stopped, then added, 'So you're the oldest member of your household?'

'Aye, sir.'

Lachie, no doubt stung by the inference that there was no

man of the house, came from the corner of the room to stand by Islay's elbow.

'This'll be the laddie that fought with Walter?'

Lachie took a step forward. 'He started it!'

'You're no' big enough to take on the likes of him,' Mister Todd said sharply.

'I'm growing!'

'You'll not live long enough to grow if you behave like a fighting cock every time the mood comes over you.'

Islay could feel the boy's thin body tense with anger. She pressed his arm warningly and he subsided.

Jamie Todd swung his basket and bag onto the table. 'I brought more flax and pirns. And I brought the payment for the last lot, since you didnae see fit to wait for it.'

As the coins rattled on the wooden table Islay's hand moved forward of its own volition, but before her fingers touched the money she managed to check herself and drew back. There was no need to let this man see how desperately they needed his money.

'But mind – there's to be no more fighting.'

'I'm grateful to you, Mister Todd.'

'Prove it by working well and not bringing any more trouble on my head. Is there nobody – older – in the family who could care for you all?'

Her head tilted proudly. 'My uncle and cousin went to be soldiers.'

'Your uncle would have been better to stay home and see to his bairns.'

'He couldn't find any work here. He went while his wife was alive. He doesn't know we're alone now, for I've no way of contacting him.'

'There's little enough money to be made in the Army. I know, for I spent some years in it myself.'

His criticism wounded her, and a sharp answer was out before she could stop it. 'It's better than dying of a broken heart in a place like this.'

It was obvious that his patriotism was stung. 'There's nothing wrong with Paisley, if you're prepared to work hard and learn our ways!'

'I meant this house,' she said. 'But since you speak of

Paisley, Mister Todd, I'll remind you that it's your home, not ours. We had our own land, once. We had space to move and clean air to breathe, and the water in the burns was sweet and pure –'

'It sounds bonny enough, but you must just make the best of what you have now, and stop feeling sorry for yourselves.'

'We didn't leave our home from choice,' she told him firmly. Lachie moved protectively closer. 'We were forced out by the landowners. We did nothing wrong.'

'Islay –' Morag faltered nervously, aware that there was a quarrel brewing.

Islay touched her shoulder with a comforting gesture. 'It's all right, Morag, don't fret. I just want to tell you that we're not criminals to be punished, Mister Todd, or beggars to be tolerated or whipped out of the town. We don't ask for your pity, or expect it. We just want to make our own way, without causing or receiving trouble.'

Jamie Todd's face warmed, and she feared that she had gone too far. Cold sweat beaded her forehead. If he took back his money, she wouldn't be able to bear it. She'd go down on her knees to him first, cut out her tongue – anything rather than lose those few precious coins.

For a moment there was an awkward silence, then, 'I see that you've a sharp tongue in your head, lassie, to match your sharp teeth,' he said dryly. 'And the boy?'

'Lachie's twelve.'

'What d'you work at, Lachie?'

'I run errands, when someone's willing to take me on.'

'Morag and I do some cleaning,' Islay added. 'And there's the spinning –' Her voice trailed away. She wasn't certain, any more, of the spinning.

'Mmmm.' He hesitated, then said, 'I'm in need of a drawboy in one of my loom shops.'

For a moment they all stared at him, unable to believe their ears. 'I could do it,' Lachie said eagerly.

'It would mean working in my loomshop in Wellmeadow, beside Walter Shaw. I'll have no fighting among my workers, lad, I'll tell you that here and now.'

Lachie swallowed hard, then ducked his shaggy head in mingled submission and acceptance.

'Very well, then, come and see me in the Wellmeadow shop tomorrow morning.'

Mister Todd turned towards the door, fumbling for the latch. He couldn't find it in the gloom. Islay went to his side; her hand touched his lightly, moved on, found the latch, and opened the door.

He stepped into the lane, and would have walked away if Islay hadn't followed him and touched his arm.

'Well? What d'you want now?'

The drizzle had stopped and the sky had begun to clear. A watery sunbeam fell onto Islay's uplifted face, dazzling her.

'Mister Todd – we're grateful for your kindness. You'll not have cause to regret it.' Then, as he stared down at her in silence, she asked, 'Is there something amiss, Mister Todd?'

'No,' he said at last. 'I was just thinking – there's an empty dwelling house above the loom shop in Wellmeadow that might do you better than this place –'

*

As he walked back home Jamie cursed himself for a weak, loose-tongued fool. He had had no intention of doing as Margaret asked, and letting the Highlanders live in his empty house.

But there was something about the older girl's spirited determination to survive, something about her face when the sunlight fell on it in those last moments; it was too pale and too thin, that face, but its fragility only served to highlight her flawless skin, a covering for the delicate, exquisitely fine bones beneath it; the dark, long-lashed eyes under finely drawn brows; the rich blue-black sheen of her thick hair.

She was only a child, this Highland girl who had travelled all the way from the mountains and glens of her homeland to blossom to womanhood unnoticed in the slums of Paisley. Only a child, and yet –

Again, Jamie cursed himself. But what was done was done. For better or for worse, he had saddled himself with Islay McInnes and her kinfolk.

Chapter Eight

On the following morning Islay hurried along to Jamie Todd's weaving shop in Wellmeadow, telling herself over and over as she went that Mister Todd had no doubt changed his mind, or found a better use for the rooms he had spoken of.

Years of hoping, then having these hopes dashed, had taught her that she could rely on nobody. The people of her clan had trusted the lairds who owned the land, yet in the space of a breath the habits and rights of generations had been overturned to make way for cattle and wool-bearing sheep.

In her wanderings since then Islay had seen many promises go sour, many folk who had been kindly enough in the beginning tire of the burden of homeless Highlanders and turn away from them, sending them off on their journeying again. She had seen her parents and her aunt die, her uncle and cousin grow bitter through enforced idleness.

Jamie Todd would like as not be the same as the others — regretting his talk of empty rooms almost as soon as the words were out of his mouth.

Islay couldn't understand why the man had made the offer in the first place. She had a feeling that he couldn't understand it, either. Which made it all the more likely, she told herself, walking faster as though by reaching him quickly she could forestall it, for another change of mind.

She stumbled over a raised stone and almost fell against someone.

'Mind your feet, lassie,' the man said roughly, in a hurry himself, and passed by without giving heed to her apology.

She went on, paying more attention to the path now. Four years before, the Council had forbidden the townsfolk to toss their household refuse out of their street doors onto the path; now, each family had to keep its midden at the back of the house. So at least there was no longer any danger of the passer-by being tripped up by a pile of stinking rubbish extending from the house wall to the roadway. But the footpaths, particularly in the town's older wynds and streets, were still rough and muddy and treacherous underfoot.

Islay reached the loom shop without any further mishap. A pend, an open, arched passageway, ran from the street to the back yard. A door in the wall of the pend led to the weaving-shop; she timidly knocked, then went in.

The second of Jamie Todd's loom shops was large enough to accommodate two handlooms and two drawlooms. The intricate drawloom harness, reaching to the ceiling, dwarfed the others.

The room was a confused clutter of sound – the clack of the handlooms, the louder clatter and thump of the harness looms as the upper mechanism lifted to raise the warp threads, then fell back to lower them again, the musical skirl of the caged birds by the window, a sudden rich deep bellow as one of the weavers raised his voice in song.

Islay's eyes fell first on Lachie who, bare feet planted solidly on the earthen floor, was already working the harness, his small face intent on what he was doing. It was humid in the shop, and the sleeves of his over-large shirt had been rolled up to just below the shoulder.

Muscles corded on his scrawny arms as he pulled with all his might on the gut cords that lifted alternate groups of warp threads in an intricate and carefully-worked system, allowing the weaver to create a more elaborate pattern than the handlooms could ever achieve.

She was relieved to see that Lachie's weaver looked cheerful enough. She had heard stories of weavers who treated their drawboys cruelly, but at least the lad seemed to be working with a kindly man.

Jamie Todd was sitting on the side windowsill studying a sketch. He looked up as Islay went to stand before him.

For just a moment, as he recognised her, his jaw tightened and his blue eyes went dark. She felt her heart constrict, tensed herself for the dismissal that was sure to come.

Then he tossed the piece of paper down and rose, brushing past her, indicating with a movement of the head that she should follow him back into the pend.

As she did so she saw that Walter Shaw was working at one of the looms. The youth looked up, caught her eye, and ducked his head again quickly, faint colour staining his cheekbones.

'You've come to look at the dwelling house,' Mister Todd said almost coldly when they were outside, away from the noise.

'Aye, sir, if it's not too much trouble.'

'Now's as good a time as any, I suppose.' He led her through to the back and up a flight of wooden stairs fastened to the rear wall of the building.

Then he unlocked the door of the dwelling house and motioned her to go on ahead of him.

Islay stepped past him, and found Paradise on earth.

The first, and larger, of the two rooms was easily twice the size of the one room she shared with Lachie and Morag in Jenny's Wynd. The floor was good strong wooden timbers, sound and free from dampness.

The walls were of white-washed stone, and two glazed, deep-silled windows, one looking out over the busy street, the other to the back, provided ample light. The open fireplace had a hinged 'swee' to enable a kettle to be swung over the flames to heat, then swung out into the room for easy access. There was a wall-bed recess, and a door that stood ajar in the corner revealed a deep-shelved larder.

Tiptoe-ing, afraid to make a noise in case the spell broke, or she woke and found herself huddled in the bed in Jenny's Wynd, Islay pushed the inner door open and found herself in a smaller room, this one with a single window looking out onto the street.

An impatient clearing of the throat from outside reminded her that Jamie Todd was waiting. When she rejoined him he was at the outer door, looking down over the yard.

'There's work needing done down there –' He swept an arm out to indicate the over-grown area beneath. 'I'd expect you to tend it.'

'I could grow kale, and potatoes. And mebbe keep some bees – and some hens, if you'd not mind.'

'Do as you wish, as long as you look after things.' He started down the stairs.

'Mister Todd.'

He stopped, looked up at her with irritation darkening his face. 'Aye? You want the place, don't you?'

'Oh, I do! But – how much would the rent be?'

'No need to think about that.' He continued on his way. Islay stood her ground.

'But I do. I must.'

'Confound it, lassie, either take the house or stay in that stinking hutch you inhabit now! Don't go fretting me with talk of rent. Now – are you biding, or are you going?'

Her heart sank like a stone. She cast one last look at the roomy, light-filled interior of the house, then closed the door slowly. The click of the latch was like the tolling of a death-knell.

'I'm going.' She picked up her skirts and began to descend the stairs. 'Thank you for letting me see the rooms.'

'But – what's amiss with you now?'

'We cannot live here without paying you rent.'

'I don't want your money!'

'If we pay nothing, you can put us out whenever it pleases you. I've Lachie and Morag to think of – I couldn't let that happen to them.'

He gave her a sapphire-hard look, then asked abruptly, 'What d'you pay to the creature that cries himself a landlord to the place you live in now?'

When she named the sum, he gave a short angry laugh. 'I might have known it would be twice what the place is worth. Very well then, pay me the same.'

'It's not enough!'

'Can you afford more?'

'No, but – it's not enough, not for a place as fine as this.' She drew herself upright. 'We don't ask for charity, Mister Todd – or accept it.'

'You may not be a fool, but you're a nuisance,' said Jamie Todd in heartfelt tones. 'Listen to me. Pay me the same as you're paying in Jenny's Wynd, and in addition you can tend the yard and keep the weaving shop clean. In return, you'll have my oath on it that I'll not put you out on the streets. Will that satisfy your stiff-necked Highland pride?'

She considered, then nodded.

'Thank the Lord that's settled,' he said.

Then he went back to his weaving shop, and left her in possession of her new home.

*

Two days later she was down on her knees in the Well-meadow kitchen, singing softly as she scrubbed the kitchen floor, when a shadow darkened the open doorway and she looked up to see Mister Todd hesitating on the wooden landing.

She jumped to her feet, drying her hands on her sacking apron. 'Come in, sir.'

For a moment she thought that he was going to refuse, then he came slowly through the doorway, ducking his head beneath the lintel.

'Is the other lassie not helping you to prepare the place?'

'She's sorely troubled with her lungs today. I made her stay in bed.'

'Has she been ailing for long?'

'Since our first winter away from our own home.'

'Has a physician seen her? No, of course not,' he answered his own question.

'Physicians cost silver, Mister Todd.'

'I've a friend, Thomas Montgomery, who'd have a look at her. I'll speak to him.' Then he added, as Islay opened her mouth to argue, 'Or is your pride more important than the bairn's health?'

She flushed hotly and said nothing.

'That's settled, then.' He looked about the empty room. 'What are you going to do for furniture?'

'Mistress Knox came to Jenny's Wynd yesterday to see me. She has some pieces we can use, she says.'

'No doubt,' said Jamie Todd dryly, and left as suddenly as he had arrived.

Plunging the scrubbing brush back into the basin of

water, Islay puzzled over the man's strange blend of antagonism and kindness. It was almost as though Mister Todd was helping her family against his will.

It was as though Mister Todd was fighting an inner war with himself, and in some way that she couldn't fathom, Islay McInnes had become his battlefield.

Chapter Nine

'I'll go along today to see how the Highlanders are settling in. I knew I'd get Jamie to see things my way,' Margaret said with smug self-satisfaction.

Gavin, tying his stock about his throat, glanced at her reflection in the mirror. 'You always do.' His tone was mocking, but affectionate.

'Well, it's a mortal sin, letting two good rooms lie empty when the lanes down by the river are fair crammed with folk in need of a good roof over their heads and solid walls to keep the wet out.'

He turned away from the looking glass and picked up his jacket. 'I'd like to see these hovels pulled down. They're a disgrace to the name of Paisley. Most folk wouldn't keep their dogs in places like these.'

'My father would tell you – and so would my Aunt Mary – that it's up to the people down by the river to make something of their own lives, and not expect others to do it for them.'

Gavin grunted in reply. He and Margaret had fought many a battle with the older generation over that sore issue.

When the day's housework was done to her satisfaction Margaret left Ellen in charge of small Daniel and set off for the Wellmeadow house with Christian, who had clamoured to accompany her.

Islay greeted the two of them with a radiant smile. 'Morag, we've got a visitor,' she called, and her young cousin came shyly from the inner room.

Margaret stepped inside, casting a swift eye over the place. The house was spotless, and the pieces of furniture that she had managed to gather from all over the town were already in place.

'It looks grand!' She ran a hand over the back of a chair,

noting the high polish on all the woodwork, the gleaming black range, the fresh curtains at the window. 'You've been working hard.'

'We all have. You'll take some tea?' Islay asked, and this time Margaret was able to accept, and to sample some freshly-made scones. Christian was clamouring to be allowed to go into the back yard, and Morag timidly offered to take her.

When the two girls had gone out, Margaret asked, 'Is your cousin's health any better for the move?'

'I'm sure it is. Mister Todd asked a friend of his, a physician, to have a look at her.'

'That'll be Thomas Montgomery, my brother.'

'He says it was the damp house that caused the trouble, and that this place, and good food, will be the saving of her. I'm so grateful, Mistress Knox. I think another year in Jenny's Wynd would have been the death of Morag.'

'And how's your brother getting on with Walter?'

'Och, they're fine together. Walter's not a bad soul – laddies always enjoy fighting. Mister Todd's warned them both well – any trouble and they'll have to find another employer. And Lachie well knows,' the soft Highland voice added ' – that we can't afford to lose our new home.'

Margaret watched the girl as she moved about the room with the springing energy of youth. Happiness and free- dom from anxiety had already brought about changes in Islay. Her long black hair was glossy, her eyes shone, her face had begun to fill out.

Her shabby, ill-fitting clothing had been replaced by a full-skirted dark red gown that Margaret had given her, with a white fichu over her shoulders, and a plain white linen cap sat neatly on her smooth dark hair.

Margaret, suddenly aware that she herself had left her youth behind and was now approaching her thirties, envied the natural grace of the girl's movements. One day in the not too distant future Islay McInnes was going to be a beautiful woman.

Someone knocked at the outer door. Islay opened it, and Margaret saw that Walter Shaw stood there.

'The surgeon's waiting downstairs for Mistress Knox.'

Margaret rose and went to the door. 'Tell him I'll be down directly.'

Walter ducked his head in answer, then lifted it and looked again at Islay before turning away. The intensity of his glance struck Margaret forcibly, but Islay didn't seem to notice it.

Perhaps, thought Margaret as the two of them began to descend the wooden stairs, the girl was still too young and naive to be aware of the attraction she held for the young weaver.

*

Islay's work was evident to Margaret as soon as she walked into the loom shop. It was accepted in Paisley that the drawboys should keep the machines clean and in good working condition, and sweep the floors each morning.

But some strange tradition that had subtly established itself said that drawboys didn't have to be responsible for the hearths. That was woman's work. As a result, the fireplaces in most of Paisley's loom shops, other than those with drawgirls, were messy, ash-ridden areas, tended now and then, with much grumbling, by the weavers' wives. Margaret had always felt that it was an unfair tradition.

In this loom shop, the fireplace that had always been an affront to a self-respecting housewife was clean and sweet, shining from the same vigorous polishing that Margaret had seen upstairs. She looked it over, and nodded in silent approval.

The drawloom Lachie worked at had stopped while the weaver untangled some yarn. As he went about his task, the man sneaked puzzled glances at Gavin and Lachie, who were over by the window.

Gavin was examining the boy's arm closely. Lachie looked worried, and bit his underlip as he looked down on the surgeon's bent head. Jamie, also puzzled, stood by. 'Margaret, here a minute –' Gavin called.

When she and Islay joined him he said absently, 'I thought I might find you here, so I looked in in the passing. See here –' He indicated a white puckered scar that marred the skin on Lachie's upper arm.

'Is there something wrong with Lachie?' Islay asked swiftly, her eyes large with apprehension.

'No – far from it. Tell Mistress Knox how you came by that scar, laddie.'

'It's –' Lachie, worried at finding himself the centre of so much attention, looked at his cousin for support, swallowed hard, then said, 'It's only the kindly pox, mistress.'

'The –?'

''Tis only the way to keep the pox at bay, that's all,' Islay's voice sang with relief. 'All the bairns at home have it done.'

'How did your physician go about it?' Gavin wanted to know, and the girl looked at him pityingly.

'Och, we'd no need of physicians. One of the old men had the way of it, and the womenfolk took their wee ones to him.'

Margaret listened, appalled, as the girl casually explained how the old man had used a sharp knife to ease a piece of the outer skin free, then rubbed the area with what he called the 'kindly pox', a substance obtained from diseased cattle. To her, it sounded barbaric. Gavin, however, paid rapt attention to every word, making Islay repeat one or two pieces of information.

'Didn't your arm bleed?'

'Not at all. He put a wee bit leaf over the place and it soon healed.'

'What happened next?'

'After that the fever comes, and the bairns have to be kept abed, away from everyone else, till they're better. It passes after a few days,' Islay said casually, and Margaret shivered.

'It's a wonder you didn't die of it!'

'Och, we never would. Nor the bad pox either. We can't catch that now.'

Then Jamie, not interested in the talk and impatiently aware of the time being lost in his weaving shop, curtly sent the young Highlanders back to their work, and Gavin and Margaret collected their daughter and took their leave.

After walking down the High Street they paused for a moment to rest before commencing the uphill climb to their home. The Cross offered a grand view of the busy stalls in the market place and the River Cart, with the Abbey ruins and the houses of the New Town sitting cheek by jowl on the opposite bank.

As she surveyed the scene Margaret was aware of a great feeling of contentment. The inkle loom she had had installed at the Poors' Hospital and the two other looms at the Todd's house were doing well. At the moment, unknown to Gavin, who would have disapproved, she was secretly looking out for a larger workshop so that she could bring in more of the ribbon-weaving looms and provide work for more of the Poors' Hospital women. When she had found it, Gavin would come round to the idea – she had no doubt of that.

Life was good, Margaret thought complacently, and put her hand on her husband's arm.

He didn't notice the caress. His face, she saw, had that closed pre-occupied look that she called his 'physician's face'.

After a moment Christian became restless, and the three of them turned their back on the Cross and continued their way home.

Chapter Ten

'No! I forbid it!'

'Margaret –'

'I'll not talk about it! How could you even think of doing such a thing to your own bairns, Gavin Knox!'

'Whose, then, if not my own?' Gavin asked in a maddeningly reasonable tone.

'How could you think of taking the knife to any child?'

'The Highlanders do it, and their bairns come to no grief.'

'The Highlanders –!' Margaret said, with Lowlander scorn for the folk who lived far from civilisation, and practised strange customs.

'Would you sooner see Christian and Daniel falling sick of the pox and dying as Kate's bairn died?'

'If they should fall sick it'll be God's will, and we'll do all we can to save them. But I'll not stand by and see it happen to them through your will!'

'I tell you I've spoken to a number of Highlanders over the past weeks, and so has Thomas. All their bairns've had the inoculation done. They're all healthy, Margaret.'

'So you and Thomas have decided that my wee ones should be made use of, have you?'

'It was nothing to do with your brother. He's no bairns of his own, and I have, so –'

'They're not just yours!' she rounded on him. 'I carried them and bore them. I nursed them and I've had the raising of them. You minded me yourself not four weeks past of the time we near lost Christian to the croup.'

'Now, Margaret –'

'You were sore vexed with me then for taking her down to the lanes by the river where the air's bad. And now –' Her voice broke with rage and she had to struggle to bring it under control again ' – now you and that heartless brother

52

of mine want to cut her arm and put poison into the wound and make her sicken and mebbe –'

'I want to save her from the pox!' he insisted. 'A surgeon's work should be to stop folk from falling sick as well as trying to cure them. And it's my idea, not Thomas's, so keep your tongue off him.'

There was a short angry silence. Gavin stood by the fireplace, Margaret by the window. The space of the parlour lay between them, the air so thick with emotion that she felt as though she could reach out and gather it up by the handful.

'The Highlanders have been keeping their children safe from the pox for years by the same methods,' he said at last, in his most reasonable voice. 'It's here, in the Lowlands, that we're putting our bairns in danger by being slow and stubborn.'

'Slow and stubborn, is it? It seems to me that you're more willing to put Christian and Daniel in danger than I am.'

'You're being unjust, Margaret. I might be able to save scores of children – hundreds, even – with this method. But how can I persuade folk to let me vaccinate their bairns when I don't vaccinate my own?'

'And if they take the pox?'

'They won't.'

'Only God knows that, Gavin. Only He's got the right to play with lives – not you, and not Thomas. If you cut one child, and that child falls sick and dies, you'll be guilty of murder.'

'And if a child that's been denied vaccination falls to the pox and dies?'

'It's the will of God.'

His laugh was chillingly bitter. 'What a Saviour He must be, to take wee bairns in such suffering.'

'You'll not blaspheme in my house, Gavin Knox!'

'Why, Margaret, I've never known you to be so pious,' he mocked her, and she doubled her hands into fists to prevent them from picking up the fine china bowl her Aunt Mary had given them for a wedding gift and bouncing it off his thick skull. Then he added, 'And it's my house, come to that.'

'Take care then, lest I leave you in it and go elsewhere.'

The words lay heavily between them. They had been spoken in thoughtless haste, but she knew by the sudden widening of his eyes, the almost inperceptible gasp as he drew his breath in sharply, that he believed her.

When he spoke again his voice was chillingly cold. 'What would you have me do, then? Vaccinate the children in the Poors' House?'

'No, of course not! They might be poor wee unwanted souls, but you've surely not fallen so low that you'd use them like beasts to suit your own purposes – in the name of progress!'

The barb struck home. He flushed a dark, angry red, then turned on his heel and left the room. Margaret, her fists pressed tightly to her thumping heart, heard the door of the small room that housed all Gavin's books and papers and medical apparatus close with a crisp controlled sound that seemed worse than a resounding slam.

After a long moment she went upstairs and into the children's room. Christian, the hoyden, lay on her side, the coverlet tucked beneath her chin, her long lashes neatly ranged on her cheeks, her mouth primly buttoned. Margaret wondered what sort of dreams kept her daughter so still and tidy during the night.

By contrast Daniel, a sturdy, sober little boy by day, lay on his back in a tangle of sheets, his pillow on the floor, his mouth open, his strongly defined black eyebrows, which were oddly mature and seemed to be waiting for the round baby face to 'grow into them' as though they were an over-large pair of britches, twitching now and then.

As Margaret tried to ease the pillow beneath his head he opened wide blue eyes, focused blearily on her face, and gave her a sudden sweet smile before sleep claimed him again. As it did so his arm flailed above his head and knocked the pillow back to the floor.

Margaret stood between the two cots, listening to her children's breathing. They were more dear to her than anything or anyone else, even Gavin.

Not for the first time, she thought wryly that motherhood was only a way of delivering up hostages to the Fates. She would never again be free to follow her own will. And Gavin knew it.

*

They spent the night apart, Margaret in their bed chamber, Gavin downstairs. By the time she woke in the big, lonely bed, dressed, and made her way to the lower floor her husband had broken his fast and left for Glasgow, where he was due to spend the day in one of the infirmaries.

He had left word with Ellen that he would be late home.

The day passed drearily for Margaret. She irritated Ellen and the children by insisting on turning out cupboards and washing all the linen. The house was thrown into a turmoil, and by the afternoon every bush in the garden was festooned with sheets and towels and Ellen was tight-lipped at the thought of the amount of ironing that would have to be done on the following day.

Finally, having polished and scrubbed until she was exhausted, Margaret took herself off to the Poors' House to visit some of her pupils in the sick-room, where they had been laid low by what Margaret sardonically called the 'poor fever'.

The name had first come to her when, as a young teacher in the Poors' House, she had heard the master and mistress dismissing a fever that was prevalent in the place as something that 'just happened' to the poor. Margaret, to mask her anger, had flippantly suggested that the fever was attributed to some chronic carelessness on the part of the paupers, and her suggestion had been considered seriously then agreed with, much to her surprise.

Now, years later, the 'poor fever' was still around. Every inmate of the House could be sure of falling prey to it at least once during their stay.

Afterwards, still restless, she called in on Kirsty, Jamie's mother. Kate was there with her small daughter. Although she looked well, with the bloom of a healthy pregnancy adding to her natural beauty, Kate's eyes were still dark with grief over the loss of her son.

'I know I've still got Alyson, and that the coming bairn'll help me to get over my loss, but somehow –' Her eyes filled with tears that she couldn't blink back, 'I know that there's nothing in the world that can bring John back to me. And it's knowing that that makes it so hard to stop missing him.'

Margaret was in a chastened mood when she left her friend. She wanted nothing more than to get back to her own two children, and to see Gavin smile lovingly at her again. Their quarrel had been one of the worst they had ever experienced in their stormy marriage, and she wanted it to be over and done with.

A lane led to Oakshawhill from a pend in the High Street, hard by the old almshouse. At the other end of the lane Margaret emerged onto a road that was quieter and cleaner than the town streets, flanked with large houses on each side.

The air was purer here, and heavy with the fragrance of the late summer roses in the big gardens.

She slowed her walk, inhaling the scent, letting her mind empty itself of all irritations. A pleasant September day was coming to a graceful end, and the retiring sun set the sky to the west ablaze with tongues of crimson and gold.

The house was pleasantly quiet as she let herself in and hung her cloak on its peg in the hall. The children would already be abed, and Ellen preparing the evening meal in the kitchen.

The parlour was flooded with golden evening sunlight that poured in through the west-facing windows. Dazzled, Margaret paused in the doorway, then as her vision became accustomed to the light she saw the tall figure standing by the fireplace.

'Gavin! I didn't think you'd be home. Oh – I'm so glad!'

He had been studying one of the ornaments on the mantelpiece. As he turned she ran into his arms, holding him close, burying her face in his chest.

For a terrible moment he stood passively within her embrace and she thought that the anger of the previous evening was still with him. Then to her relief his arms closed about her.

'We must never be harsh with each other again,' Margaret said fiercely into his chest. 'Never, never ag –'

She lifted her head, seeking his lips with her own, and the

words died in her throat.

The man who held her in his arms said, 'Forgive me, madam – I think there's a slight misunderstanding.'

Chapter Eleven

'Oh –!' Margaret drew back sharply, pulling away from him, retreating step by step in the direction of the door. Unfortunately the bell-pull was by the fireplace, close to his shoulder, and therefore out of her reach. But one hand moved behind her, feeling for the door-handle.

'Mistress Margaret Knox?' He made no attempt to follow her, but stood still, turning both hands palms-up in a gesture of good-will. 'Your maid-servant permitted me to come in and wait for you.'

Her finger-tips brushed the door-panel. 'Who are you?'

'If, as I suppose, you're Margaret, then I'm your brother by marriage. My name is Richard – Richard Knox.'

Her hand fell away from the door. 'Richard?'

'Has Gavin never spoken of me?' His broad shoulders lifted in a faint shrug; his mouth, so like Gavin's, twisted slightly. 'Perhaps not. We parted with bad feeling and we've not had contact with each other these six or seven years now. It would be like Gavin to cut me from his life entirely.'

Margaret moved back into the room. 'I knew that Gavin had a brother who left home and went abroad.'

'Who quarrelled with all and sundry and ran off, over the seas and far away,' he corrected her, smiling now. 'And they all said good riddance to him, I've no doubt, and assumed that damnation would overtake him. But the Devil chose to look after his own and so –' His hands moved again, this time to flick their finger-tips lightly against the satin lapels of his smart blue coat. ' – here I am, come to pay my respects to my brother and his wife. Unsure of my welcome, which turned out to be warmer than I had hoped.'

The amusement in his voice brought colour surging back to her face. 'The sun was shining in my eyes. I'd naturally expected to find my husband here.'

'A fortunate husband, to have such a loving wife.'

His voice had the same rich depths as Gavin's, but there was more of a drawl to it. Margaret recalled, tardily, that the man was a guest in her home.

'Gavin's in Glasgow, but I expect him back before long. Did Ellen not offer you any refreshment, Mister Knox?'

'Richard. She did indeed, but I chose to wait until I had company.'

She indicated the corner cupboard where Gavin kept the glasses and decanters. 'Please take whatever you'd like. I must just go and see that the supper's being attended to.'

He bowed, and she fled to the kitchen, demanding angrily as she burst in, 'Why did you not send word to me that we'd a visitor? Why did you not tell me in the hall?'

Ellen, sampling a pot of broth, screamed and let the ladle go. It splashed into the simmering mixture and droplets flew up to spatter the maid's face.

A few minutes later, while Margaret busily soothed the burns with a cloth wrung out in cold water, Ellen eyed her reproachfully.

'A body could die of a fright like that!'

'D'you think I should rap on my own kitchen door, now?'

'I mean, I didnae even know you were in the house at all,' Ellen grumbled. 'You must have come from outside like a mouse. I meant to catch you in the hall and tell you about your caller.'

Margaret thrust the cloth into the woman's hand and turned her own attention to the food cooking on the range.

'Well – I found him for myself. The master's brother, it seems. Is there enough to do four of us instead of three?'

'He's got an awful dark-coloured face for a Scotsman.'

'He's been in far countries.' Margaret peered and poked and stirred, her mind swiftly dividing a meal meant for three into a meal that would do four, her inner eye picturing the servings. 'We'll manage – if you and me don't eat much. Mind that, now. You can fill your belly with bread and bannocks for once. And if Mister Knox isn't home in another thirty minutes you'd best serve the supper anyway and he can have his later. Now – do I look all right?'

Ellen cast an eye over her mistress, and nodded. 'You

look fine. Will he be staying the night?'

Margaret tutted irritably. 'I never thought to ask about that. You'd best get the wee room upstairs ready, just in case.'

'Aye,' said Ellen, adding, as Margaret made for the door again, 'He's awful like the master, is he no'?'

'Not a bit of it,' said Margaret crushingly.

Richard Knox stood by the parlour window, gazing out. He turned to face her, the firelight striking a rich red glow from the glass in his hand. The sun had set and the room was dim enough for his teeth to gleam briefly as he smiled at her.

'You've no Jamaican rum in your cupboard.'

'Gavin never developed a taste for it.' Then, as Richard raised his brows, she added in her husband's defence, 'Claret and good Scots whisky seem to suit his palate well enough.'

'I built my fortune on rum. I shall see to it that he has a half-dozen bottles within the week.'

He watched in silence as she busied herself about the room, poking the fire, using a taper to light the lamps.

When she finally ran out of things to do and settled in her usual chair he came across the room and offered her a glass that had been waiting, unnoticed, on a small table nearby.

'I don't drink spirits.'

He seated himself in the chair opposite – Gavin's chair. 'And I hate to drink alone. It's claret, not whisky. Just a sip or two, while I tell you why I've suddenly arrived on my brother's doorstep out of the past.'

Margaret was not fond of liquor, but to her surprise the claret went down very well. As she sipped, relaxing into the cushions of her chair, Richard Knox talked about four years spent in Jamaica, a fifth in America's deep south, and a sixth among the cotton manufactures of Lancashire before he finally decided to return to the land of his birth.

Margaret studied him in a series of quick glances when his own gaze was elsewhere.

He was probably a little heavier about the shoulders than Gavin, but of the same height. His clothes were both elegant and expensive, and he wore them with stylish grace.

Gavin's taste ran to dark colours, but Richard was a peacock in a vivid blue full-skirted satin-faced coat with a foam of snowy white lace at his throat, a heavily embroidered bronze waistcoat, fawn britches and brown boots. There were silver buttons on the coat and silver buckles on the boots.

As Ellen had said, his ruggedly handsome face was brown, no doubt from the Jamaican sun. His eyes were green with hazel highlights, while Gavin's tended to hazel shot through with flashes of pure emerald.

His warm brown hair, touched here and there with gold as the lamplight fell on it, was lighter than his brother's, but of the same strong springy texture. She knew exactly how it would feel beneath her fingers. He wore it tied back, but allowed it to curl crisply round his forehead and temples.

Although she knew that Richard was considerably younger than Gavin, he had an air of great maturity about him. In this man, Gavin's naturally confident bearing had become a casual arrogance which she found intimidating, and yet exciting.

Knuckles tapped at the door. 'It's gone time and he's never home yet, so I've put the food on the table,' Ellen announced with as much style as she could summon.

Richard talked on while they ate, surrounding Margaret with word pictures of skies bluer than she had ever seen for herself, cool sea breezes setting exotic blossoms a-nod, hot sands as white as fresh-fallen snow, sparkling seas and brown-skinned peoples.

The man could have been a poet, she thought at one point, then took another look at him and realised that she was wrong. Richard Knox was too world-wise, too strong in character to be a dreamer. His natural role in life was that of a leader, in full control. She sensed something almost menacing about him. He would make a formidable enemy, she had no doubt of that.

But this evening he had set himself out to charm, enchant, and amuse his new-found sister-in-law. He succeeded admirably. Long after the meal was over they sat on at the table, and the first thing Gavin Knox heard when he let himself into the hall was the sound of his wife's laughter from the small dining room to his right.

Margaret looked up to see him standing in the doorway, one eyebrow raised as he glanced from her to their visitor, who had his back to the door.

She rose and went to him at once. 'Gavin, see who's come to visit with us.'

Richard got to his feet without haste, and turned. 'Well, brother?' he said, and waited, one hand resting lightly on the back of his chair.

Gavin, drawn and exhausted after a long day walking the wards, looked and then looked again, unable to believe his own eyes. 'Richard?'

'Richard!' Margaret confirmed, putting a hand on his arm to lead him into the room. With surprise, she realised that through the thick sleeve of his jacket she could feel his muscles suddenly tense. 'Such a surprise – I could scarce believe it myself, at first.'

'But that made your welcome no less warm,' Richard put in, and she flushed, then laughed with him.

A mixture of expressions flowed over her husband's face. Shock, bewilderment, and then, of all things, anger that was quickly suppressed and replaced with the polite, formal smile Gavin, with what she always thought of as the caution of the Borderer, reserved for first meeting with strangers. After a moment he moved forward, pulling free of her touch as he went, and held his hand out to his brother.

'Welcome home, Richard. I confess that I never thought we'd set eyes on each other again.'

'And I thought to find you well settled in Dumfries, physicking the folk there. I'd occasion to come back across the water a year ago. By the looks of things, now that there's trouble started in the Americas, I've come back for good.'

'Give me your coat – I'll go and tell Ellen you're ready for your supper now –' Margaret watched Gavin's long flexible surgeon's fingers flip buttons from buttonholes, then she bounced onto her tiptoes to help him ease the coat off. She hung it up in the hall, making a mental note to sponge and brush it first thing in the morning, before he left the house, then hurried to warn Ellen, dozing by the fire, that her master was home, and hungry.

Finally, she poured generous measures of whisky into two glasses. About to leave the room with a glass in each hand she hesitated, then went back to put glasses and decanter onto a small tray which she carried carefully across the square hall to the dining rom.

Gavin accepted his glass with a brief, pre-occupied smile, emptied it in two gulps, and refilled it. Ellen bustled in with a steaming bowl in one hand and a platter of bread in the other.

As Gavin began to eat hungrily and Richard resumed his account of his adventures Margaret sat down again and looked from one to the other of the brothers.

She herself had always felt that she had two families in her background – the Todds as well as the Montgomerys – and she had pitied Gavin's solitary state. His parents had both died while he was in Glasgow studying medicine, and he had made only casual mention of the brother who had left home.

Margaret, who had first met Gavin when her brother Thomas brought him to her parents' house, knew that it was the very solidarity of Thomas's family life that had caught and held the lonely young surgeon's interest, bringing him back to Paisley again and again until eventually love blossomed and he and Margaret had married.

He had welcomed fatherhood with open delight. At last he had his own family, and she took great pleasure in the knowledge that she had been the one to bring him such happiness.

But now that his brother, his own blood-kin was sitting in Gavin's home, his handsomely booted feet beneath Gavin's table, there was something wrong. Although her husband talked and smiled and even laughed on two occasions Margaret knew that in his mind he had set up a wall between himself and Richard.

'How did you know where to find me?'

Richard twirled the stem of his glass between his fingers. 'It was a most amazing happening. After making enough money in Jamaica to satisfy my immediate needs I decided to investigate the Americas. From there my new interest in cotton took me to the big manufactories in the North of England, then to Glasgow and the exporting business.'

'Did you never think to go to Dumfries?' Gavin's voice was sharp, and Richard shot him a sidelong glance from beneath lowered lids.

'I went, of course – only to find that our parents were long buried, the old house sold and nobody about the place who knew what had become of you, except that you were a surgeon and settled somewhere near Glasgow. I had it in mind to search for you, but before I could start in earnest my business brought me to Paisley, to a weaver called Duncan Montgomery. Imagine my surprise when it came out in the course of our talk that his daughter was wed to a surgeon from Dumfries with the same surname as myself, and that they lived not a mile from the weaving shop where I stood.'

'So you're interested in the Paisley cloth?'

Richard's vivid eyes tured to Margaret. 'I'm interested, dear sister, in anything that makes money. And there's silver to be had in every throw of a Paisley shuttle. I have access to a particularly good cotton thread spun in the English manufactories. I'm hoping that your father and others of his trade will agree to use it.'

'Would this thread suit the inkle looms as well?'

'Margaret –' Gavin warned.

'The inkle looms?'

'Small looms used for weaving tapes and ribbons. I have four in operation at the moment, and I hope to have more soon.'

Again, Gavin started to say something, but was interrupted by a betraying, jaw-cracking yawn.

Richard rose immediately. 'You've had a long day, and here I am, keeping you from your bed. I'll leave you now, and hope to call on you tomorrow.'

'Where will you go?'

'I've lodgings in Glasgow. I left my horse in stables at the foot of the hill, so I've not far to go.'

'Oh, but you must stay here, with us. We'll not hear of you lodging in Glasgow when your own kin lie not five miles distant. Will we, Gavin?'

There was a faint, almost imperceptible pause before Gavin came to stand by his wife. 'Margaret's right. You must stay here tonight, Richard. Your mount'll do well enough in the stables till morning.'

'And in the morning you can send to Glasgow for your things. If your business lies in Paisley, it makes sense for you to bide in the town. Ellen got the room ready hours ago,' Margaret said decisively, and Richard shrugged in submission, and smiled.

'I'd heard that Paisley folk are the most hospitable in the West of Scotland. Now I know it's true.'

'You were over-quick with your offer of hospitality,' Gavin said coolly when they were alone in the privacy of their bedchamber.

'But he's your kin – your own brother. Surely it's natural to offer him a room under your roof.' She lay in bed watching him undress.

His hand carefully smoothed the shirt he had laid over a chair. 'I'd have appreciated the chance to decide that for myself.'

'Gavin Knox, sometimes I can't make head nor tail of you!'

He said nothing, but blew the candle out.

The mattress moved slightly beneath Margaret as his big body settled beside her. She lay for a moment looking into the darkness, listening to his breathing. After five years of marriage, it still gave her a thrill of pleasure to know that she was sharing his bed, even if, as now, they weren't touching each other.

Into the darkness, she said, 'I like your brother.'

'Do you?' His voice was non-committal.

'What's amiss, Gavin?'

'Nothing's amiss,' he said, and a few minutes later he was asleep.

Chapter Twelve

'How many ribbon looms did you say you had?' Richard asked on the following morning, after Gavin had left the house.

Christian and Daniel had been charmed with him from the first moment they set eyes on him. For an hour their new uncle had played with them, before sending them out into the garden and seeking Margaret. He found her on her knees in the parlour, polishing table legs.

'Inkle looms?' She sat back on her heels, glad of a rest. 'Only four at the moment. The women from the Poors' House weave ribbons on them, to earn a little money. See –' she opened a drawer and brought sample of the work to him. He ran it through his strong fingers.

'Where d'you get the thread? And who buys the finished product?'

'The thread comes from some of our own spinsters. My father sells the ribbons along with the linen cloth made on the looms owned by himself and my brother Robert, and Jamie Todd.'

Richard handed the ribbon back. 'The Lancashsire thread I have to offer would do very well on your looms. And I think I could find a market for it in the Americas and farther afield.'

'But we're at war with the Americas.'

Richard's eyes sparkled at her from beneath lazy lids. 'Women need cloth and ribbons, war or no war. There are ways. You only have a few of these looms, you said?'

'Two in the Poors' House, and another two in a room at one of Jamie's loom shops. I'd like fine to have more, for there's plenty of women would like the work. But it costs money to find the machinery and the premises.'

'As to money, I've more than enough to spare for a

venture that might bring in more again.' He got to his feet, took her hand, and drew her up beside him. 'Show me one of those looms, sister.'

'Now? But I've the housework to do, and the ironing to see to, and –'

'Let your servant do it,' said Richard with a casual arrogance that would have angered her in anyone else. But it was impossible to be angry with Richard.

'We'll take the children with us. This Jamie Todd – I seem to recall your father using his name too. Do they work together?'

'My father and my brother and Jamie have fourteen looms between them. My father sells the cloth that they make.'

'Indeed? Show me the looms you own in Jamie Todd's shop, then, for I've a mind to talk with him, too.'

*

They walked down the hill, the children scampering ahead, the two saddle-bags holding Richard's thread samples riding easily over his broad shoulder.

Margaret was pleasantly aware of the curious, sometimes covetous glances of the women who passed by. One or two who knew her well stopped them and managed to gain an introduction to Gavin's brother. In every case, Richard set them a-flutter and a-simper.

'I can't think why you never gained a wife during your travels,' she said dryly as they neared the High Street loom shop. 'Indeed, I can't think how you managed to avoid one.'

He grinned. 'A man travels easier without responsibilities.'

'You and Gavin are so like each other in looks, and yet so unlike each other in every other way.'

'He was born with his feet planted firmly on the ground,' Gavin's brother said. 'Whereas I, dear Margaret –'

'You were born with your head in the clouds?'

'Oh no, never that. I was born to succeed,' said Richard and then they were at the door, and the children were already racing each other up the stairs to Kirsty's kitchen.

Richard watched the inkle looms at work for some time, his eyes alight with interest.

He talked to the raw-boned, poverty-pale women who worked the looms; and as he did so Margaret noted with interest that there was no trace of the ruthlessness she had sometimes glimpsed beneath the surface. At that moment he was more like Gavin, gentle and courteous and reassuring, bringing pleasure-colour to the women's faces, making them laugh, listening with interest to what they had to say.

Standing back, content to watch and listen, Margaret decided that the man was even more of a puzzle than she had first thought.

Jamie was working at his own loom in the apartment on the other side of the passageway. He got up from the saytree – the weaver's bench – to shake hands with the newcomer. The men, much the same height and build, sized each other up swiftly before Richard turned away to give his full attention to the looms.

'I see it's hand-looms you have.'

'There are two draw-looms in my other shop.'

'Margaret tells me that you work with her father and brother, weaving linen cloth.'

'Aye. Between us we've eleven hand-looms and three draw-looms.'

'I've been spending a fair bit of time in Lancashire. They've found it of benefit to bring all their looms into big buildings in England, instead of having a few here and a few there.'

Jamie's blue eyes cooled slightly. 'I know all about the English manufactories. Here in Paisley we do fine as we are.'

'You don't produce as much cloth as the manufactories, though.'

'We produce as much as we need to.'

'Linen cloth. Have you not thought of turning to cotton yarn?'

'There's plenty Paisley weavers on it already. But there's still a market for the linen, and we're content.'

'Richard has some English cotton yarn, Jamie –' Margaret chimed in.

'I have – and I'd like fine for you to have a look at it.'

Jamie shook his red head. 'We do well enough as we are,' he said stubbornly, and cast an impatient look at his idle loom.

Margaret took the hint and removed Richard, leading him upstairs to meet Kirsty and Billy.

*

'He's a stubborn man, Jamie Todd,' Richard said thoughtfully, when they were outside again.

'He's cautious.'

'He doesn't look like a cautious man to me. More of an adventurer.'

'He has been, in his time. But now that he's got responsibilities it's a different matter.'

'Responsibilities?'

'Towards his mother and step-father – and his weavers, of course. The weaving trade's not doing so well at the moment. Billy thinks Jamie's worried about it.'

'All the more reason to try something new, surely?'

'All the more reason,' Margaret pointed out patiently, 'to be careful, and wary of change.'

'Not a bit of it. As to your father and brother – are they as cautious as he is?'

'More so, I'd say.'

'But you're adventurous, Margaret. You'd be willing to try my thread on your inkle looms, would you not?'

She had liked the look of the English cotton yarn, finer and smoother than anything the Paisley spinsters could produce. It would be ideal for the inkle looms.

'Yes, indeed I would. But then, I've less to lose than the others. My looms earn very little.'

'You said last night that you'd like more looms.'

'That would take money.'

'I have money. Find yourself a loom-shop, and the machines to fill it, and the women to work them. Could you do that?'

She stopped so abruptly that Christian and Daniel came trotting back to find out what was wrong. 'Of course I could do it! Oh, Richard – d'you mean it?'

He laughed down at her indulgently. 'Certainly.'

'But – how could I pay you back?'

'We'll draw out an agreement. A proper partnership. The decisions will be yours. All I ask is that you use my yarn, and give me the ribbon to sell where I think fit. I'll take a percentage of each sale, and we'll all make a profit.'

'I've no wish to make a profit, I just want the Poors' House women to earn some money.'

'You must earn some yourself, or else there'd be no sense to the venture,' he said firmly.

'Gavin won't be pleased. He's against me giving up any more of my time to the Poors' House and its concerns.'

'My brother,' said Richard, 'lacks imagination. Does he need to know the full extent of our plans?'

'Yes, of course he –' She hesitated. She had never deceived Gavin before, but perhaps it would be better for his own peace of mind if he knew little about this latest venture for the moment. 'Well – mebbe I'll wait until I've got the weaving shop and the machines before I say anything.'

And by then, she thought guiltily, it would be too late for Gavin to protest. The deed would be done.

By her side, Richard said lightly, 'You see? The matter is easily decided, after all.'

Then he added, 'And perhaps you can do something for me in return. Ask your father and brother – and Jamie Todd – if I might have a meeting with them, to show them the English thread and talk to them about my ideas for a cotton cloth.'

'It'll do no good, Richard.'

'Perhaps not. But I've found that everything is worth the try.'

Chapter Thirteen

The meeting Richard wanted took place in Jamie's Well-meadow shop two afternoons later, after work had finished for the day.

It had long been the custom in Paisley for the weavers to set their own hours. They always began work early in the morning, and in the winter they usually went on until dusk, sometimes lighting candles or crusies so that they could continue after dark.

In the summer they preferred to stop early in the afternoons – unless the web on their machines was urgently needed – to take advantage of the good weather. Some went bowling, others walked or fished or swam, went to the cock-fights or worked in their gardens, a good number had formed themselves into debating societies, and more than a few, in this town of weavers, spent their leisure time reading, or writing poetry.

Richard had a persuasive tongue, but even so, he found himself outnumbered. The Montgomerys, father and son, were representative of their trade – stolid, hard-working men, eminently practical, and cautious when it came to money matters. They eyed each other uneasily as Richard outlined his plans. When he had finished, Duncan was the first to speak, after a long and thoughtful silence.

'You're proposing that we should give over our looms to this English thread and grant you the right to sell the cloth wherever you should find the best market for it?'

'Aye, that's the shape of it.'

'Your thread's bonny enough, there's no denying that –' Robert's voice and manner of speech was uncannily like his father's ' – but man, we're content enough with the yarn our own spinsters provide.'

'Tell me this – d'you get a goodly supply of yarn?'

'We can always do with more,' Jamie admitted. 'If a spinster falls sick we're sometimes hard put to it to make up the yarn we need, it's true.'

'But we aye manage,' Duncan Montgomery said shortly. As the oldest of the three men, it had fallen to him to lead the partnership they had set up. He heartily disliked and mistrusted the thought of change.

'And you've no trouble in selling your cloth?'

'None. We sell to a warehouse in Glasgow. He offers us fair prices.'

'Fair, mebbe – but no harm in looking into prices elsewhere.'

'I'd not want to let the man down, after all these years.'

Richard gave a snort of laughter. 'Man, he'd let you down this very day if it suited him! Now listen to what I've got to offer –'

Skilfully, swiftly, he outlined his plan. The Montgomery and Todd looms would start using the cotton yarn he could provide, and turn the resulting cloth over to him. He would then sell it to England, Europe or the Americas – wherever he found the highest bidder.

The silence fell again after he'd finished, then Jamie said cautiously, 'It's worth thinking on, Duncan.'

The older man's blue eyes travelled uneasily from face to face. 'We'd not be able to go back to our present merchant if the scheme went wrong and we had to return to the linen cloth.'

'It won't go wrong!'

Duncan's clear gaze settled firmly on Richard. 'Laddie, I've been weaving since ever before you tasted your mother's milk, and I've seen many a good man reduced to poverty because he tried to fly too high.'

'If everyone thought as you do, Mister Montgomery,' said Richard silkily, with just a hint of impatience in his even tones, 'there'd be no need for your cloth, for we'd all be living in caves and wearing animal hides – and all too frightened to try anything new.'

Duncan let the veiled sarcasm slide from his broad shoulders. 'Mebbe so. But if everyone thought as you do, Mister Knox, we'd all be in a sorry pickle. It takes all sorts to make up the world.'

'How many looms would you need to make enough cloth?' Jamie asked.

'As many as I can get. But if need be I could start with six, or eight.'

'Then can we not put some of our machines over to the new thread and keep others on the linen? I'd be willing to use half of mine – one of your two, Robert, and two of yours, Duncan –'

There was an instant, adverse reaction from the Montgomerys. 'That's madness!' Duncan said angrily, and his son chimed in with, 'We'd not make enough of one cloth or the other, Jamie. It's all the machines or none of them as I see it.'

The red-headed weaver fingered the thread again, then took a deep breath. 'I'm for trying it.'

'Why, in God's name?'

'Because the linen industry's bound to come to an end, Robert. Mebbe the time's come for us to turn to cotton.'

'I'm not happy about the market,' Robert said, and his father nodded.

'What guarantee do we have that you'll be able to sell this cloth you want us to weave for you, Richard?'

'My word on it.'

The Montgomerys eyed each other, then Duncan shook his head. 'Laddie, you might be Gavin's brother, and a fine upstanding man, just as he is. I'm not doubting that for an instant, you understand. But cloth's not your trade. I'd need more of an assurance than that.'

'The best assurance would be to weave the cloth and let me prove that I can sell it – and bring you orders for more.'

'And in the meantime,' Duncan pointed out, 'we'd have lost our own merchant. If your fine promises came to nothing, what would happen to us then?'

From where Jamie sat on his saytree, swung round so that the intricate wooden loom was behind him, he could see over Richard's shoulder and through the window. His attention was caught by a movement in the yard outside. He shifted position slightly and saw that Islay McInnes was digging the over-grown, weed-infested kale bed, her sleeves rolled up to above her elbows, a long scarf looped over her dark head and about her throat.

The argument raged on about his head as he watched the girl work. Mention of his own name brought him back, finally, to the business in hand.

'What did you say?'

'I said, I think you're in favour of trying out the scheme,' Richard repeated.

'It's worth considering.' All at once Jamie wanted the meeting to be at an end. The weaving shop had become claustrophobic.

'And I think it would be madness, at this time, for us to consider a change,' Robert said bluntly, and his father nodded.

'No offence to you, Mister Knox, for I'm certain that your scheme has merit. Mebbe other weavers in the town would be interested in hearing about it. For ourselves – we'll go on as we have done, for it suits us well enough.'

Richard studied Jamie thoughtfully before asking, 'And you, Mister Todd – d'you agree with that?'

Jamie hesitated, then said, 'The three of us have always worked together. I have to go with what Duncan and Robert say.'

Richard shrugged, rose, picked up his three-cornered hat, and bowed, his handsome face stiff with disappointment.

'In that case, gentlemen, I must thank you for listening to me so courteously, and take my leave.'

'The plan had its merits,' Jamie said when he had gone.

'Mebbe, but it was all too full of hopes and possibilities for me,' Duncan's voice was heavy with disapproval.

'I still think we could have given over some of the looms to his new thread.'

But the Montgomerys were both adamant. 'It would have been too great a risk,' Robert said, and his father added, 'Best to stay as we are. Caution's a good watchword.'

When they were gone Jamie stepped out into the pend and closed the loom shop door behind him.

He hesitated, hearing Duncan's voice, which still carried some of the inflections of his native Ayrshire, say again in his head, 'Caution's a good watchword.'

But caution had never come easily to Jamie Todd. Indeed, in his present restless mood the word filled him with irritation.

He turned towards the street, heard behind him the clang of a spade striking a hidden stone, changed his mind, and walked through the pend and into the yard.

*

'Give me the spade – I'll see to it for you.'

Islay's thoughts had been far away, in the glens of her childhood. She jumped at the sound of Jamie's voice, and looked up to see him standing before her, one hand oustretched.

'Och, I can manage fine.' She used the force of both arms to drive the blade into the hard, root-matted ground, planted one shabby, booted foot on it to force it in further, and bent to lever up a sod of black earth.

'But it's a man's work. Can Lachie not do it for you?'

'He's gone to fetch a settle that was promised us. And I can do this sort of work as well as any man.' She retained her grip on the spade handle, and got on with the business in hand. After a moment she risked a peep at the piece of ground before her. It was empty. He had gone.

Then, at the sound of another blade thunking into the ground nearby, she lifted her head to see that he hadn't gone any further than the house wall, to pick up an old rusting spade that leaned there.

It had been far too heavy for her, but Jamie Todd's muscles drove it hard into the ground, up to where the wooden handle joined the blade, then levered a solid mass of soil and roots free easily, turning it over, splitting it with the blade so that the earth crumbled and the pale strangling roots were exposed to daylight.

Then he straightened up and grinned at her. 'Two can make lighter work of it.'

She smiled back, and they worked on together in companionable, contented silence.

Chapter Fourteen

'So you've come home for good, Mister Knox?'

Mary MacLeod, Margaret's aunt, handed a teacup to her guest. Richard, who had learned impeccable drawing-room manners from somewhere during his travels, passed the cup to Margaret.

'Perhaps. If the trouble in the Americas eases I'd like to go back there, at least for a while.'

Mary tutted. 'That's a sorry business.'

Richard took his cup and sat down. 'It is indeed. It's going to hit trade badly if it isn't brought to an end soon,' he agreed blandly.

Then, to Margaret's amusement he flinched back, almost slopping tea into his saucer, as his hostess barked, 'Man, it's not trade I'm fretting over, it's folk that used to be friends spilling each other's blood! Why men never seem able to put an end to an argument without turning to swords or guns is beyond me!'

'But – if we let the American colonies dictate to us –' Richard made a valiant effort to rally, and was vocally beaten back against the wall and pinned there.

'Tuts, give the matter a bit of thought, can't you? It's like raising a family,' said Mary, who never had, but who knew better than most how it should be done. 'There comes a time when you've to stand back and let your bairns go out into the world on their own. It's the same with colonies.'

'I fail to see –'

'Aye well, you're a man,' she excused him kindly. 'So of course you'll not be able to follow my way of thinking. But it seems to me that if you were to picture Britain as a woman, and the Americas as her great lump of a bairn –'

'With respect, ma'am, I still cannot see –'

Mary shook an admonishing finger. 'With respect, sir,

that's because you havenae the patience to listen when you're being told. If you were to picture Britain and the Americas as a woman and her bairn – as I was saying – then you'd see that it's pure foolishness to suppose that we can go on leading it by the hand – or through a ring in its nose, depending on the way you look at it,' said Mary, mixing motherhood, which she had never experienced, with the farmyard where she herself had been raised. Then, having swept magnificently up the final stretch to the winning line, leaving Richard to come in a very poor second, she said, 'Are you ready for more tea, Mister Knox?'

'Your aunt's a lady who follows very – convolvulated thinking,' he said ruefully when he and Margaret left the house together an hour later.

'There's nobody can keep up with Aunt Mary when she's in one of her moods – except perhaps Thomas, and he does it by agreeing with everything she says.'

'All the same, I like her exceedingly well. She's got a – an air about her that pleases me,' he said approvingly, then turned to business. 'How are you getting on with your search for an empty loom shop?'

'I think I might have found one in the New Town across the river. Near to the Poors' House, but not close enough for folk to find out too much about my business before I'm ready to tell them.'

'Your business venture is having more success than mine,' Richard's voice was a trifle grim. 'There's a good overseas market for cotton cloth, and to my mind the Paisley weavers are the men to tackle it. But your father's not an easy man to deal with. And where he leads, the other two follow.'

'My father worked for Jamie's when he first came to Paisley, and it seems only natural now that the Montgomerys and the Todds work together. Robert used to be more interested in change and progress; I mind him arguing often enough with my father when I was still at home. But now that he's older, with a family to care for, he's changed his tune.'

'Your friend Jamie Todd was more willing to follow my thinking in the matter – until the other two persuaded him to change his mind and see things their way.'

They had reached the Knox house. Margaret beamed up at Richard as he opened the gate and stood aside to let her pass. 'You'll just have to find other weavers to try out your yarn.'

'Oh, I will. There's no doubt of that. But after meeting you I'd set my heart on dealing with your fam –'

The words tailed away as they reached the front door and heard the uproar from inside.

'Mercy me, that's Daniel! What's happened to him?'

Margaret forgot all about Richard in her haste to get to her son. Daniel rarely cried, and this hysterical continuous screaming was something she had never heard from him before. He was in pain, and terrified, and in great need of her.

All thought of looms and progress vanished as she ran into the hallway. The screams came from upstairs.

She had crossed the square hall and her foot was on the bottom step of the staircase when the door of Gavin's small study opened and he came out. He was in his shirt-sleeves and his hair was tousled.

'Margaret –'

He caught her by the arms and stopped her when she wanted to run up to where her baby was still screaming and screaming. She turned on him wildly.

'Daniel – what's happened to Daniel? What's wrong with him?'

He tried to take her into his arms, but she fought him.

'Daniel's all right, I promise you. Nothing bad has happened to him. Listen to me, Margaret –'

'All right?' she screamed at him. 'Listen to the wee soul! How can you tell me he's all right, and him making a noise like that?'

'He's frightened, not hurt. Now just listen to what I'm trying to tell you,' he said insistently. But now she was looking past his sheltering arm to the open door of the study. Within, she could just see a part of her daughter's skirt.

'Christian?' Torn between her two children, blocked from the stairs by Gavin's body, she pushed past him and ran, as best she could since her joints suddenly seemed to be fashioned out of wood, to the door. She pushed it open.

Thomas, on his knees, in the act of wrapping a cloth about Christian's bared arm, looked up at his sister, his round face drawn with guilt. Christian beamed cheerfully.

'Look, Mother –' she boasted, pulling away from her uncle, drawing the bandage down and twisting her arm to show the small bloodless incision that had been made in her soft skin.

Margaret looked, and heard a roaring sound as her world tumbled about her.

'It didn't hurt,' the little girl prattled on. 'I didn't cry one single wee tear, and now Uncle Thomas is putting a bandage on me, just as if I was a soldier in the wars.'

Now Margaret understood what had been going on while she was out of the house and out of the way. Ignoring Thomas, she turned to her husband, who stood in the doorway.

Inside, she was screaming, and yet her voice came out flatly, quietly, 'You've given her the pox.'

'No, I've vaccinated her with cowpox to keep her safe, Margaret.'

'I told you!' Her voice began to shake. 'I told you, Gavin, that I'd not have my children used like this!'

His face was white. 'I had to do it, Margaret. I had to prove that it worked.'

'There's no danger,' Thomas said uncomfortably. 'They're quite safe.'

'Are they?'

Christian, aware that something was badly wrong, lost her broad, proud grin. She brushed past Margaret and went to stand by her father, slipping a hand into his. His fingers lay slack in her trusting grip.

'I said they could cut me, Mother. I wasn't frighted, not one wee bit.'

'Margaret, it was as much my fault as it was Gavin's.'

She ignored her daughter and her brother, and spoke only to Gavin.

'I told you I'd not have it!'

'We didn't think you'd be home till after it was all by.' Christian's tell-tale tongue rattled on; then, as her parents stared at each other, ignoring her, she tugged at Gavin's hand. 'I didn't cry, did I, Father? I was more brave than a soldier ever could be.'

He dragged his eyes from Margaret's at last, and smiled down at his daughter. 'Yes, you were very brave.'

With a trusting gesture that was beyond Margaret's comprehension at such a time, Christian lifted her arms to him and he stooped and gathered her up.

She nestled her dark head into the hollow beneath his chin and told Margaret complacently, 'Daniel wasn't like a soldier. He was like a baby. He cried and cried.'

The sound of her son's name brought Margaret out of her trance and into action. The little boy's terrified wails were still ringing the house. 'Daniel –'

'I tell you he's all right, Margaret!'

'How do you know?' she said furiously to her husband. 'How can you tell?'

For the second time she tried to push past him, and this time he stepped aside and let her go. Richard, hovering in the hall, was only a hazy figure to her as she sped up the stairs to the children's room.

The noise in there was indescribable. Ellen, with Daniel struggling and kicking in her arms, was pacing the floor. The little boy's face was puffed up, scarlet, tear-streaked, distorted with fear and pain and outrage.

'Oh, mistress, I'm that glad you're back –' The maid turned a flushed, frightened face to her mistress. And at last Daniel, his upper arm bandaged, was in Margaret's arms, close against her racing heart.

'Oh, my love, my wee birdie! Don't fret, I'm here, and I'll not let them touch you ever again –' she said over and over again into his silky dark hair as she carried him downstairs to where the three men waited in the hall with Christian, who was obviously puzzled by the to-do.

Margaret paused on the bottom step and held out her free hand to her daughter. 'Christian, come to me.'

Christian hesitated, glanced at her father for guidance. He, looking sick and white, put her down and gave her a gentle push forward.

The hall suddenly began to slide and surge around

Margaret. The hand that had been outstretched to Christian groped for a support and fastened on the carved polished newel post. Dizzily, she clutched at Daniel and wondered if she, who had never fainted in her life before, was about to make a fool of herself.

She saw all three men move towards her, but to her relief, for she could not have borne to be touched at that moment by either Gavin or Thomas, it was Richard who reached her first.

Carefully, gently, he steadied her within the circle of his arm until the hall stopped revolving and became its usual steady, unmoving self again.

Then he said, 'Come, Margaret –' and led her past the other two to the parlour.

At the door she turned, still within Richard's embrace.

'Christian –?'

Gavin, ashen to the lips, watched as Christian obediently went to her mother.

Margaret and her children, escorted by Richard, went into the parlour, and the door closed behind them.

Chapter Fifteen

A few hours later the children were settled in their cots; Christian puzzled, guilty without knowing why, but defiant, Daniel swollen-eyed, hiccupping, clinging to his mother's hand until sleep loosened his hot fingers.

Margaret sat on in their room, watching them, listening to Daniel's snuffling and gasping breaths.

Her eyes felt as though they were hot rough stones in her skull's sockets. Her hands moved restlessly in her lap all the time, even when she tried to lock the fingers together to still them.

She had sent Ellen to bed, and Richard, after making sure that Margaret wanted nothing more from him, had retired to his own room. Thomas, she supposed, had long since gone, though no doubt Gavin was somewhere in the house.

At last, when she was certain that both children slept soundly enough to be left, she rose and left the room silently, suddenly aware that she hadn't eaten or drunk anything since taking tea in Mary's parlour.

The kitchen was a warm peaceful haven. Margaret poured some ale into a cup, and ate some cheese and bannocks. She was draining the cup when she realised that she was no longer alone, and turned to see Gavin standing in the kitchen doorway, his eyes haunted.

'Margaret –'

She put the empty cup down, staring at him bleakly.

'The decision was mine, not Thomas's, so don't take your anger out on him. I needed assistance and he gave it. That's all.'

Carefully, ignoring him, she put the utensils she had used on the board by the stone sink and went by him, towards the door.

His hand caught her shoulder, whirling her round to face

82

him. 'For the love of God, woman, don't look at me as though I was the devil incarnate!'

'If anything happens to my bairns, Gavin Knox –'

'Nothing will happen.'

' – I'll kill you with my own bare hands,' she concluded, and saw by the sudden tightening of his jaw that he knew she meant what she said. At that moment she hated him, hated the man who had been the mainstay of her life, the father of her children, the guardian of her future and the reason for all her happiness during the past five years.

'Nothing will happen to them, I tell you!' He shook her slightly to add emphasis to the words. She stood within his grip, making no attempt to free herself, the hot coals of her eyes burning into him.

'Go away, Gavin. Go out of this house and leave me to see to my bairns in peace.'

'I can't go, even if I would. I must be here, with them. For a day or two – a week at most – they're going to have a fever. They'll have to be kept abed. I must stay with them.'

A panic-stricken wail from upstairs brought both their heads jerking round towards the open door.

'Daniel!' Margaret wrenched herself free of Gavin's hands and ran into the darkened hall and up the stairs, hearing Gavin close behind.

Daniel was sitting up in bed, scream after scream pouring out of his wide-open mouth. Christian, raised on one elbow, blinked like a baby owl as Margaret scooped the little boy into her arms.

The howls began to subside; then as Daniel, his head resting on her shoulder, opened his eyes and saw Gavin standing by the door, they redoubled. Margaret felt the small body in her arms curl into a ball as the child tried to burrow deeper into the safety of her body.

She turned to her husband so that the child's face was averted from him. 'Stay away from him, Gavin.'

'Daniel –' he said, taking a step into the room. But at the sound of his voice the little boy's wailing immediately increased until the room rang with ear-splitting shrieks. Christian clapped her hands over her ears, eyes screwed up tightly. Gavin shrugged helplessly and went out, closing the door quietly behind him.

'Daniel's being a baby,' Christian said.

'Hold your tongue!'

Christian's eyes, so like Gavin's, were hurt. Without a word she turned over in her bed and hunched her shoulders, her back to the room. Then she drew the coverlet right over her head, and said no more.

Margaret spent that night in Daniel's low narrow cot, cramped and uncomfortable, soothing him every time the nightmares wakened him again, waiting for the long hours of darkness to pass and give way to grey dawn.

*

She got very little sleep over the next week. As Gavin had predicted, both children developed a fever. Their arms, where he and Thomas had cut into the top layer of skin and deposited minute amounts of matter obtained from the pustules of cows sick with cow-pox, became swollen and painful. Even Christian, flushed and fretful and feeling very ill, stopped looking on the whole business as a game and wept and whined and fretted along with Daniel.

Margaret, convinced that both her children were going to die of the pox, was almost out of her mind with worry. She refused to leave the house, spending her days and nights with the two of them, sponging them down with cool water, coaxing them to swallow broth or gruel, watching over them as they slept, ever-vigilant for the first signs of the virulent disease to appear on their bodies.

People came and went – her mother, her Aunt Mary, Kirsty Todd. But she refused to let anyone else stay with the children. Ellen brought food to their room, and when they slept, Margaret dozed on a truckle bed the maidservant had brought in for her, waking with a start every time one of the children whimpered.

Much as she would have liked to insist that he go far away and leave them all to see to themselves, she had need of Gavin's help and advice. Christian, who worshipped her father and was firmly convinced that he could save her from all ills, gave herself up readily to his examinations and his treatments, but Daniel screamed and fled into

Margaret's arms every time Gavin tried to touch him.

Gavin looked as though he, too, was going without sleep. On the few occasions when she looked fully at him Margaret saw the man he would become when middle age reached out and claimed him. Once, glancing in a looking-glass during that terrible time, she saw the same indication of things to come in her own face. Her eyes had dulled and become sunken, her face was almost grey, her mouth was thinner, with a new downward droop at the corners.

Then one night the fever broke and in the morning, just as Gavin had predicted, both children were clear-eyed, hungry, and clamouring to go outside into the garden to play. The tender swellings on their arms had subsided, and when the bandages were taken off the small wounds had begun to dry and scab.

Gavin, his face radiant with relief, tried to take Margaret into his arms when the two of them met on the upstairs landing. He had shaved and changed into fresh clothing and his hair was neatly brushed and tied back.

'I told you they'd be fine.'

She drew away from him. 'But you'd no right to take the risk.'

'If I'd thought it was that much of a risk, I'd not have taken it.'

'Are you sure of that, Gavin?'

'What does that mean?'

'Mebbe being a surgeon's more important to you than being a father.' Then, as he flushed, she added dryly, 'I suppose you'll be persuading other folk to let you and Thomas cut their bairns now?'

'Aye, since it'll help to save them from worse harm. You can't deny, now, that it's safe. Listen to the two of them.'

The children, eating their porridge in their bed-chamber, were chattering to Ellen like a couple of magpies. A smile curved Margaret's mouth for the first time in a week as she heard them. But when Gavin reached out again to hold her she took another step back, shaking her head. She couldn't forget the horror of the past days. She couldn't yet find it in her heart to forgive him for his betrayal.

His face changed as he recognised the rejection in her

swift movement. 'You've surely more sense, Margaret, than to nurse your anger like a spoiled child.'

'I've more sense than to trust you ever again, Gavin Knox!'

Anger settled on his rugged features. He gave her a small, stiff bow and said tightly, 'Then behave as you wish. You always have. I must be in Glasgow for the rest of the day, for I've been too long away from my work.'

'Very well.' As she followed him downstairs Richard came out of the parlour.

'Ellen tells me that they're fully recovered – quite well again.'

'Aye, they're well.'

'I'm pleased to hear it,' he said, and took her hands, smiling down at her. 'Now we must set about putting you to rights. You look over-pale. Gavin, would you permit me to take the bairns and Margaret out for a carriage ride this afternoon?'

A muscle jerked in Gavin's jawline as he looked at Richard, still holding Margaret's hands.

'Aye, if the children are warmly wrapped up and don't catch a chill.'

'No fear of that. I'll take care of them. You'll not refuse me, Margaret, will you?'

'Indeed not.'

'I'll mebbe not be home until late tonight,' Gavin said abruptly, then he turned on his heel and left the house.

Chapter Sixteen

Early each morning Islay's eyes seemed to spring open of their own volition and she rose from her bed, luxuriously spacious now that she only had to share it with Morag, ready to begin a new day.

After waking Lachie and stirring the fire into life she prepared breakfast for herself and the boy, letting Morag lie abed a little longer.

Then Lachie went off to waken the other weavers and Islay made her way into the weaving shop to clean the fireplace and sweep the floor and give the linnets fresh seed and water and tend to the pinks that grew in pots on the deep window-sills, and make everything ready for the day's work.

In the few short weeks since moving from Jenny's Wynd she had grown to love the atmosphere of the weaving shop.

In the morning, before the men arrived, the looms waited quietly, the hand-looms squat and stolid, the harnesses of the two great draw-looms, with their intricate arrangement of pulleys and lashes, towering overhead in majestic splendour.

At that time of the day the only sound came from the caged birds, already trilling their music into the room. Later, as the men tramped in one by one, rubbing sleep from their eyes, the place took on another feeling altogether. The looms sprang eagerly to life, shuttles clacked to and fro like the tongues of gossips, the webs began to grow, the men talked and laughed and sang, giving the linnets competition – and in the space of a few minutes the shop took on its day apparel.

She liked the men who worked the Wellmeadow looms. They were a kindly group, even Walter Shaw, who wasn't nearly as bad as she had thought in the days when he used to come to Jenny's Wynd to fetch the pirns and taunt Lachie into fighting him.

Indeed, more than once Islay had turned her head suddenly to find him watching her as she went about her work. At first she had looked away again quickly, as embarrassed by the brief contact as he was. But of late Walter had taken to greeting her by name if she was still in the loom shop when he arrived. He had a nice smile, when he took the trouble to give it an airing.

Not as nice, though, as Jamie Todd's broad, blue-eyed grin. She looked forward to the days when he called in at the shop, although he scarcely had a word for her, other than a swift greeting.

When the place was as clean as she could make it and the men had arrived and started work she went back upstairs to where Morag was breaking her own fast before going off to the dress-making shop on the bridge, where Margaret Knox had managed to find work for her. Nothing too strenuous, Thomas Montgomery had said, and not long hours.

So Morag, who was to learn the dress-making trade, was excused an early start until such time as Thomas decided that she was strong enough to manage it.

Once Morag had gone Islay was free to see to her own housework before she went out to collect pirns for the loom shop. Then she settled down at her wheel and got on with her own spinning, with the steady thump of the looms below and the occasional faint sound of one or more voices raised in song to keep her company.

It was when she was bringing back the collected pirns that she first met Richard Knox. She was setting her loaded basket down to open the loom shop door when a voice said, as courteously as if she was a grand lady instead of just an ordinary lassie, 'Allow me, ma'am.'

The door whisked open, the basket was lifted as though it contained no weight at all, and Islay found herself looking into a pair of appreciative hazel eyes set in a pleasing, bronzed face.

'Thank you, sir, but I can manage well enough.'

'So can I.' He ignored her outstretched hand. 'I'm

looking for Mister Jamie Todd. Is he inside?'

'He'll be at his loom in the High Street weaving shop.'

'Ah.' He made no move to return the basket to her, or to take it inside. Instead, he leaned one shoulder comfortably against the wall. 'And who might you be?'

'Islay McInnes, sir. I live in the house above.'

'Do you indeed?' He sketched as graceful a bow as his burden would allow. 'And I am Richard Knox, at your service.'

'A relation of Mistress Margaret Knox?'

'Her husband's brother. You know Margaret?'

'She and I are — friends.' It might have been presumptuous of her, but all the same it gave her a great deal of pleasure to say the word aloud.

'Then it follows that you and I will be friends too, Mistress McInnes.'

'We're Mister Todd's lodgers — my cousins and myself,' she added breathlessly, for the sake of having something to say.

There was something disconcerting about the man's gaze. It wasn't improper, or objectionable. But nevertheless it troubled Islay. She ducked by him and stepped over the sill, saying over her shoulder, 'If you'll just bring the pirns in, sir —'

'The —?'

'The pirns. In the basket.'

'Ah —! Of course, ma'am.' He followed her into the shop, setting the basket down and watching as she transferred the filled pirns from it to the box used by the weavers. As she straightened up she caught a glimpse of Walter's eyes, heavy with resentment, fixed on the well-dressed visitor who stood watching her so attentively.

Richard Knox followed her as she went outside again. 'Have you more — pirns — to collect? If so, I would be happy to accompany you and help to carry them.'

'No more today. Now I've got my own wheel to attend to.'

'Some other time, then.' He sounded quite disappointed. 'The High Street weaving shop, you said?'

'Aye sir. Not far past Townhead. Anyone can tell you where it is.'

'I've already been there. I can find my way easily enough again.' To her astonishment he captured her hand and raised it to his lips. 'Goodbye, Mistress McInnes,' he said, and left her.

At the entrance to the pend he looked back and saw that she was still standing where he had left her, watching him. He raised one hand in a light salute, and disappeared from view.

Confused and flustered, Islay went upstairs, where she sat at her wheel for some time before starting work, her hands lying idle in her lap, one stroking the other, where the touch of Richard Knox's lips could still be clearly felt.

*

'The bairns might be right as rain again, but you're looking awful out of sorts yourself these days, Margaret.' Mary MacLeod peered at her niece. 'What's amiss?'

'Nothing.'

'Tush! It's that quarrel you had with Gavin, isn't it? Have you never made it up yet, the two of you?'

Then, when Margaret stayed stubbornly silent, her aunt went on, 'I'll grant you that he and Thomas behaved badly, but the bairns came to no harm, did they?'

'They might have died!'

'Tush – the sky might have fallen in on us yesterday. Bailie Menzies's wife might not have liked the new bonnet I made her,' said Mary, who still maintained her little millinery shop at the Sneddon, despite the fact that she had no need of its support. 'The world's full of things that might have happened. Gavin did what he thought best, the bairns are fine, and that's an end of it, surely.'

'D'you think so?'

'I never took you for a fool before, Margaret Knox.' Mary sighed, and gathered up her gloves. 'Well, I must go.'

Then she sat down again and glared at Margaret. 'All this nonsense between you and Gavin's addled my wits. I clean forgot why I came here in the first place.'

'Why?' Margaret asked dutifully, but with little interest.

'You know that Caroline Cameron's managed to find a man for that elderly daughter of hers at last?'

'No,' said Margaret, who had never cared for local gossip.

'Well, she has. A man who bides in Perth, with more money than sense if you ask me, though the lassie's pleasant enough. But she's got no conversation in her at all. Anyway, nothing would please Caroline but that she should hire the assembly rooms in the Saracen's Head Inn and hold a big gathering to show the man how well-set-up the Camerons are in Paisley.' She settled herself more comfortably in her chair and Margaret, aware that there was a pile of ironing awaiting her in the kitchen, wondered how long her aunt was going to take to tell her story.

'And, of course, it never occurred to her until the thing was settled that the Camerons don't know all that many folk in the town when it comes to it – being a family that likes to keep themselves to themselves. And most of the people they do know are so old they'd drop dead in a strathspey, let alone a reel. So Caroline came running to me in a panic and asked would I see to the gathering for her. Now, there's you and Gavin and Richard – he'll make a handsome addition to the festivities, and the Paisley women like to have their hearts set a-flutter now and again –'

Margaret moved in swift protest. 'Oh no, I don't think I could go to a gathering just now!'

'Of course you could. It's just what you and Gavin need. There's the two of you, and Robert and Annie, and Thomas, and Jamie. Kate's too near her time to be able to attend.'

Mary ticked off names on her beringed fingers, then tutted. 'Mercy me, there's not going to be enough women to go round. D'you know of anyone you could bring?'

Margaret, realising that there was no escape, put her mind to the problem. 'There's Islay McInnes.'

'Who's she?'

'One of the people living in Jamie's house at Wellmeadow.'

'A Highlander? How old is she? Is she bonny?'

'Sixteen years old. And she's very bonny. She's going to be a beautiful woman soon.'

'D'you tell me?' asked Mary with interest. 'Then she'll do. You can see to her for me, Margaret, for I've got enough to do. Besides, I don't know the lassie.'

'She might not want to come.'

'Of course she will. Don't take no for an answer – I never do,' said Mary.

At the front door she paused and fixed her niece with a firm blue eye. 'You've got a good man, Margaret, so mind and guard that quick tongue of yours. It'll not keep you warm at night, or give you loving when your spirits are low.'

'We'll be fine, Gavin and me.'

'Hmmmphh,' Mary snorted, and went.

Margaret's farewell smile vanished as soon as she had closed the door behind her aunt's upright back. She was beginning to wonder if things would ever be the same again between herself and Gavin.

Christian and Daniel were as well as ever, and yet the stubborn streak that had often proved to be more of a curse than a blessing in the past refused to let her forgive him, or forget the way he had risked their children's lives in order to prove a medical theory.

She bit her lip, and sighed; then she went to the kitchen to deal with the ironing.

*

'Me? Go to a gathering?' Islay's eyes were large and bright with panic. 'Oh, Mistress Knox, I couldn't!'

'Tush,' said Margaret, and winced when she realised how like her aunt she must sound. 'You can dance, can't you?'

'Yes of course, but – but I'm not gentry!'

'Neither am I. And neither are most of the folk who'll be there. It's time you met people, Islay. You're a young woman now.'

'I'd not know what to say to them!'

'As to that, you've no need to concern yourself. You could recite nursery rhymes in that lovely Highland voice of yours and folk would listen quite happily.'

'And I've nothing to wear –' Islay was tossing as many objections as she could find in the way, while Margaret caught and demolished them with an efficiency that had been inherited from her Aunt Mary rather than from her own placid, easy-going mother, Meg Montgomery.

'I've more than enough clothes for the two of us,' she said, lifting Daniel, who had begun to grizzle, onto her knee. Christian, who couldn't stay still for a minute, had gone down to the loom shop to see the linnets.

'And I won't know anyone there!'

'You'll not get to know them if you don't attend gatherings. You'll be with me and my husband, and his brother Richard. And my brother Robert and his wife Annie will be there. And my brother Thomas – you've met him. And there's Jamie of course. It's time you found out for yourself that the Paisley folk aren't so bad after all.'

The last name caught and held Islay's attention. She hadn't thought that Jamie Todd would be going to the gathering. Here was a chance to see him in a different setting, among his own folk. Here was an opportunity to try to unravel the enigma of this man who was, in turns, abrupt, aloof, kindly – but always remote, refusing to let Islay close enough to see what lay beneath the surface.

'Well? Will you come?'

Islay's mind was made up for her in the space of a few seconds.

'I'll come,' she said.

Chapter Seventeen

On the evening of the gathering Islay stood in the middle of Margaret Knox's bedchamber, revolving slowly, trying to take it all in at once – the polished, beautifully crafted furniture, the hangings at the windows, the carpet underfoot, the elegant long framed mirror.

'It's – it's so big!'

Margaret, laying the gowns she had selected out on the bed, looked round the familiar room in her turn, seeing it anew through her guest's eyes.

'I mind the first time I was in a fair-sized house.' She sat on the edge of the bed, her face soft with memories. 'It was on the day my Aunt Mary was wed, and we were in her new house, here on Oakshawhill. I'd been raised in a weavers' cottage, and I fair affronted my mother by saying out loud that it was wrong that some folk had so much space, when others had none at all. D'you know, Islay – for all that I've got a big house myself now, I still think the same.'

Then she blinked the past away, and laughed. 'But we're not here to talk – we must get ready, or the menfolk'll be girning their heads off.'

*

As she came downstairs behind Margaret, her stomach tense with excitment and fear and anticipation, Islay found herself looking for approval in Richard Knox's eyes, and finding it.

She knew as soon as he came forward and stood waiting for her to reach the hall that she would do, and her relief was so great that she gave him a dazzling smile.

Margaret had chosen a dress in deep rose pink trimmed with dove-grey for Islay. The tight-fitting bodice was cut low, but not immodestly so. Down the front panel foamed delicate bunches of grey ribbon.

The sleeves, tight to the elbow, ended in a series of grey, rose and pink layers that fell back from Islay's smoothly rounded arms when she raised her hands to her throat, where a small ruff in the same rose shade fitted neatly about her neck.

Her hair had been brushed until it was a sheet of night-black satin, and pinned at the back of her neat head, fastened there with a spray of pink rosebuds. It had been drawn back tightly from her face to allow her neat features and wide, thick-lashed dark eyes to be seen to best advantage.

Her work-roughened hands had been pampered and creamed and massaged, and the nails trimmed then polished with a soft cloth to make as much of them as was possible.

'I thought you'd never be ready,' Gavin said abruptly, taking his wife's arm.

'But you must admit,' said Margaret, in a gown the same deep clear blue as her eyes, 'that we're worth the waiting.'

Gavin smiled down on her, the first real smile she had seen on his face since the whole sorry vaccination business began.

'I'll admit it gladly. But I'm not so sure the coachman who's been kept waiting would agree with me, for it's cold outside.'

*

It was largely due to Mary's endeavours that the main assembly hall of the Saracen's Head Inn at Paisley Cross was filled almost to overflowing. As well as being a local businesswoman and the widow of one of the town's wealthiest and most respected textile manufacturers, Mary MacLeod had been popular, despite her outspoken manner, since the day she first arrived from her parents' farm in Beith, a beautiful and ambitious young woman. An invitation from Mary was looked on as more of a summons, and few had the courage, or the inclination, to defy her.

She stood now at the door with the Camerons and their daughter, a plain, awkward young woman not much younger than Margaret, pathetically grateful at having been rescued by marriage at the last minute. Her intended husband, a little younger than she was, but just as plain and awkward, hovered uneasily by her side.

Mary's eyes swept over Islay when they were introduced, and liked what they saw.

'Have a good time, lassie,' she instructed.

'I intend to see that she does, ma'am,' said Richard, magnificent in a loose plum-coloured coat and white ruffled shirt, with blue waistcoat and breeches. Like his brother, he wore his thick hair unadorned, tied back with a blue ribbon.

Mary, never one for feminine modesty, eyed him with the open admiration of a woman who appreciates a fine-looking man, 'I've no doubt you will, sir. But the lassie's here to meet folk, so I'll be grateful if you'll not take up every minute of her time yourself. And I'll be looking to you to claim my own hand for at least one dance.'

As they advanced into the crowded hall Islay saw an unpowdered red head almost at once. Jamie Todd, his back to the door, was deep in conversation with a group of men.

The evening was almost over by the time she and Jamie met. Earlier, she had caught his eye once or twice; on the first occasion he had clearly not recognised her, though he gave a courteous, formal bow in response to her tentative smile. The second time his brows had dipped in a puzzled frown, then lifted with startled recognition.

His red head had begun to forge its way towards her, then someone—there had been so many folk, apart from Richard himself—claimed her and led her onto the dance floor.

She had had no option but to go with her escort, and later she had seen Jamie join the dance with his own partner, a stranger to Islay.

Towards the end of the evening she escaped to a quiet corner behind a pillar for a moment's respite. As she smoothed the skirt of her lovely gown the rough skin on her fingers caught the soft material, reminding her, as she had been reminded every time Richard Knox took her hands in his during the dance, that however white and smooth her throat may be, her hands were those of a worker.

Islay bit her lip with humiliation. She had never had occasion to think of that before. After all, only the gentry could afford to have soft, smooth hands. But it would be nice to feel her fingers slide over beautiful materials instead of rasping over them, Islay thought longingly, wondering if Mistress Knox might be persuaded to tell her what oils or lotions she could make up to use on her red, rough skin. She was examining her fingers closely when Jamie Todd said from behind her, 'Islay?'

She turned, flushing guiltily as though caught in some wrong-doing. 'Mister Todd.'

'What's amiss?' Before she could put her hands behind her back he had taken them in his and was examining them, brows knotted. 'Have you hurt yourself?'

'No.' She tried to draw away from him, but he tightened his hold slightly.

'I thought when I first came on you that there must be something wrong with your hands.'

She squirmed uncomfortably under his glance, then confessed, 'I was just wishing that they were as soft as – as the other women's.'

He looked impatient. 'Who's been worrying you about such nonsense? Is it Richard Knox? I saw that you were dancing uncommonly often with him.'

'He said nothing! They were my own thoughts.'

'I didn't think that vanity was part of your nature.'

'It's just that –' She managed to reclaim the offending hands and put them out of sight, behind her back. 'I only wished –'

'You earn your living with your hands, as I do. Most of these women you see fit to envy –' he jerked his head towards the vivid, chattering throng on the other side of the row of pillars where they stood – 'expect others to do their work for them. I'd not want to be of their persuasion, and neither should you. Enjoy their company, by all means, for they're congenial folk, and decent enough. But never envy them. You're worth just as much as they are in the scale of things.'

His eyes touched briefly on her upswept hair, the tiny milky Scottish pearls Margaret had affixed to the small neat lobes of her ears, the rich stuff of the gown she wore, and he gave a short, half-apologetic laugh. 'You must forgive me my poor manners earlier. I didn't recognise you. You look so –' He paused, and she waited with rising hope. Would he say that she looked beautiful? Would he at least say that she looked pretty? 'Grown up,' he said, at last, and her hopes were dashed.

'Mistress Knox loaned me the dress. And it was she who invited me.'

'It was only right that she should. I should have thought to ask her to in the first place. Are you having a pleasant time?'

'Oh yes. Everyone's been very kind.'

'There's no reason why they shouldn't be.' His mouth twisted wryly. 'The Paisley folk aren't all ogres like myself.'

'You're not! You're –' She hesitated, then said lamely, 'You've been good to us, Mister Todd.'

He brushed the words aside with an impatient movement of the hand. 'Will you dance with me, Islay?'

It was one of the more sedate of the Scottish dances. Islay moved through the steps with confidence, for she had learned them as a youngster in the glens of her birth. Jamie danced competently, but without Richard Knox's natural sense of rhythm. Even so, his was a style that suited her, and she floated around the hall like a puff of thistledown, twirling and stepping, parting from him and rejoining him, putting her work-roughened hands into his without so much as a thought for the white smooth fingers she had been longing for so passionately.

At the end of the dance he offered her his arm, and led her over to where Margaret and Gavin were sitting. Before Islay could take her seat beside Margaret the musicians struck up again and Richard arrived to claim her for the next dance.

She hesitated, glancing at Jamie Todd, but he merely moved aside, so she put her hand into Richard's and let him lead her away.

*

Jamie watched the two of them take their places among the

dancers then said abruptly, 'Your brother seems to be very interested in Islay McInnes, Gavin. He's scarce allowed her to dance with anyone else all night.'

The surgeon shrugged. 'My brother's activities are none of my concern – and never were.'

'All the same, I gather from Islay that she's with your party tonight.'

'I invited her,' Margaret said. 'It's time the girl met some of the townsfolk. Richard's only making her welcome. Would you be happier to see her sitting alone and unwanted all evening, Jamie?'

'Of course not,' he said stiffly. 'But the man's much older than she is. Attention from a man of the world such as Richard could turn the child's head and set up all sorts of unhappiness.'

'Jamie's right, Margaret. Richard's altogether too aware of his own charm and the effect it can have on women.'

'Oh – tush!' Margaret glared at both men. 'I'm just grateful to him for making Islay's first evening in Paisley society so pleasant. And as for her being a child, Jamie – she's a woman now, as you've surely noticed for yourself.'

Jamie said nothing, but watched unsmilingly as the rose-pink gown and its attendant plum-coloured coat wove their way in and out of the dance.

Chapter Eighteen

Somehow, whether by design or by chance, Islay found that Jamie was her partner in the final dance of the evening.

'I'll walk back to Wellmeadow with you,' he offered as the music came to an end, adding, 'Or mebbe you'd prefer to travel by carriage with the rest of your party.'

She beamed up at him. 'No, indeed. It would be pleasant to walk in the night air.'

Richard was waiting at the edge of the dance-floor, holding the warm cloak that Margaret had loaned Islay. Jamie took it from him and put it about her shoulders. 'I'll escort Islay back to Wellmeadow.'

'That's not necessary. A carriage is waiting outside for us.'

The men loomed over Islay, one on either side. She put a hand on Richard's arm. 'I'd like to walk, truly.'

'Then it's my place to escort you.'

'It would take you out of your way, Mister Knox.'

'But –'

'Besides,' said Jamie with cool finality, 'Islay and I have to discuss some matters to do with the loom shop as we walk.'

Richard hesitated, then shrugged gracefully, kissed Islay's hand, and went off to join his brother and sister-in-law.

*

Although autumn had arrived the night was unseasonably cold. The chill struck home after the warmth of the Inn, and Islay drew the borrowed cloak close about her shoulders as she and Jamie walked through streets that fell quiet once they had left the bustle of departing guests about the Saracen's Head's doorway.

Now and again they passed a lighted window and heard sounds from within of a child crying, an adult coughing, men's voices raised in the lengthy debates that the Paisley weavers loved, whatever the subject. But most of the houses were dark, their inhabitants long a-bed.

Jamie said nothing, and Islay was happy enough to patter along by his side, her hand resting as lightly as a flower petal on his arm, letting her thoughts roam around the evening she had just spent, carefully listing and preserving each moment.

The rose pink dress rustled about her legs; tomorrow it must be carefully wrapped and taken back to Mistress Knox, but for tonight it was Islay's, and she relished the feel of it, the whisper of silk, the snug way the bodice cupped her breasts and fitted to her waist, the soft kiss of the flounces against her forearms as she moved.

In no time at all they had passed the house where Jamie lived. From there it was only a matter of minutes to the building in Wellmeadow.

When they reached it, Jamie paused and looked up at the night sky. Clouds had formed a thin veil before the moon, shutting out most of its clear cold light.

'Will you see to find your way up the stairs?'

'Yes, indeed.'

'In that case, I'll bid you goodnight.' Jamie Todd wasn't one to kiss a woman's hand, and Islay hadn't expected it of him.

She ducked her head in farewell and turned to go through the pend. Beneath the stone arch the place was as black as pitch, but she had walked it often enough to know just where to set her feet. Confidently, she moved into the dark area, angling slightly to the right as she neared the other end of the archway. The wooden staircase was just a few steps round the corner.

She was almost out of the pend when her foot struck against something soft and she stumbled.

Someone – or something – grunted, there was a scrabbling, then a hand closed about her ankle and she cried out in fright, taking a swift, involuntary step back, wrenching herself free but losing her balance in the process.

She staggered, and for a moment she felt herself falling

back, then one shoulder hit painfully off the far wall of the pend.

'Islay?' Jamie Todd called sharply from the street. The pend was suddenly filled with a flurry of sound as whoever had startled her fled towards the street and collided with Jamie as he came running in. There was a short scuffle, then Jamie said breathlessly, urgently, 'Islay – in God's name where are you?'

'Here. I'm here –' She put her hands out and almost at once felt them grasped in his.

'Are you hurt, lassie?'

'No –' But her voice trembled with shock, and so did her hands, still trapped in his. He put one arm about her and supported her weight easily.

'I'll take you up to the house.'

'No! I don't want to fright Morag and Lachie.'

'Then we'll go into the loom shop.'

He found the door without any trouble and half lifted Islay over the raised wooden sill and into the room. Then he lit the candle that was always kept on a shelf just inside the door.

In its glow the loom shop was a place of elongated shadows; the looms stood silent, unmoving guard round the pool of light that cupped Jamie and Islay. The place smelled faintly of the oil that was used on the machines.

Jamie held the candle up so that he could see Islay's face. 'Are you certain you're not hurt?'

'Just frightened. He caught my foot and I didn't know what was going to happen to me. Who was it?'

'Some drunken vagabond sheltering in the pend for the night. He'll not do that again in this town,' said Jamie savagely. 'I'm going to hand him over to the town watchmen, and tomorrow the magistrates'll run him out of the place.'

'No!'

He stared. 'The man's a danger to the community, Islay! You said yourself that he caught hold of you. There's no knowing what he might have done if I hadnae been there to hear you cry out!'

'He was probably just sheltering for the night. He'd have

got as much of a fright as I did, poor soul. Oh – don't hand him over to the militia – they'll like as not flog him before they run him out.' She shivered, remembering what it was like to have nowhere to sleep, no knowledge of where the next meal was coming from, the continual fear of being forced out of towns or villages with nowhere else to seek shelter.

'He probably deserves a good flogging.'

'That's a wicked thing to say!'

'God's teeth, lassie! The man gives you enough of a fright to stop your heart – and heaven only knows what other mischief he had in store for you – and you accuse me of being wicked just because I want to see him being taught a lesson? I'll never understand you Highlanders!'

That was the trouble, Islay thought wretchedly. Nobody in this town understood her people. And not being understood was almost as bad as being rejected altogether.

Then she suddenly thought of the gown and jumped to her feet, twisting round in an attempt to examine the back of the skirt. 'Mistress Knox's fine dress! I've mebbe dirtied it against the wall –'

'No matter if you have,' he said, 'As long as you're not hurt.'

Then he gave that wry smile she had seen on his lips before. 'Mebbe you'd have done better to accept a lift home in the carriage instead of trusting yourself to me. Now – I'd best bring in that ne'er-do-weel that's lying out in the pend.'

While he was gone Islay had time to reassure herself, at least by the candle's light, that the lovely dress seemed to be unharmed. Tomorrow morning she would have a better opportunity to study it in daylight.

Then Jamie was back, dragging with him a slightly built man who lolled in his grip, only half-recovered from the blow Jamie had dealt him. His head rolled on his chest, his feet stumbled as they tried to walk. He tripped over the sill of the door, and Jamie jerked him roughly inside, deposited him on the settle by the fireside, and went back to shut the door.

'Is he hurt bad?' Islay forgot her worries about the dress as she went to the settle.

'If he is it's no more than he deserves.'

She touched a limp hand. It stirred beneath her fingers and the man groaned.

'He's so cold!'

Jamie brought the candle over and set it down. Then he caught a fistful of the long, lank black hair that hung round the stranger's drooping head and jerked on it, pulling the man's head back and exposing a gaunt face, white beneath its grime. Dazed brown eyes blinked in the light, trying to focus.

Islay's own eyes opened wide in disbelief.

'Ross!'

'Eh?' asked Jamie blankly.

'Dear God! It's my cousin Ross MacInnes – Morag and Lachie's brother! Oh, Ross –!'

Her cousin's eyes cleared at the sound of his own name and he made an attempt to pull himself upright, shaking his head to clear it.

'Islay?' he asked wonderingly in the Gaelic.

'Yes, it's Islay. What are you doing here – where did you come from? Is my uncle with you?' The questions poured from her.

He put a hand to his face and probed his jaw, then winced and looked round, still groggy. 'Islay? How did you come to be here?'

'We live in the house above, now – Morag and Lachie and me.'

'They're safe, then?'

'They're safe – and well.'

'Mother?' He said the word reluctantly, as though he knew the answer already.

Islay took one of his hands in hers. 'She died some time back. I'm sorry, Ross.'

He was silent for a moment, then said, 'I thought she might be. Mebbe she's better off. Where is this place?'

'Jamie Todd's loom shop. Oh, Ross, I never thought to see you again! How did you know where to find us?'

He began to talk, haltingly at first, then more easily as his head cleared. Islay, sitting beside him, still clutching his hand, couldn't take her eyes from him. As far as Morag and

Lachie were concerned, she had never given up hope that Ross and her uncle would return; but in her own mind, she had never thought to see either of them again.

She was only dimly aware of Jamie Todd's presence. At first he leaned back against one of the looms, surveying the cousins, his hand absently stoking the wooden roller that held the yarn.

Then he began to prowl restlessly, and finally he came to stand before them, interrupting the flow of words.

'Islay – what in the world's going on? I can make neither head nor tail of your gibberish!'

It was only then that she realised that she and Ross had been speaking in their native tongue.

'He's out of the Army now, and he's walked all the way from London to find us. He went to Jenny's Wynd and someone told him Lachie worked here. He was sheltering in the pend until morning, waiting for Lachie to come to work.'

'What of his father?'

She bit her lip, then said, 'He knows no more about my uncle than I do.'

'Well –' said Jamie, at a loss. 'And now what do you plan to do with him?'

Ross dragged himself upright and stood by Islay, clutching with one hand at the back of the settle, swaying slightly from weakness and exhaustion.

As she glanced swiftly from one man to the other Islay's heart was wrenched with pity for her cousin. When she had last seen him Ross had been a strong, well-set-up young man.

But lack of nourishment and hard usage had turned him into a pathetic, shabbily dressed shadow of his former self.

Jamie, on the other hand, had never known what it was like to be destitute. Although his garb for the evening was much less elaborate than Richard's he looked, in his dark green jacket with silver buttons, and black britches, like nobility compared to her cousin.

Ross's eyes, as he faced the sturdy, well dressed man before him, were hostile. So, Islay noted with some dismay, were Jamie's.

'What d'you plan to do?' Jamie repeated.

'I must take him upstairs and give him some food, for a start. Come, Ross –' Islay said in the Gaelic, and put her arm about her cousin.

Jamie brushed her aside. 'I'll see to him. You go ahead with the candle.'

Ross drew back slightly, but Jamie ignored the movement, putting a strong arm about the other man and half carrying him out of the shop and up the stairs after Islay.

At the house door he hesitated, releasing Ross. 'Will you manage on your own now?'

'Yes. Thank you for your help, Jamie.'

'I'll see you in the morning,' said Jamie, and departed without a backward glance.

It was only then, as she watched him disappearing from the pool of candle-light, that Islay realised that during the excitement his first name had come to her tongue – as naturally as if she had always used it.

Chapter Nineteen

As Mary MacLeod had prophesied, the gathering at the Saracen's Head Inn had gone some way towards easing the situation between Margaret and Gavin.

For one thing, it had brought back memories to both of them of the time when Gavin formally invited Margaret to be his partner at a public dance there.

It was on that night that he had first kissed her, she thought as they walked into the hall with Islay and Richard. And giving Gavin a sidelong glance, she caught him doing the same to her. They smiled, then laughed together, and set out to enjoy the evening.

Later, much later, Gavin made love to her in the privacy of their bed-chamber and as she drifted off to sleep with his head pillowed on her shoulder and his bare arm wrapped about her, Margaret knew a sensation of deep, healing peace.

But trouble erupted only two days later, proving that the chasm set up by the original quarrel still existed, and had only been hidden for the moment beneath their new-found contentment with each other.

It started when Gavin, finding Margaret in the parlour, proposed that she and the children should ride out with him on his country rounds that day.

'We'll not have much more sunshine this year, and it's time the four of us had a day to ourselves.'

She bit her lip. 'I must go to the Poors' Hospital school-room this morning, then I've to see how the inkle looms are doing –'

'Och – confound the schoolroom and the inkle looms!' Gavin said with a sudden spurt of irritation. 'Margaret, I'll not have these folk at the Poors' Hospital taking up time you should be giving to me and to your own bairns. When was the last time we all were together properly? When are things going to go back to the way they should be in this house?'

She kept on folding the table-cloth in her hands, matching side to side precisely, smoothing each fold meticulously. 'There's nothing wrong with the way things are.'

'You can say that, when Richard's forever under my feet and I never seem to have a moment alone with you? When Daniel still draws away whenever I go near him, and cries out if I put a hand on him?'

'It was you that frighted Daniel, Gavin. You can't deny that.'

His voice sharpened. 'And you've encouraged him to keep that thought in his mind. You've made a baby of him again.'

He turned to the door, put a hand on the handle, said over his shoulder, 'You'll turn the lad into a timid wee creature frighted of its own shadow if you're not careful. It's high time I put a stop to it.'

'I scarce think you've the right to tell me how to treat my own bairns – not after what you did to them!'

He left the door and was across the room before she realised what his intentions were. The table covering fell to the floor as he caught her upper arms, his face dark with anger.

'Listen to me, Margaret. You didn't produce them entirely on your own, for all that you're such an able creature,' he said between clenched teeth. 'They're mine too, and what I did I did for love of them. Mebbe one day you'll come to see that for yourself. As for the Hospital and the inkle looms – I've stood by long enough, Margaret. Let someone else see to them for you from now on.'

'I'll not be ordered about like a servant!'

'You'll do as I –'

Gavin stopped short as the door opened. Richard stood on the threshold, looking from husband to wife.

'Still here, Gavin? I thought you'd gone long since.'

Gavin opened his hands and released Margaret as his brother advanced into the room.

'I've arranged to meet Jamie Todd later, but I'll walk down to the Hospital with you, Margaret. We'll mebbe have time to inspect the new loomshop first –' he added before she had the chance to stop him.

'What new loomshop?' Gavin asked swiftly, suspiciously, looking from one face to the other.

Margaret laid the neatly folded cloth on the table and smoothed it before turning to face him.

'Richard and I are setting up more inkle looms for the women in the hospital.'

Her husband's eyes were blazing agates. 'Richard may do so, if he wishes. But not you.'

'It's all been decided. We hope to move the looms in to the new weaving shop next week.'

'I forbid it, Margaret!'

Even if she had wanted to, there was no changing her mind after she heard that. 'And I've decided, Gavin.'

He rounded on Richard. 'This is all your doing!'

'Mine? Surely you, of all men, should know that nobody forces your wife to do anything against her will.'

'Get out of my house.'

'Gavin!'

'I may not hold any authority over you, Margaret. I may not even be allowed to be a father to my son. But by God, this is my house and I'll have my say as to who's welcome in it and who isn't!' Then he turned his attention back to his brother.

'You were never done causing trouble and mischief as a laddie, Richard, and you've not changed. But from henceforth you won't do it under this roof!'

'Gavin Knox, have you taken leave of your senses? Richard's done nothing to deserve this treatment!'

'Not yet, mebbe. But he will, Margaret, he will, if he's given the least chance for mischief.'

Richard's eyes had narrowed slightly, but his face was still and untroubled. 'I've done nothing to be ashamed of, Gavin, but since you –'

'Nothing? You call causing the death of your own mother nothing?'

Richard went white to the lips. 'You're lying!'

'Am I, Richard? You know the truth as well as I do! Always, from the moment of your birth, you were the centre of her universe. And what reward did you see fit to give her?' As the bitter words poured from Gavin in a torrent, Margaret, appalled, realised that they must have lain within him for years, rankling and festering.

'She had to lie for you, to protect you from the consequences of your mischief-making,' he raged. 'And you repaid her by running away – leaving her without a backward glance, never sending her word of your whereabouts. She sickened from that day. She died of a broken heart, Richard, and it was you who broke it!'

He stopped, and for a moment there was silence. Then Richard lifted one shoulder in a faint shrug and half-turned away. Gavin, maddened by the gesture, lunged across the short space of carpeted floor between them and caught at his brother's arm, spinning him round so that they faced each other.

Richard's hands came up in a self-protective move just as Margaret took hold of Gavin's arm and pulled him away from his brother.

'Gavin! For pity's sake, the man's a guest under our roof!'

As soon as he was released Richard stepped back, slipping his fingers distastefully over the crumpled material of his sleeve.

Gavin drew a long ragged breath then said coldly and steadily, 'I've told you – you're no longer welcome beneath my roof. If you're not out by the time I come home tonight I'll take you by the neck and run you out!'

Neither of them spoke until they heard the front door crash to behind Gavin. Margaret found that she was clutching tightly at the back of a chair, so tightly that the skin stretched over the knuckles of both hands was bone white.

Shakily, she released her grip and sat down.

'Richard –'

He shrugged again. 'Don't concern yourself, sister. Gavin was always given to sudden bursts of rage, as I recall. I shall easily find suitable lodgings in the town.'

'But all these accusations – are they true?'

'Oh, I doubt it. I'll not lose any sleep over them, I can assure you. Gavin always had a possessive love of our mother, as I recall. Clearly he needs to lay the blame for her death at someone's door. But never at his own. And, as the family scapegoat, I must accept any blame he chooses to cast.'

Margaret, remembering the white-hot rage in Gavin's face, began to shiver, though the room was warm enough. All at once the future, usually predictable and safe, was like a dark endless corridor, a fearsome place that she was afraid to enter.

'Richard –' she said. 'Oh, Richard – what's to become of us? What's to become of Gavin and me?'

Chapter Twenty

Gavin was right about one thing – winter was fast approaching and there wouldn't be many more lush warm late autumn days to come.

After she and Richard, accompanied by Christian and Daniel, had inspected and approved of the new loomshop, Margaret went back to the Poors' Hospital to conduct the morning class.

Her own children often attended the classes with her, working diligently on their slates, enjoying the novelty of being with the others.

Today, too pre-occupied to concentrate on the lesson, Margaret led her young charges out of the high-ceilinged cheerless school-room and into the fields by the river where they could run about and play in the sunshine.

On the way through the large entrance hall they encountered the hospital mistress. The woman's nostrils flared slightly with disapproval as she watched the youngsters scampering past her and out of the door, heading gleefully towards freedom; but she said nothing, acknowledging Margaret's greeting with a painfully manufactured smile.

Margaret had been the first ever teacher to be appointed to teach the pauper children, and she had done her work well over the years. The board of directors, Mary MacLeod among them, approved of her work in general, although there had been many clashes between them when their views on the treatment of the wretched, dependent inmates under their care were at variance with hers.

Now, of course, she enjoyed extra powers as the wife of a respected surgeon and the sister of a local physician, both known to have given their services, unpaid, to the hospital on numerous occasions.

She sat on a fallen tree and watched the children at play, their pinched little faces lifted to the sun, their under-nourished bodies seeming to fill out and blossom in its meagre autumnal warmth.

Beside these pauper children Christian and Daniel appeared to be both overfed and pampered, Margaret thought, and knew that she couldn't abandon the hospital inmates, no matter how much Gavin railed at her.

She bit her lip, recollecting his face earlier that day – the face of a stranger. He hadn't asked her to give up her work, he had demanded it. And Margaret Montgomery – not for the first time since her marriage Margaret fully understood and appreciated the Scots custom whereby a married woman was perfectly entitled to retain her own name instead of being obliged to use her husband's at all times, as in England – Margaret Montgomery, she repeated to herself defiantly, didn't take kindly to demands.

*

A carter had just finished loading bales of linen from Duncan Montgomery's loom shop later that day when Margaret and the children left her mother's house. The man, an old friend of her family's, gave her a nod, and on the impulse she asked, 'Are you going to the bleachfields?'

'I am that.'

'Will you take us up to the braes?'

His eyebrows climbed. 'Bless us, Maggie Montgomery, you're surely past the stage of riding on the bleachfield carts!'

'My bairns aren't.'

'You'll have to walk back.'

'I always did.' She lifted Daniel up, and deposited him on top of the bales. The man shrugged and swung Christian, squealing with excitement, to a seat beside her brother. Then as Margaret gathered up her skirts he gave her his hand and the past five years vanished like snow in the sun as she stepped, sure-footed, onto the cart to join her children.

When the three of them were settled in a nest among the bales the man clicked his tongue at his horse and the patient beast set off, the cart joggling and bumping along behind it.

Margaret wrapped her arms about the giggling children and for the first time in years savoured the pleasure of riding in the back of a linen cart, looking down on the pedestrians.

Now and again she waved to familiar faces among the folk on the footpath. Some, after their first puzzled stare, recognised her and laughed and waved back; others looked shocked. Margaret was thankful that she had left her mother safely out in the back garden, tending to her bees. She could just imagine what Meg Montgomery would have had to say about a grown woman, a wife and mother too, disporting herself on the back of a linen cart for all the town to see.

Jamie, coming out of the Wellmeadow pend as the cart drew level with him, didn't notice its occupants. His head was lowered, his eyes fixed on the ground.

'Hello, Jamie! Stop a minute –' Margaret appealed to the driver, who obediently reined in his horse as the red-headed man looked up.

'Margaret, now what are you up to?'

She laughed down at him and reached out her hand, 'We're off to the bleach-fields. Come with us, Jamie.'

'The bleach-fields – the bleach-fields –' Christian began to caper about on the linen bales, chanting, and Margaret locked a firm hold on her skirt and dragged her down again.

'Come on, Jamie!'

As the carter shook the reins and the vehicle began to move again Jamie made a sudden decision, caught at the tail of the cart, and swung himself up beside them.

'It's a while since you and me last used this form of transport,' he said breathlessly.

'Too long.' Margaret settled back against the bales, and gave herself over to enjoying the ride.

*

The driver stopped his horse about a mile beyond the town, just before it reached the bleach-fields. There, the linen would be stretched out on the ground, exposed to the sun and doused with pure burn water until it was bleached from its original coarse grey shade to as near white as was possible. 'Will this do you, Maggie?'

'It'll do me fine!'

Jamie got down and lifted the children to the ground. Then he reached his arms up to Margaret, who dropped lightly into them.

Christian and Daniel, drunk with the excitement of this most unexpected treat, were already racing over the short tufted grass, swerving in and out of the whin bushes. Margaret and Jamie, after a word of thanks to the carter, turned to follow the children as the cart moved away.

At first they walked in silence, each occupied with private thoughts. Then Jamie said abruptly, 'I've decided to throw in my lot with Richard Knox.'

'Use his cotton yarn to weave cloth for him?' She stared at him with astonishment and a little dismay. 'But what about my father, and Robert?'

He had the grace to look uncomfortable. 'Och, they're set on continuing with the linen yarn. Richard needed six or seven looms, and I thought that perhaps we could have spared that many between us. But Duncan and Robert are determined to keep all their machines on linen cloth. So, today I told him I'd turn my eight looms to cotton and weave his cloth for him.'

Margaret could scarcely believe it. Ever since her father had come to Paisley as a young, newly-wed man and been taken on by Peter Todd, Jamie's father, the Todds and Montgomerys had worked together. Jamie's move put an end to all of that; to Margaret, it represented more than just a change of cloth. It meant a split between the two families.

'Jamie –'

'I know, I know!' he said angrily. 'But it's time for a change, Margaret. The linen's not bringing in enough money. I've got seven weavers and two drawboys to think about, as well as Kirsty and Billy to support. I must think ahead!'

'But what if the new cloth doesn't sell? What if Richard's wrong when he says he's got a good market?'

'It'll have to sell, Margaret. That's the truth of it. If not – well, I'll give up the whole business and get out of the town.

We're at war in the Americas – I could go back to being a soldier.'

'You said you'd never do that!'

Jamie's hair seemed to flame belligerently. 'Is it only women that are entitled to change their minds?'

'Anyway, you're getting too old to fight.'

'I'm too old for many things,' he said bitterly. 'But not too old yet for soldiering. Not quite.'

She put a hand on his arm. 'Don't go, Jamie. Don't leave us again.'

'Lassie, if this cloth doesnae work, I must leave, before I'm laughed out of the town!'

Beneath her touch the muscles of his arm were corded and rock-hard with tension. 'There's more than the cloth troubling you, Jamie Todd. What's amiss?'

'Nothing,' he said, and pulled away from her, striding ahead as the ground suddenly dipped into a small hollow.

Margaret picked a grass head and began to strip it of its seeds as she followed. Ahead, the children's voices rang like bells in the clear cool air.

On the opposite side of the hollow Jamie slowed to let her catch up. But his face was still averted, and she knew better than to say any more about the cloth.

'How are the Highlanders coming along?' she asked instead. 'Have Lachie and Walter managed to keep their hands off each other?'

'Aye. They know what they'd get from me if they tried to make trouble in my loom shop.'

Margaret twirled the grass stem. 'I think there's more on Walter's mind than fighting. If you ask me, he's smitten with Islay.'

'Nonsense!'

'I'm telling you. A man never notices these things, but a woman does.'

'They scarce know each other.'

'What's that got to do with it? I saw the look on his face when she opened the door to him once, when I was visiting with her.'

'Walter?' He said the name as though she had just mentioned the most unlikely candidate possible for Islay's hand.

'Aye, Walter. He's a fine-looking laddie, and Islay's fast growing into a beautiful woman now that she's got enough to eat and she's wearing better than those poor rags she used to have. And they're both of marriageable age. She could do a lot worse than to settle for Walter.'

There was a pause, then, 'Islay's cousin's back from the Army,' Jamie said.

'Oh? I didn't know that. I must call on her. What's he like?'

'I can't take to him. For one thing, he persists in speaking in his own tongue – though he can probably speak English as well as the next man – and I can never tell what he's saying. For another, there's something in his eyes when he looks at me –' He stopped, and swiped irritably with his boot at a bush. 'I'll be glad when he's out of Paisley. It seems to me that he's of no use to Islay. But she fawns over him as if –' He stopped again, then finished, 'I don't care for him at all.'

Christian and Daniel, some distance in front of them as they walked back down to the town, reached the top of a slight slope and began to disappear from view. First Daniel's dark head, then Christian's, vanished from Margaret's sight. All that was left of them was the sound of their laughter carried back to her on a breeze.

Then she and Jamie topped the rise and saw that the children had thrown themselves down on the grass and were rolling down the hill, bumping from tussock to tussock, screaming with amusement as they went. Christian's skirts had wrapped themselves round her knees, and her legs kicked free.

'Times I wish,' said Jamie, grinning, 'that I was their age again.'

'Oh – so do I!'

He stopped, turned her round, and looked down into her face. For the second time that day a man held her shoulders, compelling her to look up at him.

But this time the face above hers was compassionate and concerned. It was his turn to ask, 'What's amiss, Margaret?'

If he had been anyone else she would probably have denied that anything was amiss. But she and Jamie had always had a special relationship. If he had had his way, they would have been man and wife. Margaret wondered, bleakly, if that might not have been a good idea after all.

'It's Gavin and me. Everything's gone wrong, Jamie, and I don't know what to do to make it right again.'

'I can't advise you, for I've no experience of marriage – nor likely to have now.'

'For goodness' sake, Jamie Todd!' She felt tears of self-pity prickle the backs of her eyes, and chased them away by forcing a mock frown. 'You're not as old as all that – there's plenty of good marriageable years in you yet. All you need to do is to find the right woman.'

He released her and they began to walk again. Below them, now, lay the town, blurred beneath a soft blue haze of smoke from its chimneys. The children had picked themselves up and were racing on.

'I'm not so sure about that,' said Jamie. 'Sometimes it seems to me, Margaret, that I've made a right confusion of being an adult.'

She slipped her fingers into his and gripped his hand tightly.

'Sometimes, Jamie, I think the same about myself,' said Margaret.

Chapter Twenty-One

By the time Gavin returned that night Richard Knox had found lodgings in St Mirin's Wynd, near to the Cross, and moved his belongings out of the Oakshawhill house.

Gavin made no comment about his brother, and neither did Margaret. When the children noisily wanted to know where Uncle Richard was, and when he was coming home, their father silenced them with a look that cowed Daniel completely and even caused Christian to find the sense to close her mouth.

Neither of them mentioned Richard in their father's hearing again.

The business over Richard not only re-opened the chasm between Margaret and Gavin, but made it all the wider.

She went about the work of setting up more inkle looms in the new weaving shop, and finding capable women from among the hospital inmates to take on the work. She attended to her Hospital duties and to her household duties, and made certain that Gavin could find nothing to complain of; and she did it all with an unhappy heart.

'Your mother's getting worried about you,' Mary MacLeod told her at last.

'There's nothing amiss with me.'

'Oh, you put a very good face on it – and so does Gavin. But Meg and me aren't daft altogether, Margaret. We can tell when a marriage has soured. Is it not time you and Gavin agreed to forget about this smallpox business?'

'It's nothing to do with that. It's the way he's treated Richard.'

'Margaret, you're the man's wife, not his owner. You'd not thank him if he interfered between you and Robert, or you and Thomas. Leave him and his brother be.'

'I'll not stand by and watch Richard ill-used and insulted!'

'It's not worrying him half as much as it's worrying you. I saw him in the town this morning, looking even more handsome than ever. For all that Paisley's air's damp, it seems to be doing Richard good. But then,' said Mary dryly, 'Richard's getting everything his own way these days.'

She was right. Richard Knox had come to Paisley in search of looms to weave his cotton yarn. He had them – and in addition he had some eight inkle looms using up the yarn he bought from the English manufactories, and turning out ribbons and tapes for him to export abroad from the Glasgow docks while he waited for the first consignment of cloth to roll off Jamie's looms.

He had found himself comfortable lodgings and taken on a manservant; during that winter he became a familiar sight, riding about the town on the fine chestnut horse he had bought for himself, his dour-faced servant riding behind him on a sturdy grey.

He was very popular with the local people, and much in demand at the flurry of gatherings and dinners that took place during the dark winter months.

Each time Margaret and Gavin encountered him at these social events Gavin was formally courteous, treating Richard as though he was a little-known acquaintance. His manner didn't seem to trouble his brother one bit.

Margaret, curious to see Islay's cousin, found time to visit the house above Jamie's loom shop. She wasn't long in Ross McInnes's company before she had decided that Jamie was right. There was something almost menacing about the youth, something that made it impossible to chatter with Islay in his company.

Normally Margaret would have felt a quick, warm sympathy for him, for he carried the stamp of someone who had seen and experienced a great deal of suffering. But Ross, embittered by his experiences, clearly didn't want anyone's sympathy.

When he spoke to Islay in the Gaelic before Margaret, the girl flushed and said sharply in English, 'Ross, you must speak the Lowlander tongue before our guest.'

His dark eyes rested briefly on Margaret, then moved away again. 'I said I'll away out for some fresh air.'

He picked up a carefully patched and darned jacket, gave Margaret a mocking bow, and left. Islay watched him go with troubled eyes.

'He's had a hard time,' she said apologetically as the clatter of his feet on the wooden stair died away. 'He should have gone to the Americas with the rest of the soldiers, but he was very ill, and like to die. They left him behind, and when he was well enough he walked here from London.'

'Does he have to go back to the Army when he's strong again?'

The girl shook her head. 'It seems not. Or he's made up his mind not to go. I don't know the truth of it. He's talking of going to Edinburgh to settle once he's well enough.'

'And leaving you alone again?'

Islay looked down at the hands twisting together in her lap, then up at Margaret. 'He wants us to go with him, all of us. He – he wants me to wed with him.'

'Oh? And what do you want, Islay?'

'I don't know. You've all been kind to us – you and Mister Todd, and the others. I like Paisley well enough. But Ross is set on leaving the place. He'd not settle here.'

'Islay, if you don't want to marry him you don't have to. He seems –' Margaret hesitated, searching for the right words, and the girl said swiftly:

'It's not his fault that he's bitter and suspicious. Bad things have happened to him. You should have seen Ross before – when we were all at home together. He was strong and able and willing. He was good at everything he turned his mind to.'

She smiled faintly, remembering. 'He was the best dancer and the fastest runner – and there wasn't a thing Ross couldn't do with the beasts. That's what he has in mind now – to work on the land, with mebbe a wee farm cottage for us all to live in. The way it would have been, if things hadn't changed for the worse for us.'

The smile faded, to be replaced by a sadness far beyond her years. 'But then we were thrown off our land, and there was all the hardship, and seeing folk sicken and die, one by one. The old ones and the littlest bairns, then the others. Not knowing where we were going to lay our heads, not knowing if we were going to eat, or be made welcome, or stoned. Not finding work, when we finally arrived in Paisley. Then the Army – so many things to change him.'

'Most of these things happened to you, too. And you've not let them turn you to bitterness.'

'But it's different for us, isn't it? Men take it badly if they can't look after their families. Men have their pride.'

'And you think women don't?' Margaret asked tartly.

The girl flashed her a sudden mature, sharing smile; a smile that bound them together, once and for ever, as friends and confidantes. 'Oh yes, women do – but we know how to temper our pride, don't we? It's something we have to learn early in life.'

As she was taking her leave, Margaret said again, 'You don't have to marry with Ross if you don't want to, Islay.'

'I'll see – when he's well enough to move on. I'll see.'

'Is there someone else?' Margaret thought of Walter Shaw, and was sure she had hit on the truth when sudden colour stained the girl's face.

'Who else would there be?'

'Nobody special – I just wondered,' said Margaret, and left.

*

When she had closed the door behind her guest Islay leaned her forehead against it for a moment. Margaret Knox's words echoed in her mind. 'Is there someone else?'

Fleetingly, she thought of a man with very blue eyes and a thatch of blazing red hair. A man of changing moods, a man she longed to know and understand. A man, she thought, her brow knotting with worry, Ross disliked. A man who returned that dislike, measure for cold measure.

Morag, returning from an errand, clattered up the wooden stairs and lifted the latch. Islay put all thought of Jamie Todd firmly from her mind and stepped aside to let her cousin in.

*

Towards the end of the year Gavin received an invitation to work in his home town of Dumfries for a short while with a surgeon he had known in his youth.

For the first time in many weeks his face was animated as he told Margaret his news. 'It was that man who decided me to take up medicine in the first place. I'd like fine to have the chance to work by his side.'

It pleased her to see him come to life again. 'Then you must certainly go.'

'Will you come with me – you and the bairns?'

'Gavin, where would we stay?'

'I could find a house to rent easily enough.'

'But I don't know anyone there,' she said in dismay. 'And it would be an awful upheaval, taking Ellen and the bairns all that way for a short while. At this time of year, too, when it's so cold and the weather's bad for travel –'

'Then leave them here. Ellen can look after them, and there's your Aunt Mary and your mother to help her. Come yourself.'

'Oh no, I couldn't leave them –'

Gavin's face was suddenly cold. 'You couldn't leave your looms and the Poors' House, you mean.'

'I don't mean that at all! See reason, Gavin – you'll be in the hospital most of the time. I'd be alone, in a place where I don't know anybody.'

'You'd meet folk. It's not just in Paisley that people are friendly. I was a stranger here myself at one time, but it didn't stop me from settling when you wanted to stay.'

'It was different for you. You didn't have a family, and you didn't have bairns –'

Gavin got up abruptly and made for the door. 'I'll go alone.' He threw the words over his shoulder.

'How long will you be gone?'

He stopped at the door and looked at her with angry eyes. 'I don't know. Does it matter?' he said, and walked out of the room.

*

Meg Montgomery eyed her daughter closely when Margaret walked into her kitchen and announced that Gavin was off to Dumfries.

'Should you not go with him?'

'It's not worth it for all the time he'll be away.' Margaret loosened her bonnet strings and put her cloak aside. 'I'd only have found myself in a strange town, with Gavin at the hospital all the time.'

'All the same, a woman's place is with her man. And the way things have been with you two –'

'The way things have been, a wee spell away from each other might be just what we're needing. Anyway, I'm busy with my new inkle looms.'

'I suppose you know what they're saying in the town –' Meg said unhappily. 'That Gavin and Richard had words, and Gavin put his own brother out of the house. It's a shaming thing, Margaret, to hear such talk of my daughter's man.'

'It's none of your concern, or mine, what falls between brothers.' Margaret unblushingly made use of Mary's words. 'Besides, who pays heed to the town gossips?'

'Plenty do. Specially where Richard Knox is concerned. That man's set the fox among the hens as far as your father's concerned, I can tell you.'

Margaret flapped an impatient hand. 'It's nothing to do with me. I've no wish to hear about it.'

Meg gave a loud sniff. 'You'll hear about it all right, if Duncan has his way of it.'

Almost as though husband and wife had pre-arranged it, the door opened and Duncan Montgomery walked in and caught the last few words.

'If I've my way of what?'

The women eyed each other before Margaret, realising that there was no getting out of it, said, 'We were talking about Richard Knox.'

Duncan's strong square face was normally cheerful. But at the mention of Richard's name it settled into dour lines. 'Him! That man's a trouble-maker!'

'He's a man of business, that's all.'

'Oh aye, I heard he'd got you on his side – against your own husband's wishes, too.'

She felt her anger begin to rise. 'I'm not on his side – he's helping me to set up the inkle looms I need, and we're using his cotton yarn. As for Gavin, that business is for him and me to settle between us.'

'I don't know what's possessed you, Margaret. And I don't know what's possessed Jamie Todd, agreeing to turn all his looms over to cotton weaving.'

'He thinks linen's on its way out. The man has a right to use his own looms in whatever way he thinks fit.' Then, as her parents said nothing, she pressed on, 'I don't know why you and Robert wouldn't agree to trying the yarn on some of your machines.'

'Richard Knox isn't a weaver, and never has been. He knows nothing of the looms. I'll not trust my livelihood to a man whose only interest is in buying and selling and making money for himself.'

'And for the weavers.'

'As to that, Robert and me'll wait and see what happens. The man's full of high notions and promises, but they've yet to be proved,' said Duncan darkly, and try as she might, Margaret could find no way of shifting him from his pessimistic view of Richard Knox's business in the town.

Chapter Twenty-Two

The old year had ended and 1776 had settled in before Ross McInnes was well enough to consider moving on, out of Paisley.

Islay had been in no hurry for him to make a full recovery. She dreaded the time when she must make a decision about her own future.

In some strange way she now felt more secure in the loomshop than in the house above. Each morning as Lachie scampered off along the dark empty streets to waken the weavers she looked forward to the time spent alone with the silent, waiting looms. There was a good feeling about the place, a sense of security and timeless peace.

All too soon Lachie would come hurrying back and begin squirming his thin, agile little body beneath the machines, cleaning out the threads and fluff and snails that sometimes found their way into the pits left in the floor to make room for the set of foot treadles.

Then the others arrived, yawning and sleepy-eyed, filling the place with their talk.

Islay usually found some excuse to loiter until the first weaver settled himself on his saytree, running his hands over his loom in the way that the weavers had, as though re-affirming the bond between man and machine. Eventually the man would press his foot down on a treadle and the loom would lumber into action, the harness that held the weft threads lifting to form the 'shed'.

The weaver would skilfully throw the yarn-loaded shuttle through the shed from one end to the other, the yarn stretching out behind it. The treadle was released, the harness fell back into place, the newly-thrown weft thread was firmly tapped into its place on the cloth with the weaver's 'pooking pin', and the day, for Islay had begun.

Although Jamie Todd's looms were no longer using linen yarn he found weavers willing to take all the yarn that his own spinsters had formerly spun for him, and so Islay's wheel was kept as busy as ever.

As she went about her housework, or settled at her wheel, Islay was continually aware of Ross's dark eyes fixed on her. He tended to follow her about the house, or hovered restlessly by the window if she had to go out, watching for her return. He himself rarely went further than the back yard.

With each day that passed, she sensed his growing restlessness. Finally, on a mild day in early February as he was sitting by the fire, watching her work at her wheel, he announced abruptly, 'It's time we were moving on.'

Islay's fingers tightened on the yarn, almost snagging it, then deliberately relaxed. 'Why should you want to move?'

'I told you,' he said impatiently. 'I'm going to find work on the land.'

'There are farms round here. No doubt you could find work on one of them.'

'No, not here. We're going to the other side of the country, by Edinburgh way.'

'But Ross, we've got a good house, and Lachie and Morag have work.'

'I can't settle in Paisley,' he said impatiently. 'I don't like the place.'

'You'd come to like it if you'd just give it some time.'

'We'd be better somewhere else – anywhere else,' he went on, without heeding her.

'When did you have it in mind to leave?'

'As soon as we can.' It was always 'we', she noticed, and felt her heart begin to thump.

'You're not well enough to travel yet.'

'I'm as well as I'll ever be. It's doing me no good to sit here day after day.' He got up and began to pace the floor, his lithe body jerky with his impatience to be out of the town.

'But Lachie and Morag have work now.'

'They'll find work elsewhere.'

'Ross, will you stop and think –'

'No!' He glared at her, his eyes stormy. 'I'm the man of the family – I decide what we do. And I've decided that we're leaving.'

'Lachie and Morag –'

' – will want to be where I am.'

It was true. The youngsters were overjoyed to have their brother back with them. They would follow him to the ends of the world without question, rather than be left behind.

'And you, Islay, you'll come with us?'

The words were shaped as a question, but a question that didn't need an answer. Ross took it for granted that she, too, would follow where he led.

The moment Islay had dreaded ever since his arrival had come. She stilled the wheel, studied it for a moment, head bent, then looked up at him.

It needed all her courage to say, 'No, Ross. I want to stay here.'

For a moment his jaw sagged in sheer astonishment. Then his mouth snapped shut and immediately opened again to say, 'Of course you'll come with us!'

'I don't want to go wandering again. I've found a home here. I like the folk. I want to stay.'

'I'm your kinsman. I must care for you – and you must do as I wish.'

'I can see to myself well enough.'

His eyes narrowed. 'Is it some man – is that it? Has some Paisley man got a hold of you?'

'Does there need to be a man? Can I not just decide to stay because I'm happy here?'

'But Islay, we'll marry – you and I.'

'No, Ross.'

'Yes! It was always known that we would, even when we were children!'

She twisted her hands together in her lap. 'That was when we thought we'd be living a different life. No doubt we'd have been wed by now, if things had gone on as before. But everything's changed now.'

'I've not changed, and neither have you. Islay –' He came to her, lifted her to her feet, his hands urgent on her. 'All the time I was soldiering, all the time I was making my way here, I had the thought that once I found you again we'd be wed, then we'd always be together – all of us.'

The desperation in his voice shook her to the centre of her soul. She was consumed by pity for him. But pity made poor soil for the long, strong roots of a good marriage.

'It was what our people wanted, Islay –'

'Our people are dead now,' she heard herself say stonily.

'It's what I want!'

'But not what I want. Not now. I can't marry with you, Ross.'

'Islay –' He pulled her roughly into his arms and kissed her. She submitted to his embrace, but when his hands began to fumble at the fastenings of her gown she tried to push him away, realising what his intentions were. Once he had taken her she would be his, with no right to refuse to marry him. 'No!'

'Islay!' He wrapped his arms about her, held her closer so that she was trapped within the circle of his embrace. She hadn't realised that he had gained so much strength. The spinning stool fell over as the two of them struggled silently, Ross intent on winning his own way by force if necessary, Islay determined that he should not.

She was losing ground, being forced step by step towards the wall-bed, when someone rapped at the door.

The sudden unexpected noise tore the cousins apart. They stared at each other, both breathless from the struggle. The angry colour that had flared in Ross's thin face suddenly fled, leaving him white and sick-looking, his eyes bright with terror. 'Who's that?'

'How should I know?' Hurriedly she pulled her gown straight and tucked in hair that had become unloosened from beneath her cap in the struggle, then went to open the door.

Jamie Todd stood outside. 'I'm going along to Maxwellton, Islay. If you've got some pirns ready I'll take them along for you.'

His eyes flickered over her, then beyond, narrowing as they settled on the overturned stool.

'Yes –' She tried to calm her breathing, certain that he must realise what had been going on. 'I'll fetch them for you.'

'Tell the interfering fool to go,' Ross said sulkily in Gaelic. She ignored him, going to where the basket of pirns lay. When she picked it up and turned, she saw that Jamie had stepped into the room and was waiting just inside the door.

Ross looked from the newcomer to Islay, then snatched up his jacket and went out, ducking his head as he passed the Paisley man, slamming the door behind him.

Jamie picked up the fallen stool and put it neatly back in its place. 'Is there something amiss?'

'No.' She held out the basket. For a moment she thought that he was going to persist in his questioning. But instead, to her relief, he took the basket and left.

*

Ross stayed away until it was almost dark and Islay was beginning to worry about him. He returned just in time for the evening meal and ate it in silence, not looking once in her direction. Immediately afterwards he retired to the inner room, where he was sleeping on a mattress supplied by Margaret Knox.

The household was accustomed to bedding early and rising early. Once the meal was over and the dishes cleaned and put away Lachie and Morag went to their beds; Islay, after spinning for a short while by candle-light, took off her blouse and skirt and cap, brushed her hair, then blew out the candle and slipped into the wall bed, falling asleep almost at once.

She was wakened by a draught of cold air as the bedclothes were lifted back.

'Wha –?' The sleepy question was cut short as a hand clamped over her mouth.

The mattress beneath her dipped under the weight of someone climbing into the bed, and Ross's voice hissed in her ear, 'Hold your tongue! D'you want to wake the lassie?'

Then his hand left her mouth as he settled in the bed beside her, his body clamped urgently against hers from shoulder to toes. Morag, always a heavy sleeper, stirred and mumbled something, then settled again.

'Ross! Leave me be, Ross –' She tried to fight off the marauding fingers that tore at the fastenings on her chemise but she was hampered by the blanket that covered her, and by her fear that her young cousin would waken and realise what was going on.

'Be still, will you!' he panted into her ear. There was a soft ripping sound as the material of the chemise gave beneath his strong, determined onslaught, and she felt his chilled hands cup the soft warmth of her breasts.

'No!' She put her own hands against his chest and tried to push him out of the bed, but he was spurred on by lust as well as a grim determination to bend her to his will, and too strong for her. His mouth found hers and claimed it just as his hands were busily claiming her body.

Now he had her half-pinned against the mattress, his thigh thrown across her hips so that she was prevented from moving freely.

Outrage at being used against her will gave way to fear as Islay realised that there was little she could do to stop her cousin, other than to scream at the top of her voice and waken Lachie and Morag. But she couldn't bring herself to rouse the youngsters, no matter what happened to her.

Ross chuckled breathlessly, as though reading her mind. The hem of her shift was dragged to her thighs, then his hand groped between her legs.

It seemed that there was little else to do but to stop struggling and let him have his way with her. But some part of Islay, the part that had kept her alive during the terrible time after the Clearances, refused to let it happen. She whipped her head round on the pillow and sank her teeth into his wrist, just as she had bitten Walter Shaw on the day he had tried to throttle Lachie.

Ross cursed sharply in English, a foul obscenity that had no place in his own language and must have been learned from his companions in the Army, then as Islay's teeth released him he balled his fist and hit her.

A burst of stars flared before her eyes and she struck out with clawed fingers, her nails finding and digging into the flesh of his cheek.

He cursed again and drew away sharply. But he was already on the edge of the bed, and with flailing limbs he fell out, landing on the floor with a bone-jarring thump.

Light as a startled deer, Islay sprang from the mattress, leaping over him and landing on the middle of the floor. Sure-footed even in the dark, she ran the few steps to the range, blessing the instinct for tidiness and order that caused her to put the heavy iron soup ladle away on the same hook each time she used it.

She whirled, moving her hand so that the dim glow from the range gleamed dully on the metal implement she held. 'Get back to your own bed and leave me be, Ross,' she whispered, 'or I'll –'

'Islay?' There was movement from the bed, and Morag sat up. Her voice was peevish and clogged with sleep.

'I – I'm just coming to bed. Go back to sleep, Morag.'

'I heard a noise –'

'I tripped over a stool in the dark.' Islay drew the torn chemise across her breasts, her other hand keeping a tight grip on the ladle. If she had to, she would use it. 'I'll be with you in a minute.'

Mercifully, Ross stayed where he was, out of the girl's sight. Now that her eyes were accustomed to the little light that the range provided Islay could see his eyes glittering at her from the floor like an animal's.

Morag sighed, turned her back on the room, and lay down again, curling into a ball and falling asleep at once.

Islay stepped to where her clothes had been placed over the back of a chair. She put the ladle quietly down on the table and began to dress hurriedly, ready to snatch the improvised weapon up at the first sign of movement.

'What are you doing?' her cousin's voice hissed out of the dark corner by the bed.

'I'm going outside, away from you.'

'You're not going to get the militia?' There was sudden terror in his voice.

'Not this time.' She fastened her skirt, picked up her woollen shawl. 'But if you ever touch me again, Ross McInnes, I will get them! I swear before God that I will!'

His sudden silence assured her that she had managed to cow him. Even so, she picked up the ladle again before letting herself silently out of the door and closing it behind her.

For a while she sat on the wooden stairs, huddled into herself, intending to stay there until morning came. But the cold quickly struck through her clothes. She got up, already stiff with the night chill, but hesitated with her hand on the latch. What if Ross tried again to get into her bed when she was asleep? What if he hadn't gone back to the room he shared with Lachie, but was waiting on the other side of the door, knowing that she must eventually return?

Slowly, she backed away from the door and went down the stairs into the inky black pend, fumbling along the wall until she found the door of the loom shop.

Although the fire had gone out long since the room seemed warm after the night's chill. Islay, afraid to light the candle in case the town watchmen saw the glow in the window and came to investigate, made her way slowly across the room, stumbling against the looms. Then she crouched over the grate, holding her hands close to the grey ashes in a search for the last vestiges of fire.

After a while she drew her shawl tightly about her shoulders and sat down on the saytree of one of the looms. The long narrow bench, made as part of the machine, was polished and shaped by many years of constant use, and comfortable enough.

Islay leaned her elbows on the beam directly before her and pillowed her head on her arms. Her face throbbed where Ross's fist had struck against her cheekbone. She recalled her cousin as he had been in the old days, her childhood companion, her friend, her protector.

In those days she had happily expected to join with Ross in marriage, to share a home with him, to bear his children. But not now, not now that hardship had embittered and warped him and brought him so low that he was prepared to treat her with as much respect as an indifferent farmer would show to the animals beneath his care.

Not now that she had ventured into the world, and had come to know a different life from that of the glens and mountains.

Not now that she had met with Jamie Todd.

The thought of Jamie comforted her. She held him close in her mind until finally, without realising it, she slept.

Chapter Twenty-Three

She wakened early in the morning to the tread of a man's boots on the footpath outside. Startled and confused, she stared for a moment at the angular grey outlines of the looms about her, and put wondering fingers to the side of her face, which felt strangely stiff and clumsy.

Then she winced as pain shot through her cheekbone, and remembered where she was, and why.

Almost crippled with cold, she made her way up to the house, to find everything as it should be – Morag sound asleep in the wall-bed, and no sign of Ross. Moving silently, Islay took her shawl off, put the ladle by the bed, where it was close at hand, and slipped beneath the coverlet fully dressed, trying to draw some warmth from Morag.

Five minutes later, hearing Lachie stir in the next room, she rose and put the ladle back on its accustomed hook, then tidied her hair and began to make his breakfast.

The boy's eyes widened when he saw her. 'What happened to you?'

She looked into the little mirror that hung on the wall, and saw that there was a swelling bruise high on her cheek, just below her left eye. 'I tripped over a stool in the dark last night and fell against the table.'

Lachie accepted the explanation. But later in the loom shop Walter Shaw eyed her sceptically when she gave her story.

'Are you certain?'

'I should know how I hurt my own face!'

'I'd not put it past that cousin of yours to lift his fist to you.'

'He'd never do that!'

Walter scowled and settled himself at his loom, the same loom Islay had pillowed her head on during the night. A change had come over him in the few months since the

Highland family had moved into the dwelling house above. He kept his tongue and his hands off Lachie -- although Islay sometimes thought shrewdly that her young cousin wouldn't mind a good fight. Lachie had his elder brother's enthusiasm for the sport; it was an enthusiasm that was inbred in their race, and the reason why Highlanders made formidable and fearless soldiers. But at times such as the times they found themselves in, and in places such as Paisley, the lust for blood was out of place and more of a curse than a virtue.

Walter had become quite considerate towards Islay herself, helping her to carry well-water or pirns if he chanced to come across her in the street. Often, if she was working around the loom shop while the weavers were there, she looked up to see his eyes fixed on her. At first he had ducked his head with quick embarrassment when she met his gaze, but in the past few weeks, since Ross's arrival, he had smiled at her before turning his attention back at his work.

Now, when Islay had set the fire burning to her satisfaction and went out of the room with a bucket of ashes for the midden, Walter left his saytree and caught her at the door. 'I'll carry that for you.'

'It's the lassie's face that's bruised, no' her hands,' one of the other weavers said with a grin, but Walter, cheeks reddening, took the bucket from Islay's fingers and followed her out into the back yard.

The midden was over in the far corner, in an angle of the wall that shaped the back yard. Several times a year, when it grew too large to be manageable, a refuse cart came and took the assorted rubbish away. In the heat of summer the house windows in the town often had to be closed against the stench arising from these domestic middens; when that happened, the refuse carts were called more often than usual.

Walter tossed the ashes onto the heap with less care than Islay would have shown. A fine cloud of pale grey ash lifted into the air and was blown back in their faces by the cool moist breeze, setting the two of them coughing.

Islay briskly swept the worst of it off herself, took the pail back, and was about to return to the loom shop when he detained her with one hand on her arm.

'Islay, wait a minute.'

She stopped, her head still turned away from him so that the bruise on her cheek was hidden. She wanted no more questions about that – she had trouble enough without the likes of Walter Shaw causing more.

But he had other things on his mind. 'Will you go walking with me later, when the work's done?'

Sheer surprise brought her chin up swiftly. 'Walking with you –?' she started to say, then she saw that a covering of grey ash had landed on his brown hair and his eyebrows, turning him prematurely into an old man. The sight was so funny that she burst out laughing, wincing when the movement hurt her bruised face.

Walter flushed scarlet under a fine speckling of ash, and his brows drew together fiercely. 'What's so amusing about that?' he asked stiffly.

She tried to sober herself. 'Nothing. It's just – oh, Walter, you've gone grey!' And then she lapsed back into the comfort of helpless laughter as he put a hand to his head and brought it away to stare at the grey powder on his fingers.

Then he looked up at the sky, completely mystified.

'It's the ash from the grate, you daft gommerel! You threw it onto the midden against the wind. You should have stood over there, and avoided it,' Islay managed to explain, between giggles.

Gradually a smile broke over his face, developing into a broad grin as he ran his hands vigorously through his hair, surrounding them both with another, smaller cloud of powder.

'Is that better?'

'Here, bend down –' She whisked a hand over his head, restoring him to his own youthful colour again. 'That'll do – but think what you're about next time you throw out the ashes.'

'I will. You've not answered my question, Islay. Will you come out walking with me?'

'Why me?'

'Because –' Walter floundered, then said, exasperated, 'Lassies are nae supposed to say that! Just tell me – will you or won't you?'

Something – not a sound, but a sixth sense – made her look up, to where Ross stood on the landing outside the dwelling-house door, watching the two of them. Both his fists gripped the flimsy wooden railing tightly.

Walter hadn't noticed him. 'Islay?'

'It's kind of you to ask, Walter, truly it is. But I – I can't.'

'Can't? What sort of an answer is that?' he began, aggrieved. Then seeing that her attention had left him completely he swivelled about and looked up, too, taking in the sight of Ross. 'Is it because of him?'

'No!' The way men took a refusal to mean that there must be another man in a girl's life infuriated her. 'I just don't want to go walking with you, Walter Shaw!' She thrust the pail back into his hand. 'I've got work to do, even if you haven't. Here – you can put that back by the grate for me.'

Then she walked away from the sight of his hurt expression and went up the stairs, brushing by Ross and stepping into the house, where Morag was up and dressed and preparing the morning meal.

The girl's mouth fell open at the sight of her cousin's swollen cheek.

'I fell against the table in the dark last night,' Islay snapped, forestalling the inevitable question.

Morag said nothing; but as Ross came into the room to sit sullenly at the table, she looked from one to the other, from Islay's bruised cheek to the scratches on Ross's gaunt white face, and for a moment her own small features held a knowing expression that was far older than her years.

*

Islay kept the kitchen knife close by her after that, leaving it on the table while she worked about the house, or sat at her spinning, and putting it beneath her pillow at nights. But Ross never again tried to lay a finger on her.

But the incident couldn't be forgotten. The air in the little house seemed to vibrate with Ross's smouldering anger and Islay's apprehension. She scarcely slept, and only toyed with

her food. She stayed indoors as much as she could, sending
Lachie and Morag out with the pirns, and rose early to make
certain that her work in the loom shop each morning was
over long before the weavers arrived, so that she didn't have
to face Walter's resentment.

It was a relief when Ross told his brother and sister after
supper a few nights later that they were about to leave the
town.

Islay had thought that the youngsters might resent being
uprooted as much as she herself did. But the two of them
glowed at the prospect of being with Ross.

'Lachie, it means giving up your place as drawboy,' she
said, and Ross shot an angry glance across the table at her,
the fading red marks of her fingernails suddenly standing
out against his skin like whip-lashes.

'He'll find other work. Paisley's not the only place in the
world.'

'You'll come with us, Islay?' Morag asked, her eyes
darkening with apprehension.

'If she's got any loyalty to the dead she will,' said Ross.

Islay swallowed hard and looked at the two children who
had been her care and her support during the long lonely
months of exile. 'I must stay here.'

This time the glance Ross shot at her was positively
malevolent. Then he spread out his arms so that he
embraced Morag on one side, and Lachie on the other. 'So
it'll be just the three of us.'

'The three of us,' Lachie said enthusiastically, face alight
at the thought of fresh adventures. Morag took a moment to
ponder, then nodded slowly, her choice made.

'The three of us, Ross.'

But that night in bed, she snuggled up to Islay and put her
thin arms about her neck. 'Please come with us.'

'I can't.'

Morag raised herself on one elbow, her face a pale
glimmer, her soft straight hair tickling Islay's cheek. 'Is it
because of Ross?'

'What makes you say that?'

There was a silence, then, 'I don't know,' said Morag, and
lay down again with a sigh. After a moment her moth-wing

whisper said in the darkness, 'I had a sort of dream – about you and Ross. It frighted me.'

'It was only a dream.'

'When I woke up you had a sore face, and so had he. Dreams can't do that, can they?'

'I told you – I fell against the table. Go to sleep, Morag.'

'He's kind, underneath,' Ross's sister said. 'And he wants you to come with us, Islay. I know he does.

Islay said nothing, and after a while she heard her cousin's breathing deepen and slow.

She put a hand beneath the pillow and felt the hard smooth knife handle against her fingers. Then she, too, fell asleep, comforted by the proximity of Morag's body.

Chapter Twenty-Four

Ross spent the next few days away from home, reappearing on the Saturday afternoon, just when Islay had begun to wonder if he was ever coming back.

He took Lachie and Morag away very early the next morning, loading their possessions onto a cart that arrived, apparently by prior arrangement, while the town was still asleep.

Islay, roused from her bed to make a meal for them before they left and prepare some food for the journey, hugged Morag tightly when the girl was ready for the journey.

'You'll take care, now, and not let the damp air get to your lungs?'

Morag, bright-eyed and pink-cheeked with excitement, and healthier than she had ever been since the days when they were thrust from their Highland homes, nodded vigorously. 'Don't worry about me, Islay. I'll be fine.'

'You'll look after her? She shouldn't sleep out in the open in weather like this.' Islay turned to Ross, who was impatient to be away.

'D'you think I'd neglect my own blood kin? There's folk I know along the way – houses where we can find shelter at nights until we get to our destination.' Then he said swiftly, urgently, 'Come with me, Islay. I need you by my side.'

For a moment the true Ross, the Ross she had trusted and loved, the Ross she had been ready and willing to marry, looked out of the pale thin face at her. For a moment, Islay wavered before she drew back, shaking her head. 'No, Ross. My destiny lies here, whatever it may be.'

His eyes turned to clear glass in an instant. 'Then may you rot along with the rest of this God-forsaken town,' he said with soft menace, and turned away, leaving her without another glance.

*

When the cart had rattled off into the gloom and she was alone again, Islay went back upstairs and surveyed the empty, silent house.

Then she rolled her sleeves up and began to give the place a thorough cleaning, unable to bear the prospect of sitting down and letting her thoughts take over.

Several times during the day she almost put her shawl on and went along to tell Jamie Todd that he had lost one of his drawboys. But, grieving as she was over the loss of the only family that was left to her, she couldn't face his anger. So she did nothing, and left the matter lying until the morrow.

The loom shop was scoured and the fire set very early on Monday morning. After that, Islay set off on Lachie's duties, tramping the streets in the cold grey dawn, hammering at doors until a sleepy, querulous voice from the other side of the panels or from an upper window assured her that the weaver was awake and about to get ready for his day's labours.

On her way back to the house she stopped a small boy who was out early on an errand of his own and gave him some money to take a message to Jamie Todd. Then she went home, made some food, forced herself to eat it, and sat down at her spinning wheel.

*

She had to wait almost until noon before he came tramping up the stairs and thundered his fist against the door. By that time she was in such a state of nervous anticipation that she couldn't trust herself to walk across the short space of floor between her stool and the door.

So she called out, 'It's on the latch –' and kept working as the door was thrust open and Jamie erupted into the room.

'What's this I hear? Is it true?'

'If you mean Lachie going off with Ross – aye, it is.'

'Without so much as a word? And me left without a drawboy? This is what comes,' said Jamie wrathfully, 'of putting my trust in Highlanders!'

She tried to speak, but couldn't. Instead, she slowed and stopped her wheel, and sat with bowed head, letting him spill out his justified anger on her.

'Oh, I was well warned at the time. You can't put faith in them, some said. They'll use you and leave when it suits them, others said. But daft fool that I am, I gave the laddie his chance, and emptied my store rooms so that the pack of you would have a place to live – and what's my reward? Eh?' he thundered as she still said nothing. Then he asked, with a sudden change of tone. 'Why aren't you with them?'

'I – I chose to stay.'

He stopped his pacing and stood before her, feet planted firmly on the floor. 'Speak up, lassie! I cannae hear a word when you mutter at the floor like that!'

She drew a deep ragged breath and lifted her face to meet his. 'I said – I chose to stay.'

He was no longer listening to her.

'In Heaven's name!' He grasped her shoulders, lifting her from her seat, making her stand before him. One hand took her by the chin and tilted her face to the light. She stood mute beneath his hands, although her heart fluttered at his touch.

'Who did this?'

'I fell against the table in the dark.' She had said it so often that she had begun to convince herself.

But Jamie Todd took more convincing than most.

'You fell against that scoundrel Ross McInnes's fist, more like. Is the rascal coming back? Because if he is I'll have a few words to say –'

'He's not coming back. None of them are coming back.'

'Then why did you not go with them?' he asked puzzled.

'I want to stay here.' Islay said, and felt her throat suddenly tighten. She closed her eyes against Jamie's look, but two tears, determined not to be held back, forced themselves beneath the lids and slid down her cheeks. All she wanted to do at that moment was to rest her head on his broad chest and know that at last she had found a home.

Someone walked in at the open door. Jamie's hands fell away from Islay, and she whirled, convinced for a panic-stricken moment that Ross had come back and that he and Jamie would have a confrontation there and then. But the newcomer was Margaret Knox.

The surgeon's wife took one look at Islay's tear-wet face and said crisply, 'Jamie Todd, what have you been doing to the lassie?'

'Me? It's not me that did this, that's for sure!'

He tried to take hold of Islay's face again and turn it to the light. She pulled away from his grasp as Margaret said, 'For goodness' sake – that's not a horse you're trying to harness, it's a lassie! Have some care!' Then, as her eyes fell on the large fading bruise, she went on, 'Mercy me! Was it Ross?'

'It was,' Jamie did the answering. 'And now the ne'er-do-weel's fled the town. I knew from the moment I saw him that he'd cause nothing but trouble. I'll not weep tears over his going, I can tell you.'

'What about the bairns?'

'Gone along with him, without a word of warning – and left me missing a drawboy, confound them!'

Islay dried her eyes on her apron and faced up to him. 'I'm sorry, Mister Todd, for what Lachie did. I'll move my things out of the house as soon as I can.'

'Eh?'

'Well, Jamie? Isn't that what you wanted – to get rid of the lot of them and get your nice store-room back?' Margaret asked with sarcastic sweetness.

'Of course it's not what I want!'

'Then why go on at the girl? It's not her fault if her kinfolk have left town without telling you. Does it mean nothing to you that she's shown her own gratitude by staying on – and taking the rough edge of your tongue into the bargain?'

A wave of crimson swept over the weaver's rugged face. He looked helplessly at Islay, then said, awkwardly, 'Lassie, I'd no intention of punishing you for your cousin's misdeeds. From the look of you, you've had punishment enough.'

'Just so. Now off you go and find yourself a new drawboy,' Margaret instructed him. 'I'll see what I can do to help Islay.'

When he had left them she said, 'Well now, Islay – what's to be done about you? Would you like me to make enquiries as to suitable employment in the town? My aunt, Mistress MacLeod, might be interested in taking on a new companion. I know she misses Beth sorely.'

'Thank you, but I'll manage fine between my work in the loom shop and my spinning wheel. There's only me to feed and clothe now, so I'll not need much.'

Margaret's eyebrows rose. 'You mean you're staying on here? I thought after the way Jamie behaved you'd want to get out of his way altogether and find somewhere else to live.'

Islay shook her head. 'Oh no,' she said. 'I've done with moving on and trying to make a new life for myself. I'm staying.'

Chapter Twenty-Five

Gavin Knox stayed in Dumfries for longer than he had originally planned. As February passed by and gave way to March Margaret missed him more and more. But her pride wouldn't allow her to admit that, to Gavin or to anyone else.

So she wrote formal little letters giving him news of the household and the town, and received equally formal little letters which, like hers, gave no indication whatever as to his true thoughts and feelings.

'He seems to be quite content, working with his old friend,' she said to Richard.

'Gavin was always a single-minded man,' his brother said easily from where he sprawled in Gavin's favourite chair. Today he was dressed in a sky-blue coat that contrasted with the dark winter clothes worn by the Paisley men. Richard, who had spent so many years in a warm climate, seemed quite impervious to the cold.

'He seems to be too preoccupied to think of returning home.' Margaret kept her voice light and brisk. 'As to that, I'm so busy myself that I've scarce noticed the time passing. I was thinking of asking Islay McInnes if she'd take on the task of visiting the inkle loom shop each day. I've more than enough to do with the school-room and this house to run.'

'Islay –?' He repeated the name thoughtfully. 'Is that not the pretty little girl who lives above Jamie Todd's weaving shop?'

'Yes. She's reliable, and sensible – and she could do with the extra money, I'm sure of that.'

He shrugged. 'Whatever you decide.'

'I'll call in on her the next time I'm at Wellmeadow – or mebbe I'll send word to her to come up here, then we can make a social visit of it.'

Richard got to his feet. 'I'm going to Wellmeadow myself

today. I'll ask her to call on you.'

'I'd be grateful. Are things going well with the new cotton cloth?'

He smiled down on her. 'Oh yes,' he said. 'Very well indeed.'

*

'It's an unlikely friendship, but it seems to be firm, for all that,' Richard said a few weeks later in Mary MacLeod's parlour.

'What makes you call it unlikely?'

He shrugged. 'Margaret's well-to-do, married to a surgeon. Islay McInnes is a nobody, rescued from a pauper's life.'

Mary gave an unladylike snort. She and Gavin's brother had become fast friends. Mary loved Richard's worldliness; Richard appreciated the older woman's honesty and knife-sharp wit.

'My dear man, you've got a lot to learn! Margaret's from common stock the same as Islay, or me – or you, if it comes to it. Oh, I'll grant you that your father was mebbe more of a gentleman than mine, but that makes no odds in Paisley. It's what you are that counts, not who birthed you.'

'Indeed, ma'am?'

'Aye – indeed, sir,' said Mary firmly, refusing to let his amused bating divert her. 'Of course Margaret and Islay have become friends – they're much alike, these two. They're both strong-minded and independent – and they're both lonely. Margaret because that man of hers seems set on staying away for as long as he can, first in Dumfries, and now in Edinburgh,' said Mary, a worried furrow appearing between her brows for a moment, 'and Islay because some pompous jumped-up nobody of a landlord in the Highlands knows no more than to treat folk like insects. I'm glad the lassie's found a good friend in Margaret.'

'Mmm.' Thoughtfully, Richard took a sip of the excellent rum he had presented to Mary. A bottle was kept in the corner cupboard specially for his visits. His hostess watched with indulgent approval as he rose and refilled his glass with the air of a man who felt completely at home.

'You know, a parlour's always the better of a man's presence. Thomas comes to visit me now and again, but like Gavin, he's too busy with his physicking and his visiting to call more than once a week.'

'You should marry again.'

'Oh – tush! I said I like to see a man in my parlour now and again. I didnae say that I'd care to have one around for all the hours in the day and night, getting under my feet and wanting to rule the roost,' she retorted. 'No, no, laddie, I'm happy enough as I am. But you could do worse than take your own advice. It's high time you found yourself a wife and settled down.'

Richard laughed. 'I manage very well as I am. I'm more interested in making money than in marriage.'

'Have you not made enough of that to do you?'

He lifted the glass, studied the colour of the liquid within it with satisfaction. 'I'll never make enough.'

'D'you say so? I hear the first of your new cloth's off the loom now.'

'Aye, the first shipment goes out in April. Jamie Todd made the right decision when he agreed to weave my yarn. He'll not regret it.'

'It's to be hoped not, for he's lost two good friends through it.'

'There's no quarrel between Jamie and the Montgomerys, surely? None that I'd heard of.'

'No quarrel, but a coolness. Duncan and Robert'll never forgive him for breaking away from them.'

Again, Mary's brow was furrowed for a moment, but Richard's eyes were clear and untroubled as they met hers.

'They had no contract. And I've as much time for loyalty as I have for marriage. Unless, of course, the loyalty's being shown to me.'

'Sometimes,' she said, looking at him with a mixture of affection and irritation, 'you make me think of a spider, Richard Knox. Europe and Jamaica and the Americas and Paisley, all woven into a web of your making. Tell me, have you ever had anything to do with slave-trading?'

'You think I'd stoop to that?'

'Of course I do. You're ruthless enough – and moneyed enough.'

'And you're a clever woman, Mary MacLeod.' He lifted his glass to her in laughing salute, then drained the last drop and put the empty glass on a table. 'Speaking of Jamie, I must go down to his loom shop now.'

Mary got up, moving a little stiffly and muttering a swift curse at the rheumatism that had caught her in its grasp that winter, for the first time. As she came to stand beside him a movement outside took her eye.

A slim, cloaked figure hurried along the footpath beyond Mary's small front garden, head bent against the March wind that swept down the length of the road.

'Islay McInnes,' Mary said. 'She'll be calling on Margaret, I expect.'

Richard picked up his tricorne hat. 'I think I might call on Margaret myself.'

'I thought you'd to go down the hill to see Jamie?'

'Eventually. I could escort Islay back down into the town. She's a bonny girl, is she not?'

'I'm surprised to hear you say so, her being a nobody.'

'But as you reminded me yourself, I'm from common stock too. There's no harm in friendship between commoners – is there?'

Mary surveyed him shrewdly, and he returned look for look. Finally she shook her head.

'There's no besting you, is there, Richard? Whiles I wonder why you've lingered so long in a dull town like Paisley.'

'You know why. I'm here on a matter of business.'

'It seems to me,' said Mary shrewdly, 'that you're here on a matter of mischief.'

Chapter Twenty-Six

It was late April before Gavin Knox finally returned home from his travels.

During the long weeks and months of his time away from her Margaret had pictured his homecoming over and over again. His favourite meal would be on the table, she herself would wear a new, becoming dress

She would go into his arms immediately, without allowing either of them time to set up barriers. She would, if she had to, tell him how sorry she was that there had ever been misunderstanding between them.

For some time now she had been patiently working on Daniel, talking to him about Gavin, reminding him of his love for his father. Now she was certain – well, almost certain – that the little boy had overcome the fear Gavin had instilled in him with his surgeon's knife.

But Fate tended to turn sullen when mere mortals tried to plan their own destinies. Instead of letting her know when he was coming home Gavin arrived unexpectedly, walking into the house one evening when Margaret was presiding over a dinner party made up of her parents, her Aunt Mary, her brothers Thomas and Robert, Robert's wife Annie, Kirsty and Billy Carmichael, Kate – returned to her usual slender beauty since her baby son had been safely delivered – Kate's husband Archie, Islay McInnes, Jamie Todd and Richard.

The gathering had been planned by Margaret and Mary, and was an attempt to reconcile Jamie, Duncan and Robert. It hadn't entirely worked, Margaret thought as the meal came to its close, for the three men had had very little to say for themselves, and had tended to avoid each other's eyes.

The other guests, however, were in light-hearted mood, particularly Richard and Mary.

When the door opened Margaret, seated at the head of the table, looked up, expecting to see Ellen marching in to chase them all into the parlour so that she could clear the plates away.

Instead, the doorway was filled by a tall, familiar figure, clothes rumpled by hours of travel, face pale with fatigue, hazel eyes darting with quick surprise round the crowded table – then cooling as they landed on Richard.

'Gavin!'

Everyone turned and gaped. Margaret, remembering her plans for his homecoming, ran round the table to him, her arms outstretched. That, at least, she could do. But he forestalled her, catching her hands in his before she could embrace him, bending to drop a light, chilly kiss on her forehead.

'Margaret. It seems that I've come home at a difficult time for you.'

'Of course you haven't!' She retained his hands, drawing him into the room, talking and talking in an attempt to cover up his coldness. 'It only means that we're all here to welcome you. Have you had any food?'

'Not since noon.'

'I'll fetch Ellen at once – I'm sure there'll be enough left. You should have let me know that you were coming –'

Thomas was on his feet, coming forward with hand outstretched and a broad welcoming grin on his round face. Mary followed, stretching up on tiptoe to kiss Gavin's cheek, and one by one the others followed, clamouring round him, drawing him back into the fold.

Faced with so much open affection Gavin began to thaw – until at last Richard got to his feet and came forward. 'Well, brother – you've become almost as travelled as I am.'

Gavin's face closed again, and he barely touched the hand his brother offered. 'Scarcely, Richard,' he said, and turned to Margaret, presenting his broad back to Richard. 'I'll eat in the kitchen, and join you all in the parlour presently, when I've had time to change my clothes. Where are the children?'

'In bed and asleep. You'll see them in the morning.'

His face was suddenly hungry with love – a hunger that she had hoped to see when his eyes first fell on her,

Margaret thought bleakly. 'I can't wait until tomorrow. I'll go up to them now.'

Before she could stop him he had turned on his heel and left the room. Panic seized her. If Daniel was to wake suddenly from sleep and see his father without benefit of the careful preparations she had planned –

'Mother, take everyone into the parlour. I'll see to Gavin and join you all there –'

She sped from the room, almost bumping into Ellen in the hallway.

'The master's home – put out food for him in the kitchen at once.'

'But there's little left. That lot ate everything I prepared.'

'Find something!' Margaret gathered up her skirts and ran up the stairs. By the time she reached the children's room he was there, candle in hand. Christian, with some sort of sixth sense, opened her eyes at once, leaping from sleep to wakefulness in one easy bound, and shot upright in bed, with a gleeful scream of, 'Father! It's Father!'

Daniel's small body gave a convulsive leap as he was startled out of a deep sleep. He, too, sat bolt upright, eyes staring, just as Gavin, dimly-seen in the flickering candle-light, bent over his bed, stooping down to embrace him and kiss him.

With a shrill animal-like scream of terror Daniel threw himself away from what he saw as a monstrous attacker. Caught up in the bed-coverings, he struggled in total panic, and rolled right off the other side of his narrow bed, landing on the floor with a thump.

Margaret reached him first, scooping him up, holding him tightly.

'It's all right, Daniel, you're all right!'

Recognising her voice, the little boy clutched at her and buried his face in her neck, his body trembling violently.

Christian, still whooping, 'It's Father, it's Father!' shot from her own bed to wrap her arms about Gavin's legs. He stroked her hair, his eyes fixed on his wife and son.

Margaret, half-strangled, looking at Gavin over Daniel's silky head, felt her heart sink as she saw the bewilderment and anger in his eyes.

The home-coming she had prayed for and planned so carefully had become a shambles. And Gavin's absence, it seemed, had done nothing to resolve the troubles that still threatened their future together.

*

When Gavin had put on fresh clean clothes and eaten in the kitchen he joined his wife and their guests in the parlour.

Thomas immediately drew him aside and started asking him about his work in Dumfries and Edinburgh. Margaret, glancing over at the two of them now and again, saw that Gavin was talking cheerfully, though every so often he would shoot a sidelong glance of pure dislike at Richard, who seemed quite unaware of it.

Gavin looked drawn and tired, she thought with compassion. Mary, insisting that she had come to enjoy herself, not listen to physicians talking about death and disease, tried to draw him into the general conversation. But once he and Thomas had been separated Gavin lapsed into silence, staring at the floor, giving brusque answers to any questions that were put to him.

He only became animated again when Kate asked him outright if he would go to Barrhead and vaccinate her children against the smallpox. Gavin agreed swiftly, casting a look of thinly veiled triumph at his wife.

Margaret was relieved when Kirsty and Billy rose to go, and started a general exodus. Richard went off into the hall, and came back with Islay's cloak. He tucked it carefully about her shoulders.

'I'll see you safely home.'

The girl flushed becomingly. 'But it would take you out of your way –'

'In that case I think I'll just take the evening air before I go back to my lodgings,' he said with an attractive, half-mocking and half serious smile, 'Will you grant me the pleasure of your company along the road, Mistress Islay?'

She laughed, and nodded.

Gavin stood beside Margaret at the front door, bidding their guests a courteous good night. When the last had gone and she was closing the door he left her side.

She went into the parlour to find him already there, pouring some whisky into a glass. Then he took up his favourite stance by the fire and said without wasting time on formalities, 'I thought I made it clear that my brother is not welcome beneath my roof?'

'While you're away from home the domestic responsibilities fall on my shoulders. This time you were gone for so long that I confess I'd begun to think of it as my roof – or, at least, ours.'

'Nevertheless –'

'I shall not invite Richard here when you're in residence, Gavin. But when you're away from home I shall do as I think fit.' Then she added, as his face tightened dangerously, 'Richard is my business partner, after all. I must offer him some hospitality when I'm in the position to do so.'

'Ah, yes, the inkle looms. How are they coming along?'

'Very well.'

'No doubt you'll soon be in a position to become completely independent. How gratifying that will be for you – and for Richard.'

'Gavin, I cannot understand why you bear such malice towards the man!'

'You know very well that he was responsible for my mother's death.'

'He didn't strike her down with his own hand. And you were away from home when she died, from what I heard. I fail to see how you can lay her death at his door with such confidence.'

'My mother,' said Gavin slowly and clearly, 'was a gentle woman, with no interest or concern in her life but her home and her husband and Richard – and myself.'

The final two words, Margaret noticed, were added on as an afterthought. He seemed to read her thoughts.

'She lost two children in early infancy after I was born, so naturally Richard was especially dear to her. He was a pretty child, with an endearing manner, whereas I was perhaps too solemn and serious. My mother worshipped him, but unfortunately Richard had a tendency to fall into every sort of mischief a small boy could find. As he grew, the mischief became more serious. He was – the cause of trouble among neighbours and friends on more than one occasion, and my parents were grievously upset when this happened.'

He drained his glass, and stared down at the final golden dregs. 'I did my best to talk to Richard, to reason with him, but it did no good. Finally, when I was in my first year at University, he – fathered a child on a young girl, the ward of my father's best friend. They weren't much more than children themselves, but even so, the girl was more than willing to marry my brother, and her guardian and my parents would have approved of the match.'

'But Richard didn't want it?'

'He didn't want it,' Gavin agreed. 'And it's not in Richard's nature to do anything against his own wishes. He ran away, and that was the last my parents ever heard of him.'

'So he has a child in Dumfries?'

'I've no doubt that he has at least one child somewhere in the world,' said Gavin dryly. 'But none in Dumfries. The girl died in childbirth, and her baby with her. Fortunately my mother never knew of that final tragedy, for she began to decline from the day he left. She passed away within a few months, still hoping to her last breath that she would hear from Richard. My father died not long after that. From heart trouble, his physician said. But I suspect that his heart stopped from shame.'

There was a long silence before he spoke again, with a bite in his voice. 'Now you know why I'll have nothing to do with him, and why I would prefer you to have nothing to do with him.'

'It's not a pretty story. I'll grant you – but Richard is still my business partner, and Jamie's. Even if I wished to have no more to do with him, it's not possible.'

'I see. I'll bid you good night, Margaret, for I must go to Glasgow tomorrow and it's getting late.'

'Gavin,' she said as he put his empty glass down and moved towards the door, 'why did you stay away for so long?'

He stopped, but didn't turn to look at her. 'There was a lot to be done, in Dumfries and then, as fortune would have it, in Edinburgh. I was needed.'

She got to her feet. 'And you thought that there was no need of you here?'

When he turned to her his eyes were hazel pools, so deep that she couldn't read them. 'You were always too independent to have need of any one person, Margaret. And it seems that your independence is growing, and therefore your need is diminishing.'

'I do need you.'

Gavin raised one eyebrow mockingly. 'Prove it, my dear,' he said. 'Give up the Poors' Hospital, give up the inkle looms.'

'I can't. I won't.'

'You see?' He inclined his head slightly. 'Good night.'

When she followed him upstairs some ten minutes later he seemed to be asleep. She moved around the bed-chamber quietly so as not to disturb him. Each time she glanced at the bed, his dark lashes were peaceful on his cheeks, his breathing unchanged.

She blew out the candle and slid between the sheets. His hand, strong and sure, closed about her shoulder, turning her to face him. His lips sought and found hers in the darkness.

He made love to her with stormy insensitive hunger, and she responded with a need and passion as strong as his.

Finally, sated and exhausted, they fell away from each other and slept in the tangled, dishevelled battleground of their marriage bed.

Margaret woke in the morning to find Gavin dressing swiftly.

'What time is it?

'Early. No need for you to rise yet.'

She lifted herself on one elbow. The sheets fell back from the upper half of her body and she saw him throw one burning glance at her breasts, naked as he had left them in the night, before he turned away. 'Gavin, must you go to the wards today?'

'Yes,' he said, and went out without looking back.

Chapter Twenty-Seven

Although Islay was living alone for the first time in her life there was little danger of her feeling lonely.

Her work in the loom shop and the house, together with the hours she put in at her spinning wheel each day, took up most of her time.

In addition, she crossed the bridge every afternoon to visit Margaret Knox's loom shop in the New Town, checking that the inkle looms were all in operation and that there was a good supply of yarn for them.

More yarn had to be ordered if it was needed, and she had to keep a tally of the amount of ribbon that was being woven.

She also paid a daily visit to the two inkle looms that were still housed across the passage from Jamie's High Street loom shop. Sometimes, especially if she had to order more yarn, she saw Jamie himself. But never for long. The red-headed weaver seemed to become more and more abrupt with her, and more incomprehensible.

Now that spring had arrived there was the garden to tend to as well as her other duties. She had expected that Ross would have been there to help her with the digging and the planting, but now there was nobody but herself to see to it.

Quite often, when the loom shop finished early for the day and Islay was working in the garden, Walter came through the pend to help her. He was a strong willing worker, and with his help she gradually gained control of the whole area.

Afterwards, she gave him ale and home-made oatcakes in her kitchen.

Jamie had never again worked alongside her as he had done that day in the autumn, although once or twice when she was away from the house in the lengthening evenings she came back to find a stretch of earth that had been waiting for the spade neatly turned over and ready for planting, or some weeding done.

When she asked Walter outright if he had done it the young man shook his head firmly. 'Not when you weren't there – there'd be no pleasure in that. I'd have to be daft to do the digging then.'

One day he plucked up the courage to ask her along to his house to take tea with his mother, a thin, over-worked woman with far too many children and little liking, Islay soon realised, for Highlanders.

Sometimes she and Walter walked out along the river bank, or over the moors – Islay's favourite walk because it reminded her a little of home.

And, of course, there was Richard Knox. He had taken to calling at the house if he happened to be at the Wellmeadow loom shop on business, sitting for a while in the pleasant warm kitchen, talking on and on as Islay worked at her wheel.

He was amusing and charming, she realised as her initial shyness wore off. He knew how to put folk at their ease, and he always treated her with courtesy.

Summer arrived unheralded and unexpectedly at the end of April. Islay woke to a soft quiet dawn that seemed to hold the promise of a warm fresh day out to her in cupped hands. She sang as she worked about the looms and the linnets, newly freed from their shrouding night-cloth, chirruped in answer.

The housework done, she went down to the yard and, for want of bushes to dry her washing on, stretched a piece of rope between the house wall and the wall at the back of the yard. Then she dragged out the fair-sized wooden tub she had found during earlier explorations in the ramshackle shed, and scrubbed it out.

It took some time to heat enough water for the tub, and several trips up and down the stairs, lugging the heavy big kettle.

But at last the tub was ready, and Islay knew great satisfaction as she deposited the last armful of washing into it and stripped off her stockings before hoisting her skirt and high-stepping in on top of the blankets.

As she worked her way round and round the tub, treading the washing down vigorously so that the winter's grime was forced out, warm water bubbled up between her toes. A cool breeze lapped pleasantly round her bare legs.

Treading blankets on a warm sunny day was one of the most pleasant occupations Islay could think of, and she sang as she worked, treading to a song she had learned from her mother as a small child.

Her singing came to a sudden stop when she revolved to face the pend and saw that Richard Knox, hat in hand, was standing on the rough flagstones watching her, a broad grin on his handsome face.

'Oh –' She stood facing him, confused and embarrassed, suddenly aware of her bare legs but unable to drop her skirts because then their hems would land in the water.

'A very pretty sight, Mistress Islay.' He bowed, then came forward. 'And a pleasant way of spending a warm afternoon. I'm tempted to join you.'

'I doubt if there would be room, Richard,' Jamie Todd said curtly, stepping from the shade of the pend. 'Islay, have you nothing better to do with your time than disport yourself in this fashion?'

He looked from Richard to Islay, taking in her kilted skirts, her flushed face framed by silky black hair that had loosened itself from the knot she had pinned on the top of her head before she set to work.

His eyes, she noted miserably, were a deep cold blue, with none of their usual sparkle. For a moment she quailed before those eyes, then she rallied, fingers gripping her skirt tightly.

'I'm only washing the blankets, Mister Todd. Would you have me leave them as they are, after a winter's use?'

'Of course he wouldn't – and nor would I,' said Richard smoothly.

'Surely they're done by now. You've been in that tub for near enough half an hour!'

Richard raised an amused brow. 'You've been keeping time, Jamie?'

The weaver's face flamed, and he took a step forward, holding out a hand. 'Come on out.'

Richard, too, held out his hand. Islay, unable to take both hands because it would mean letting her skirts dip into the water, hesitated, looking from one man to the other, wishing that she had never decided to wash the dratted blankets.

She was saved by the clatter of feet in the pend. Thomas Montgomery burst from its shadow.

'There you are, Islay – I've need of your help.'

'What's amiss?' It was Jamie who asked the question. But Thomas's eyes were on Richard as he gave the answer.

'It's Gavin. He's down with the pox. He fell sick in hospital in Glasgow yesterday.'

They stared at each other, sick at heart. It was Richard who spoke first. 'At least he's in the best place.'

'He was,' Thomas agreed grimly, 'before Margaret insisted on fetching him home.'

Richard's face paled. 'In the name of God, why? What about herself, and the children? What about the rest of the folk in the town?'

'As to that, nobody can go in or out of the house until the matter's resolved one way or the other,' Thomas said rapidly. 'The children and Ellen are with Aunt Mary. Margaret refuses to give a thought to her own safety. She's alone in the house with him, and determined to stay until –'

He broke off, then said directly to Islay this time, 'She can't nurse him all on her own. You've been protected against the pox. I thought you might help her.'

She was already scrambling from the tub unaided, heedless of how much slender bare leg she showed in the process. 'I'll go at once.'

'No!' Jamie said violently as she brushed past him to sit on the bottom step so that she could dry her feet and legs. 'No, I'll not allow it, Thomas. The lassie might sicken.'

'She's been vaccinated.'

'When she was a child! Who's to know if she's still protected? Islay –'

She finished drying her feet and began to draw her stockings on, aware with some part of her that Richard, for all his shocked silence, was watching her, and yet not caring about his gaze. 'I must go to Oakshawhill, Jamie.'

'I'll not allow it!'

'You've no right to stop me.' She finished putting on the second stocking and nodded to Thomas. 'I'll just fetch some things and close the range down. I'll not be a minute.'

When she came back down Richard had gone. Thomas and Jamie waited for her at the pend opening.

The weaver put a hand on her arm as she brushed past him. 'Islay, what if you fall sick?'

She looked up at him. 'There's nobody to care if I live or die now.'

'I'll not allow it!'

'What's amiss with you, man?' Thomas asked in angry amazement. 'You don't own the lassie – Margaret and Gavin need her help, and she's free to do as she pleases!'

Jamie's white teeth bit into his lower lip. the detaining hand fell from Islay's arm, and let her go.

Hurrying up the hill by Thomas's side, she realised that once again, in a moment of stress, she had used Jamie's Christian name.

And once again it had lain naturally on her tongue, as though it belonged there.

Chapter Twenty-Eight

On the night before summer came to Paisley Margaret had dreamed of the road that stretched from Glasgow.

Along that road, in her dream, came the smallpox in the form of a malevolent, horribly disfigured old man riding a black cart, whipping a black horse on in its mad gallop towards Paisley, getting nearer with every swift turn of the flaying hooves and iron-bound wheels.

She woke to the echoes of her own muffled scream. The room was in darkness, her body was damp with sweat, her heart hammering. She was alone, for Gavin had stayed in Glasgow for the past few days, with not enough time to come home at night.

Small-pox was rife in the area where his hospital stood, Margaret already knew that; but he and his colleagues had hopes of containing it.

It hadn't, as yet, reached as far as Paisley. The wizened, hideous old man in Margaret's dream hadn't galloped his black horse and cart along the road, between fields and hedges sprouting the summer's fresh green growth. But there was still time, she thought, collapsing back onto her pillows. It could still happen.

And despite what Gavin and Thomas had told her over and over again, despite the fact that Kate and Archie had had enough trust in the new method of vaccination to have it done to their older, surviving child, and would have it done to the new baby whenever Gavin considered the boy old enough to undergo the knife, Margaret feared for her own children. She got up, moving sure-footed in the dark, and crept into the next room, listening to their soft, even breathing.

Then she returned to bed, praying that the white puckered patch of skin on their chubby upper arms, the only reminder of the day Gavin had taken the knife to them, and had in doing so cut the bond between himself and Margaret, might after all turn out to be some sort of magic charm to keep Christian and Daniel safe.

The next morning the dream was forgotten – until mid-morning, when Thomas arrived at the Poors' Hospital in search of her, his face grim and haggard.

Margaret, in consultation with the Master and Mistress, emerged from the small office as her brother strode through the big front door.

'Margaret – I went to the house and Ellen said I might find you here –'

'What is it?' But she already knew; something had whispered a name to her as soon as she saw her brother's ashen face. 'It's Gavin, isn't it? He's been hurt – an accident –'

'No!' Thomas looked about the big bleak entrance hall, where some of the residents lingered, eyeing them inquisitively. 'There's been no accident. Is there not some private place where we can talk together?'

'The g – garden – ' Her lips were numbed, stumbling clumsily over the words. He cupped a hand round her elbow and they went swiftly down the corridor that led to the kitchens and the back door.

The walled garden at the rear of the Poors' Hospital was meant for vegetable beds only, so that kale and potatoes could be grown cheaply to help to feed the inmates. But a former master with imagination and a firm belief that even paupers could benefit from colour and beauty had managed to set aside a small corner for a few rose bushes and clumps of pansies and carnations.

Some men and youths were digging the kale beds; they paused for a moment in their work and looked at the man and woman who passed them and went towards the flower-beds, then returned to their task, leaving Thomas and Margaret in peace.

'Tell me!' she insisted, ready to take him by the shoulders and shake the news out of him. But when he did tell her, she would have given all she had in the world, all she held dear, except Gavin and Christian and Daniel, not to know.

'It's the pox, Margaret.'

There was a strange sound in her ears, as though she was standing down at the Cross, near where the river thundered over the small weir called the Hammills.

But she wasn't at the river, she was in the walled garden of the Poors' Hospital, and the flowers near her feet were undisturbed by any wind.

She realised, as Thomas gripped her shoulders and sat her down on a bench, and she saw his lips moving and knew he was speaking, that the noise was within her own head.

With that realisation it ebbed and died, and she could hear her brother's voice again.

'I got word last night to go up to Glasgow, to the infirmary,' he was saying. 'I've been with him all night. He asked me to tell you why – why he can't come home.'

'You saw him? Is it bad?' She remembered that Gavin had complained of a headache three evenings before. She remembered him grumbling about the cold on the following morning, how warm his lips had felt against her forehead when he kissed her. She remembered that he had gone out that day, the last time she had seen him, without breaking his fast, and she cursed herself for not realising then that he was ill.

But Gavin was never ill; he made sick folk better, as Christian was proud of boasting. He was a surgeon – sickness couldn't put its hands on him. Or so Margaret had always thought. Until now.

Thomas's final sentence hung in her mind, and finally she made sense of it. 'You've not brought him home?'

'He's got the pox, Margaret! How can he come home? He's in the infirmary, where he'll be looked after until – until –'

His eyes slid away from hers. He was too honest, and he knew that she was too shrewd, for reassuring lies to be mouthed or believed. But she wasn't thinking of that. She was recalling everything that she had heard about infirmaries from Gavin himself, and from Thomas.

The big rooms filled with folk, most dying. The women – drunken slatterns, many of them – who were paid to tend the patients as best they could. She had often thought that the sickroom in the building that loomed behind Thomas's shoulder as he stood before her was a dreary place, but from what she had heard it was far superior to anything that could be found in an infirmary for sick people.

'How bad is he?'

'There's no knowing as yet. The sickness is in its early stages.'

'Have you a carriage at the door?'

'No, I travelled on horseback.'

She was already on her feet, hurrying along the narrow earthen path towards the house.

'Then find a carriage – a cart – anything that'll take us to Glasgow.' She threw the words over her shoulder.

'Margaret, you're not thinking of going to the infirmary?'

She stopped, rounded on him so fiercely that he stepped back, away from her, and one foot sank into soft sticky earth. 'D'you think I'd stay in Paisley, safe and sound, when my man's mebbe dying only a few miles away?'

'I can't allow you –'

'Thomas!' Her voice ripped through his words. 'There's no 'let' about it! Either you'll help me or I'll go and find him on my own!'

She would have struck him to the ground if she'd had to, and he knew it. In thirty minutes they were in a small open two-wheeled gig, rattling over the bridge that spanned the River Cart. A few more minutes later the neatly laid out streets of the New Town were falling behind them, and they were on the road that led to Glasgow.

*

The infirmary where Gavin worked for part of each week was a large stone building that looked more like a prison than a house of recovery. People buzzed round it, swarming in and out of the great door like the bees inhabiting the skeps in Margaret's parents' back yard.

As the carriage drew up before the main door two men jogged past and into the building carrying the infirmary bed, a mobile cot enclosed with striped curtains to conceal the patient who had been too ill to travel to the infirmary unaided.

A twinge of horror took hold of Margaret as she saw the canopy, once boldy bright, now shabby, flutter its way through the door. She knew without being told that most folk who were admitted like that were already beyond recovery.

Gavin lay in a corner of a vast ground-floor ward. As Thomas led her towards him she only had eyes for her husband, and didn't notice the surroundings at all.

To her relief he looked much like his usual self, though feverish. He was in a restless sleep; a pattern of tiny scarlet spots overlaid his face and throat and hands.

'Are you certain it's the pox?'

'Aye, I'm certain. By tomorrow the pustules will have appeared.'

It hurt unbearably to see Gavin lying there, sick and helpless. She looked away, and was appalled by what she saw.

The ward was large, with cots all down the walls and in two lines along the middle of the room. Every one of them was occupied, and a smell of mingled sweat and vomit, blood and unclean skin and putrefaction, hung over the place like a thick blanket. The windows were tightly close and the room was stuffy, depending on the ever-open door for all its fresh air. Underlying the stench of sickness and suffering was another smell; it reminded Margaret of something, and after a moment her nose identified it as the stink of a midden heap, no doubt just outside the ward windows.

The narrow passageways between the rows of beds were crammed with people. Physicians worked over patients or conferred in twos and threes. Men and women and children, many of the men grim-faced and helpless, the women in tears, the children bewildered and terrified, crowded round cots that held friends or relatives.

Here and there a dog or a cat scavenged round people's feet or cowered under a bed. The women she had heard Thomas and Gavin talk of went to and fro, carrying jugs and bowls or with their arms filled with dirty, bloody sheets.

One of them brushed past Margaret; her grey hair hung in lank greasy ropes from beneath a cap that had once been white, her dress was crusted with dried blood and grime, and in her wake she left a smell of ancient sweat and alcohol.

Margaret felt her stomach move, and swallowed hard, turning back to her husband so that she needn't look any longer at his surroundings.

Now she saw that the pillow beneath his dark head was filthy and the blanket tissue thin and completely inadequate.

'I must take him home!'

Thomas stared. 'Margaret, see sense!'

'If he stays here he'll die.'

'If he goes home,' said Thomas with brutal candour, 'He'll likely die anyway, and you with him.'

'At least he'll die in comfort, in his own bed.'

'For God's sake –!'

The sound of their quarrel roused Gavin. His lids fluttered and opened and his eyes, bright with fever, fixed on Thomas. Dry lips shaped themselves into a smile.

'You've –' His voice was hoarse, and he cleared his throat and tried again, ' – you've been to Paisley?'

Then his gaze travelled on and found Margaret. Immediately his face suffused with horror.

'No!' He pushed himself up on one elbow, shock giving him a surge of unexpected energy. 'Margaret, get away from here!'

'I will, as soon as I can. And you'll come with me.'

'No, I must stay – and you have to go! You should never have allowed her to come, Thomas,' he fretted weakly.

'I couldnae stop her,' her brother said wretchedly.

The surge of energy left Gavin and he fell back, coughing and gasping for breath. A jug stood on the floor by his cot; Thomas lifted it and supported Gavin's head so that he could drink from it.

Then Gavin collapsed onto his thin dirty pillow, his eyes anguished as they fixed on his wife's face again. 'You must go away from here!'

'We must both go away from here, Gavin.'

'I can't!'

Margaret drew a deep shaky breath, more afraid than she had ever been in her life. 'Then I'll stay and tend to you.'

'Margaret!' Both men spoke together, Thomas's voice sharp and horrified, Gavin's a weak groan.

'Look at the women that work here –' Thomas indicated the room with a sweep of his arm. 'You can't stay. You'd not be safe!'

She knew that. She knew that if she didn't die of the pox in this terrible place she'd like as not be robbed, perhaps even murdered. Or she would die of cold or hunger or sheer fright. But her mind was made up.

'I'll not leave Gavin. Either I stay with him here or I take him back to Paisley.'

'And spread the pox through the town?'

'I'll nurse him myself, and not let anybody else into the house. I'll send Ellen and the bairns away and put quicklime on the walls and wash the house with vinegar and spirits of camphor and –'

'And if you fall sick?' Thomas asked, despair in his voice.

'I'll not fall sick.' How she could prevent it she didn't know, but at that moment she was prepared to promise anything if she could just get Gavin out of this dreadful place. She reached for his hand; with a whimper of fear lest she be contaminated he tried to draw it away, but she captured it in both of hers. Its unnatural heat struck through her own skin and her fingertips felt the raised pattern of the rash.

'Gavin – I'm your wife. One way or the other, I'll not leave you,' she said. 'We'll not be put apart!'

'Unless it's by death itself,' her mind added, but she left the words unspoken.

'Margaret, see reason,' he whispered painfully. 'If anything should happen to you as well as me, what'll become of our bairns?'

She bent over him, and realised that he, too, was inflicted with the stench of decay. Even Gavin wasn't invincible, after all.

'They'll never be alone,' she said steadily, her eyes on his. 'They've got my mother and father, and Aunt Mary, and a host of folk to make sure of that. But I've only got you, Gavin. I'll not leave you to fight this battle on your own!'

Chapter Twenty-Nine

She won, as she knew she must.

She had anticipated a further struggle against the infirmary's authorities and the driver of their small carriage, but she was spared.

The wards were over-crowded with new patients coming in all the time and visitors anxious to see their sick friends and relatives; nobody had the time to worry over what was happening to Gavin.

Mercifully, the shivering which he had put down to the weather but had instead been the fore-runner of his illness had caused him to put on a long warm cloak when he left Oakshawhill. This, together with Thomas's wide-brimmed beaver hat, hid the tell-tale rash from sight.

The driver of the gig, only interested in receiving payment for his work once it was done, paid no attention as Margaret and Thomas half-carried Gavin from the building and, with difficulty, helped him into the open carriage.

As the vehicle began to move Margaret drew a deep breath and looked at her brother, seeing her own tension reflected in his round face.

Between them, as the carriage lurched and jolted towards Paisley, Gavin shivered and burned and muffled his groans in Margaret's shoulder.

*

When they reached Oakshawhill Thomas waited in the carriage with Gavin while Margaret ran into the house, shouting for Ellen.

'Is the house on fire?' the servant squawked, running to the hall, the rolling-pin still in her hand, a trail of flour sprinkling the floor behind her.

'Where are the bairns?'

'At Mistress MacLeod's house.'

Margaret snatched the rolling-pin from the woman's hand and dragged her upstairs. 'Listen to me, Ellen. Mister Knox is taken sick and I've brought him home.'

'Och, the poor soul! I'll put a hot brick in his bed this minute, and make him some of my –'

'I'll see to him.' She threw open the door of the children's room and hustled the maid inside. 'You must take some clothes for the bairns and for yourself and go along to Mistress MacLeod's house. And you must stay there until – until I tell you that you can all come home again.'

'But –' Sudden understanding dawned in the serving-woman's eyes, followed by fear. 'The sickness – is it –?'

'Never mind what it is, just do as I tell you! If you're not down in the parlour and ready to go in five minutes I'll – I'll turn you out of this house and never let you back in!'

And Margaret flew back downstairs to the parlour where she scrawled a hurried note to her aunt.

As she finished it she heard Ellen lumbering down the staircase, laden with her own and the children's belongings.

'Give this to Mistress MacLeod as soon as you get there. And remember – don't let Christian and Daniel come back until I say so. Keep your eyes fast on Christian, for she's stubborn, that one.'

'I'll take the letter and the clothes, but let me come back and help you.'

'No!' Margaret said sharply, then as the woman's eyes filled with sudden tears she added on a gentler note, 'The wee ones need you, Ellen. And I must know they're being cared for properly while I'm not able to see to them myself.'

Ellen had been a part of the Knox household since Margaret's marriage. She had known and loved the children from the first moment of their lives. Standing at the door, watching the woman scurry as fast as she could out of the gate and along the footpath without stopping to look at the waiting carriage, Margaret felt as though she had just seen everything that spelled security vanish from her life.

But there was no time to let her imagination have its way. She had work to do.

Between them, she and Thomas got Gavin inside and put him to bed.

'God, Margaret, my heart was in my mouth!' her brother said as they settled Gavin against the pillows. 'If that driver had known what was amiss with one of his passengers he'd have thrown the three of us out onto the roadside – d'you realise that?'

'Fortunate for us that he didn't realise it, then,' Margaret said tersely, too worried about Gavin to fret over what might have occurred.

While she heated bricks to combat the fever that now consumed the sick man Thomas went off to warn everyone to stay away from the house and to collect medicines and vinegar and spirits of camphor and quicklime to whitewash the walls of the bed-chamber.

When she had made Gavin as comfortable as she could Margaret removed everything that wasn't needed, rolling up the carpets and dragging them out onto the landing, then set to and scrubbed the floorboards with lye.

By the time a knock on the door announced her brother's return her hands were red, and felt as though a thousand needles were being stabbed into the skin.

Islay stepped through the door first. 'I can't take the pox, so I've come to help you,' she said, and Margaret felt unbidden tears of gratitude and relief fill her eyes. She and Gavin weren't going to have to face the fight alone after all.

By evening the three of them had fumigated the room where Gavin lay, as well as the other rooms on that floor. Margaret's back ached, and the sharp smell of the agents used to fumigate the room stung her throat and her eyes.

They fed Gavin, then he fell asleep, soothed by clean sheets and a soft pillow and hot bricks.

When Thomas had gone, promising to come back first thing in the morning, Islay insisted that Margaret should eat something.

'You're going to need all the strength you can get before this is over,' she said firmly, walking into the kitchen and taking charge as though she had worked in it for years.

Margaret sat at the table, watching the younger woman, trying to concentrate on her words. The thought that Gavin might die was an insistent, clamouring black horror that must be kept at bay.

Islay, turning to put a platter of oatcakes on the table, read the fear in her face. 'He's young enough yet, and strong,' she said gently in her soft musical voice. 'He'll be right.'

As she ate, Margaret blocked the darkness in her head by repeating over and over again to herself, 'He'll be right. He'll be right.'

Later in the evening as she washed Gavin and made him comfortable she noticed with a fresh pang of fear that the rash had now unmistakeably become a mass of tiny blisters, each filled with a drop of liquid.

His eyes opened and met hers. Recognition faintly coloured the blank stare and he smiled at her. Then his heavy lids closed, and he slept.

Despite the balmy promise of the day the evening had brought rain. It pattered softly against the ground outside as Margaret turned the lamp down so that it wouldn't disturb her patient, then curled up in a chair, a blanket over her shoulders, her eyes on Gavin's face.

*

The fever had dropped slightly by the time Thomas called the next day, but the pustules were more pronounced.

'He's escaped the truly virulent pox, thank God,' he said, low-voiced, and Islay nodded wisely.

'Aye, the pustules are separate, one from another. I've seen the pox in all its forms, and helped to nurse those struck down with it.'

Thomas shot her a look of swift admiration. 'There's little to do but wait, and try to ease his sufferings,' he said as he and Margaret went out of the sickroom, leaving Islay to watch over Gavin.

'How are the bairns?' She was hungry for news of them.

'They're well. Christian wants to come and nurse her father. She says she's protected against the pox now, so she'll not catch it.' He grinned, and Margaret summoned up a watery smile.

*

The days and nights dragged by, interludes of light and darkness without number. The room where Gavin lay had to be kept dim at all times because the light hurt his eyes. The fever eased, then returned. The pustules spread into his mouth, making speech impossible. They grew and crusted, causing unbearable irritation. Even in his weak state he was too strong for the two women: they found it hard to keep his fingernails from tearing and ripping at his face and body.

It was Islay who suggested that they bind his wrists to the bed-frame. Margaret looked at Gavin, tossing and moaning in the grip of a frenzied fever, then stared back at the girl in horror.

'It's such a cruel thing to do!'

Islay met her gaze levelly. 'It's that, or have him cruelly disfigured for the rest of his life. We'll use soft cloths to spare him as much as we can. D'you have some old bedding that I can tear into lengths?'

When Margaret fetched a sheet, fragrant with lavender, from the closet, it was Islay's turn to look horrified. 'It's far too good, Mistress Knox! Have you nothing that's ready to be torn up for rags?'

'For any favour, Islay, will you call me by my given name?' Margaret said wearily, and ripped at the sheet with all her strength, knowing a certain vicious satisfaction as the material gave beneath her hands. 'And what do I care about good sheets at a time like this?'

They bound his hands to the bed-frame, then settled down to spend hour after hour by his side, sponging his ravaged face and body with cold water in an attempt to ease the itching.

They slept when they could, one in the children's room next door, the other keeping watch in the big chair by Gavin's bed.

Occasionally Islay almost forced Margaret out of doors, sending her into the back-yard to breathe some fresh cool air as she paced the long narrow path between the vegetable beds. Sometimes the sky above was blue, sometimes cloudy, sometimes night-black, studded with stars or silvery with moonlight.

It was hard to believe that in the houses nearby people entertained and baked and washed and talked and laughed and played with their children and slept and lived contented, normal lives; and all the time this was happening, she and Islay were helping Gavin to fight for his life.

Margaret's parents were staunch church-goers, of the Baptist faith. She had attended church meetings with them from the time she was a small child, and still did. Gavin's lack of interest in religion was something that until then had irritated her, but she had accepted it as part of the being that was Gavin.

One night when she was standing in the quiet dark garden, his lack of faith suddenly frightened the wits out of her. What if, lacking intervention from God, Gavin was allowed to die? What if he died anyway, and his soul was denied peace in Heaven?

'Lord,' prayed Margaret in a panic, 'Forgive him for not believing, spare him for my sake, and for Christian's, and Daniel's.'

A sudden fear caught at her heart, sending her stumbling into the house and upstairs and into the bedroom; it was a fear of being left alone, and it only eased its grip on her when she heard Gavin's harsh breathing and saw his dark head move restlessly on the pillow and knew with relief that he was still alive and she wasn't a widow. Not yet.

Islay was carefully dripping water into Gavin's sore mouth. She looked up and smiled as Margaret went to stand by the bed. 'I think he's a little better tonight.'

'Aye –' said Margaret. 'Aye, I think so too.'

But she wasn't speaking the truth, and she doubted if Islay was, either.

*

Occasionally, glancing from a front window, Margaret saw Walter Shaw hovering on the opposite side of the street, watching the house. The first time she mentioned it to Islay the girl's pretty face bloomed rose-red, with annoyance rather than pleasure.

'At your age, it's surely pleasant to have an admirer. And Walter's a fine-looking young man.'

'Aye, but – but he's not my choice.'

'So you've already got your eye on someone?'

Islay said nothing for a moment, concentrating on dampening a cloth and wiping Gavin's face gently. They were seated at either side of the bed, talking in low voices and taking it in turns to cool his brow and his crusted, swollen lips with water. The sound of their talk seemed to soothe him.

'Mist – Margaret, would you say that a woman's best to marry for practical purposes, or in answer to her heart?'

Margaret, taken aback, couldn't think of an answer right away. The Highland girl, taking her silence for a reply, nodded sagely.

'You see? You were fortunate, you followed your heart and made a good marriage into the bargain.' She looked round the room. Even stripped of its furnishings it was a handsome apartment, with large graceful windows and a decorative ceiling.

'You've got everything a woman could want. You've been so fortunate.'

She had no way of knowing that each word struck Margaret like a stone. She had indeed had everything, and she had been ready – almost willing, if it came to the truth – to throw it away for a matter of stupid pride. If Gavin were to die without their quarrel being resolved once and for all, she thought – and shivered at the prospect.

'Nothing's ever as perfect as it looks,' she said, low-voiced.

'I know that. What I don't know is –' Islay leaned over the bed, her lovely face – a woman's face now, no longer a girl's – intent. 'What should I do? Should I be practical, or should I listen to the voice inside that tells me to try to get what I truly want, even though there seems little chance?'

'Little chance? Islay, I can't think of a single man in Paisley who'd be daft enough to turn away from you. You're kindly and able, and bonny, and young –'

Islay's face twisted with sudden pain. 'Too young, mebbe.'

'You mean the man you care for's older than you?' Sudden fear touched Margaret. She herself liked Richard, but all the same, if those tales Gavin had told of his brother were true he'd not make a wise choice for a vulnerable girl like Islay. 'It's not Richard Knox, is it?'

'No, of course not.' Islay sounded so surprised at the idea that Margaret was instantly reassured. 'How could the likes of me ever think to marry with the likes of him?'

'Then who else can it be, but –'

Margaret stopped short as a rosy flood of colour stained Islay's cheekbones. 'It's nobody – nobody that you'd know,' she said swiftly, then, 'But tell me, Margaret – what should I do?'

Gavin moaned slightly and turned his head on the pillow so that his face was towards Margaret. Light from the window landed fully on his features, cruelly showing the crusted, disfigured mask that overlaid his former good looks. Margaret rested her eyes on the diseased face, and loved it with all her heart.

'You must do as the voice tells you,' she said. 'Even if nothing comes of it – you must try.'

After that, she said nothing to Islay when she happened to look out of the windows and see Walter standing outside.

*

Gavin's disease ran its course, and Thomas was cautiously pleased with his patient's progress. The pustules crusted – and then the fever came back with frightening suddenness and Gavin tossed and raved and fought against the hands that tried to ease his suffering.

Thomas came to the house four or five times that day, and stayed for most of the night. Looking into his haggard face, Margaret felt her heart contract painfully.

'If he comes through this crisis, he'll live,' her brother said.

'But you think he's going to die,' she challenged flatly, and saw his eyes slide away from hers.

'There's no way of knowing for sure, Margaret.'

He left at dawn, promising to come back later. Islay insisted that Margaret, who had been by Gavin's side all night, should go to the kitchen to break her fast.

She sat at the table, staring at the food and drink that lay untouched before her. When Islay came into the room she jumped up, her eyes flaring.

'Is he –?'

'Margaret – I think you should go to him. I think we'd best send for Thomas.'

'How can we, when we can't leave the house?'

'Walter's across the road. I'll call to him from a window. You go to your man.'

Suddenly Margaret didn't want to go back into the bedroom she had shared with Gavin. She didn't want to see him draw his last breath. She wanted to stay in the warmth and comfort of the kitchen, to let the dying pass her by. But Islay's hand was on her arm, gently propelling her to her feet.

'I think,' the girl's soft Highland voice said, 'that he needs you to be with him.'

'Yes,' Margaret said, pushing back her panic and fear, forcing herself to straighten and walk out of the door towards the stairs, and Gavin, and the passing that would end all the living and the loving they had shared together. 'Yes.'

Slowly, she climbed the staircase.

Gavin's eyes, a smoky tawny yellow now that the worst of the fever was gone, were open. The skin of his face was stretched over his skull. His lips curved in the ghost of a smile as she went to the bedside.

She forced a smile in return, although her face felt as though it was frozen and she didn't know if her mouth had obeyed the instruction to turn up at the corners.

'Gavin –' Her voice was a whisper in her throat, and she coughed and tried again, fumbling for the right words, words that would comfort him and ease whatever was to come. 'Gavin, you're not to worry about anything. I'll manage fine, and I'll raise Christian and Daniel just the way you'd have done yourself. We'll be fine, the three of us. And – and –'

Her voice struggled and faltered and faded away. Islay was right. He needed her at this moment, just as she would have needed him if she had been the one to fall sick.

Only when her time came, he wouldn't be there. She would be alone. Gavin was going to leave her. She would be alone.

At that thought a sudden passionate anger surged into Margaret, shattering the stone wall that had encased her heart from the moment she accepted that he was going to die. The warmth of her rage sparkled along her veins, crackled in her sinews, brought a tingling to every part of her skin.

'No!' said Margaret. She straightened. There was no need to lean over him now, no fear that he wouldn't hear her voice. It was loud and clear, honed to razor sharpness by the anger that made her want to take him by the shoulders and shake him until he promised not to leave her.

'No!' she said again. 'We'll not be fine, Gavin Knox. We'll not be fine at all! You promised before God to be my husband and to – to care for me. And what sort of caring's this? I'll not let you turn your back on me and our bairns! It isn't near time yet for us to part, and well you know it! It's your duty to – to see that Christian and Daniel grow up. You know I'll do it wrong if I'm left to my own ways! You know what I'm like! How can you even think of going away and leaving – leaving –'

She stopped, hands fisted, then said with a passion that almost shook her apart. 'You can't! You're mine and I'll not let you die! You can't!'

'Margaret!' Islay came into the room, took Margaret by the shoulders, her lovely dark eyes shocked. 'You must calm yourself! You don't want him to go with harsh words in his ears, surely?'

'I do! Yes!' Margaret stormed. If she was going to be forced to live on alone and in misery then Gavin should know that it was his doing, and only his. She began to weep, great stormy sobs dredged up from the depths of her being. Then, angrily, she pulled away from Islay, dashing her arm across her eyes, drawing in a long shuddering breath and pressing her fists tightly to her mouth to force the tears back. The time for crying was later, when –

'Confound it, Margaret,' Gavin's voice croaked from the bed. She turned to see that the eyes still fixed on her had taken on a new, stronger lustre.

'Confound it,' he said again, and there was a faint ghost of laughter in his weak voice, 'I might have known that you'd even deprive a man of his right to die with dignity.'

Chapter Thirty

Islay walked home slowly, tired to the bone after days and nights without adequate sleep. The small bundle containing her possessions banged rhythmically against her thigh as she tramped along.

She had just turned into the familiar pend when the weaving shop door opened and Jamie stepped out to stand in her path.

It was almost too much of an effort to lift her head and look at him. For a long moment they considered each other; it seemed to her that his eyes moved from feature to feature then went on to map out the shape of her face as though he needed to convince himself that she was indeed Islay McInnes, his troublesome tenant.

Since he seemed disinclined to speak, she said, 'Mister Knox is making a good recovery.'

'So Thomas told me. And you, Islay, are you all right?'

'You needn't concern yourself – I'm not diseased. I'm not carrying the pox to endanger you all.'

He flushed angrily. 'That's not what I meant. You look bone tired.'

'Nursing a man as sick as Mister Knox was doesn't leave much time for sleep. I'm fine. If you're wanting me to clean out the loom shop I'll be down as soon as I've taken my things to the house.'

'God's teeth, but you must take me for an ogre of an employer! Go home, lassie, and sleep for as long as you need. The loom shop can wait for another few days,' he said explosively, and marched back in, slamming the door behind him.

As she emerged from the pend she saw that someone had dug and planted and tended the kale beds during her absence. The house had been dusted and swept, there was a good fire on, and the kettle sitting atop the range was gently puffing steam into the air.

Islay let her bundle drop to the floor and surveyed the room, quick tears stinging her eyes. She was home.

*

Within a week her routine had fallen into its usual pattern, and it was as though Gavin Knox's near-fatal illness had never happened to disrupt the still, placid pool of Islay's existence.

Jamie continued to avoid her, and Walter continued to ask her to go walking with him. If she refused he accepted her decision with a quiet resignation that made her feel so sorry for him that every now and then she accepted. He was good company, but not the company she would have chosen.

It wasn't long before Richard Knox began to find his way up the stairs to her kitchen at least once a week, as before. And then, one day not long after she returned from Margaret and Gavin's house, Jamie himself put in an unexpected appearance at the house door.

She stared, unable to believe her eyes, then stepped back to let him in. He stood in the middle of the room for a moment, looking round at the waxed furniture, the shining range, the twinkling windows and clean curtains.

'You've looked after the place well.'

'I like to keep it right. You'll take some ale?'

'No.' He sat down in one of the chairs that flanked the range. Islay took the other, drinking in the sight of him sitting at her hearth. She had often dreamed of it, but never thought to see it come true.

Jamie shifted in the chair as though finding it uncomfortable. For the first time she realised that his interest in the room was a ploy to avoid looking at her. Nervous apprehension fluttered in the pit of her stomach, and she folded her hands over her apron in a bid to control the strange and unpleasant sensation of panic-stricken butterfly wings deep within.

'Walter's been at me to pay him more wages,' he said abruptly.

'Aye?' For the life of her Islay couldn't see what concern it was of hers.

Jamie studied the cupboard, where her precious collection of crockery shone in ordered rows. 'He's of a mind to get wed. To you.'

'Me?' Her voice rose in an unbecoming squeak of pure shock.

Jamie ploughed on as though she had never spoken. 'I think it's a fine idea, myself. I hope you'll consider it wisely when he comes to speak to you about it.'

'But – why should I want to marry with Walter?'

'You've been walking out with him, have you not?'

'Aye, but not as his sweetheart!'

'Walter thinks otherwise.'

'Then he must change his way of thinking. I've no intention of wedding him!'

Jamie's brows lowered and met. 'Don't be a fool, lassie! You could do a lot worse than take Walter Shaw as a husband.'

'I'm not your possession, to be married where and when you think fit!' She got to her feet, glaring down at him.

'You're under my roof, and in my employ. And so you're my responsibility.'

'No need for you to think that!'

Now he rose to tower over her, his broad shoulders making the room look smaller.

'Have you heard anything from that rogue of a cousin of yours?'

'No. And I don't expect to, either.'

'So – you're alone in the world. And my responsibility, whether either of us likes it or not.'

'I can see to myself.'

'Aye, but can you? Richard Knox comes around this house more and more often.'

'He only calls to talk now and then.'

'And you like that, do you?'

His voice was scathing, and she felt her face turning warm. 'I find him pleasant enough. It little troubles me whether or not he comes or stays away.'

'Lassie, he's a man years older than you – far-travelled

into the bargain, and wise in the way of the world. It's not right for you to entertain him the way you do. If you'd a husband he'd look after you and – and protect you from the likes of Richard. It's not only him,' said Jamie, speaking now as though the words were being wrenched out of him. 'There's mebbe others that would show an interest in you if they could. Some men don't have the self-respect they should have, when it comes to women. You need to be protected –'

'When I feel the need to marry, I'll find my own man!'

'And like as not find the wrong one. Walter's –'

'I'll not wed with Walter!'

'I'll send him up to see you when his day's work's done,' he said obstinately. 'You can talk the matter out between you, face to face.'

The small insistent voice that had been clamouring within her, the voice she had told Margaret about, made itself heard to Islay. Margaret was right – she had to listen to it before it was too late and the voice was stilled for ever.

'Jamie –' She reached the door before he did and stood with her back against it, barring his way. 'Why are you doing this?'

'I told you. To protect you from the likes of Richard Knox.'

'Are you certain of that? Is it not to protect you from the likes of me?'

Jamie's eyes blazed in startled comprehension, then were swiftly masked. 'You're havering, lassie!'

'Am I, Jamie Todd? You're far-travelled yourself. You're near as worldly as Richard. You're some years older than I am. Look at me, Jamie – can you not see the truth for yourself? D'you not know that Walter isn't the man that I want!'

His face had gone so white that it was in startling contrast to the blazing sapphires that were his eyes. 'No –' he said hoarsely.

'Aye! You know it!'

'For God's sake, Islay!' He looked and sounded like a man in torment. 'I'm thirty-three years of age, and you're only a child!'

'A child? A minute ago you were all for marrying me off to Walter.'

'He's only a year older than you are! You need to be wed. You need to be looked after –'

'I don't need protecting against my own wanting.'

'You do. You're too young to realise what you're saying!'

'I'm a woman! Look at me, Jamie, and see that for yourself!'

She didn't stop to think what she was saying. She was fighting for her future as hard as Margaret Knox had fought for hers in the bed-chamber where Gavin hovered between life and death.

'No –' Jamie said again. 'No! It would be wrong!'

'The wrong lies in giving myself – or being given – against my will, d'you not see that? Jamie –' She reached out to him but he moved back, beyond her reach.

'Islay –!'

'You'd force me into a marriage I don't want? You'd do that to me?'

'It's the best way. The only way.'

The muscles along his firm jawline were corded and a fine film of perspiration gleamed on his forehead. His eyes, when they finally met and held hers, were implacable.

Slowly Islay stepped aside, leaving the door free. Jamie opened it, and looked back at her from the threshold.

'I'll send Walter up, as I said. I hope you'll see fit to tell him that you'll wed with him.'

She followed him onto the small landing. 'What if I refuse him?'

Jamie, already starting down the steps, turned to look up at her. His face was still marble-white, and set in harsh uncompromising lines.

'Then he may well find another wife. But Walter can't afford a cottage of his own and there's not enough room in his mother's house for him and a bride. I'd feel obliged to offer him this place. If you're wise, you'll take him, and provide yourself with a good man as well as a good home.'

Then he blundered off down the stairs without a backward glance, and she was alone.

*

As soon as she heard the news Margaret hurried to Wellmeadow. 'What's this I hear about you getting wed?' she asked as she walked into the kitchen.

'It's true.' Islay carefully poured boiling water onto tea-leaves then swung the kettle on its swee back over the range.

'To Walter Shaw?'

'Aye. The banns have been called for the first time. We'll marry in two weeks.'

'But Islay – what about the other man – the feelings you told me of, when Gavin was ill?'

Islay filled a cup and handed it to her guest. 'Och – that was just a silly lassie's fancy. Nothing at all.'

'No, it wasn't. And I've a good notion who you were talking about, too.'

'It was nobody –' Islay said sharply. 'Nobody at all!'

There was a short pause while Margaret considered her thoughtfully. Then the older woman said gently. 'Lassie, are you being pushed into this marriage against your own will?'

Islay lifted her head, smiled brightly. 'Of course not. Walter'll make a good husband. It's for the best.'

'Oh? And who was it said that to you?' Margaret asked dryly.

In answer, a small, genuine smile suddenly brightened Islay's pale face. 'Mistress MacLeod's already been here to offer to make me a new bonnet for the day.'

'That's my Aunt Mary for you – she doesn't consider that a bride's properly wed unless she's topped with a bonnet of her making. You'll let me and Gavin give you your wedding gown, of course.'

'Oh, Margaret, that would be too much!'

'After you helped to save his life? It's not near enough!'

'How is he?'

Margaret, easily diverted these days by the very mention of Gavin's name, experienced the sudden glow of pleasure that always warmed her whenever she saw or thought of him, ever since she almost lost him to the smallpox. It reminded her of their courting days.

'Oh, he's coming along well. The marks have almost left

him, apart from a scar he'll always carry on his chin to remind us.'

Islay's dark eyes searched Margaret's face. 'You look happier than I've ever seen you.'

Margaret blushed like a young girl. 'It's because I've been blessed with another chance. I wish you looked half as happy as I feel – nobody looking at the two of us would know that you were the bride, and not me.'

Islay's smile wavered, made a valiant attempt to brighten, then faded altogether. 'I'm content enough. Walter's a good man,' she said, in a voice that forbade any further argument.

Margaret paid heed to it, and said no more on the subject. When she was standing on the landing outside the house, preparing to take her leave, she hugged the Highland girl and said on an impulse, 'Islay – let Gavin and me hold a gathering for you in our house after the wedding. There's room for all of your friends, and his.'

The girl shook her head. 'There's no need. The wedding gown's more than enough. It's not as if I'm one of your family.'

'You are! You're part of both our families – the Todds as well as the Montgomerys. Nobody belongs to one without belonging to the other.'

'I'd as soon as leave things as we've planned them. We'll get married quietly then come back here, just the two of us.'

'Very well, if that's what you want. Now – I'll call for you tomorrow morning, and we'll go to my dressmaker to look at material for the wedding –'

Margaret's voice tailed off. Islay wasn't listening. Her eyes had slid beyond Margaret, her attention held by something in the yard below. Her face was almost gaunt, sharp-etched with hunger and loss.

Margaret turned and caught a glimpse of a fiery red head below as Jamie Todd, who had come into the yard to collect something, disappeared into the pend.

After she had left Islay, Margaret found some excuse to go into the weaving shop below to talk to Jamie. Walter was at his loom, singing cheerfully in a pleasant tenor voice as he worked. He shot her a shy smile as she stopped to congratulate him on his coming marriage.

In contrast to his young weaver Jamie looked quite ill. In his face Margaret saw the same despair, the same hopeless longing she had read in Islay's eyes.

Now she knew the truth; and she knew, too, that she had found it out too late.

Chapter Thirty-One

Islay wore a deep blue silk gown for her wedding day. The overdress was open from shoulders to waist to reveal a beribboned paler blue stomacher, and open again over a pale blue flounced underskirt.

The tight sleeves cascaded into layers of white lace at the elbows; the same lace also edged the neckline and the low bodice line of the dress.

Mary MacLeod, recognising the pointlessness of vying with her young client's natural beauty by giving her a fancy bonnet, had made one of natural straw in a simple milkmaid style, trimmed with ribbons in shades of blue to match the gown. Beneath it Islay's glossy black hair had been drawn away from her face and twisted into a knot at the back of her head.

Walter, too, looked his best. His straight brown hair had been well brushed for the occasion and tied back with a green ribbon. He was dressed in his finery – a green topcoat and brown britches fastened at the knee with silver buckles. There were silver buckles on his sturdy black shoes, and his calves were encased in brown hose.

His face shimmered with joy and pride as he led his bride to her wedding. But Margaret, who had gone with Gavin to witness the marriage, watched Islay with concern. The girl's face was pale, her eyes deep dark unfathomable pools. An occasional smile flickered nervously about her lips when she caught anyone looking at her, then faded and died.

'It's all wrong!' Margaret mourned in a whisper. Gavin laid his free hand restrainingly on the fingers clutching at his arm.

'Hush, Margaret – the lassie's old enough to go her own

way. There's nothing we can do to change things, no matter how much you might want to.'

*

Islay scarcely heard a word of the marriage service that bound her to Walter Shaw for the rest of their lives. She stood motionless within the wedding gown, beneath the lovely new bonnet, with no feeling that she was actually wearing them. It was as though they merely enclosed her.

Walter took her hand in his own warm strong clasp and slipped his ring onto her finger. It was over, she was wed; she had stepped through a door that led from one life to another and there was no turning back.

They walked to Wellmeadow alone after the small wedding party had dispersed; Islay with her hand through her husband's arm, Walter swaggering with pride as one well-wisher after another stopped them. He had been given a day off work for his marriage, and as they went through the pend the other weavers and the draw-boys swarmed out of the loomshop to greet them. Jamie wasn't among them.

When they finally climbed the stairs and went into the house Walter unbuttoned his coat and peeled it off, throwing it carelessly over the back of a chair. It half-sprawled to the floor as its owner dropped into one of the fireside chairs with a grunt of satisfaction.

'It's finally done, lass! Man and wife!'

'Aye, it's done.' She picked up his coat and put it away neatly. Then she took off her new bonnet and replaced it with a linen cap.

'You'll be ready for your meal.'

'I am that,' said Walter. 'Where are you going?'

She paused, her hand on the door leading to the inner room. 'To put on my working clothes.'

'No need to go in there. You're my wife now – have you forgotten?'

He was sitting upright now, his eyes suddenly intent on her. Heat was creeping into them. Islay swallowed convulsively, then said, 'I've not forgotten.'

Her hand fell away from the door and she moved back into the kitchen, reaching for her apron.

Walter got to his feet and took her by the shoulders as she finished tying the apron round her waist. 'Islay, you'll not regret marrying with me, lass. I'll look after you.'

His face was anxious, and absurdly young. All at once she felt years older than he was. 'I know you will, Walter. It'll be fine.'

He smiled. 'Aye, it'll be fine.' Then he bent to kiss her, his lips touching hers lightly at first, then increasing their pressure as his arms closed about her.

She submitted to the embrace, putting her own arms about him, telling herself firmly that he was her husband now, and she his wife. But as the kiss became fiercer and Walter's body began to tremble against hers, his hands moving with more and more urgency on her, she broke away. 'I'll – I'll see to the food,' she said, and turned to the range.

After they had eaten she cleared the table before picking up a bucket and going to the door.

'Where are you going now?'

'To fetch water from the well.'

He took the bucket from her. 'I'll do that. I'm the man of the house,' he said, and went out.

Alone, Islay tore off her apron and the pretty wedding gown and dressed in her working blouse and skirt, her hands trembling with haste.

After she had put her apron back on and hung the gown up in the press, letting her hands linger for a moment on the soft luxury of the silk, she looked about the kitchen that had been hers for some six months, and was hers no longer.

'I'm the man of the house –' Walter's words echoed in her head. Already his stamp was there; his good coat on the peg behind the door beside her cloak, the air in the room heavy with the smell of the pipe he had been smoking. The pipe itself lay on the range, the tobacco in its bowl dully glowing at her like a red eye within a deep black socket.

She took a deep breath and swung the swee away from the range, out into the room, so that she could tip hot water from the kettle into a bowl.

When he came back Walter glanced at her everyday clothes, but said nothing. Instead, he refilled the kettle before settling himself back into the fireside chair. He took off his shoes, picked up his pipe, and stretched his muscular legs across the rag rug, sighing with contentment.

'It's like a palace here. At home the place is full of bairns, and my mother screaming at them from morning to night. But here –' he looked around with an air of satisfaction, and settled his buttocks more firmly into the chair.

When she had finished washing the dishes Islay took her place opposite him, her sewing in her hands.

Walter reached across and lifted a handful of the light material she was working on. 'What is it?'

'A nightshift. I should have finished it yesterday, but I didn't have the time.'

'Is it for tonight?'

'Aye.'

He rubbed the ball of one thumb appreciatively over the cloth. 'It's bonny.'

Evening wore on and the room darkened until Islay could no longer see the tiny stitches she was taking in the hem of the new nightgown. She put down her work and rose. Walter reached out a long arm and caught at her skirt as she passed his chair.

'Where are you going now?'

It was the third time he had asked that in the short time they had been married. She began to feel as though her freedom had suddenly been taken from her. 'To light the lamp.'

'No need for that. It's surely time for us to go to bed now. I've to get up early in the morning.'

'I've not finished the shift. It only needs a few more minutes –'

'No need for the shift, either,' said Walter. 'Not tonight.'

He put his arms about her and his fingers fumbled at the strings of her apron. It fell to the floor between them and Walter's foot nudged it to one side as he began to unfasten the small buttons down the front of her blouse, squinting with concentration.

When the blouse, too, had been dropped to the floor and pushed aside he started working with the same dogged purpose on the ribbons that fastened her chemise. His breathing seemed loud in the quiet dimness of the room.

When Islay put her hands up to take over the work herself rather than submit to his clumsy ministrations he lifted his gaze briefly to her face and said, 'Don't!'

She dropped her hands and stood before him, feeling his fingers tremble against her skin; feeling that same tremor begin deep within herself, though she didn't know whether it was caused by nervousness or pleasurable anticipation, dread or excitement.

The chemise dropped away and Walter's hands took her breasts, claiming them as triumphantly as any explorer coming on hitherto undiscovered terrain. Fire darted through Islay as the touch of those masculine hands began to rouse her to stiff-nippled excitement.

Her own breath caught raggedly in her throat as Walter took time to unfasten the strings of her bonnet and toss it away. Then he loosed the knot of hair at the back of her head and let it fall in a black curtain about her naked shoulders.

'Your skin's like – like the softest silk that ever was,' he breathed, and bent to brush wondering lips over her throat and shoulders and, finally, down over her breasts.

Islay closed her eyes, bringing her hands up to busy themselves in his thick hair, loosening the ribbon that held it back. All at once she felt that everything was, after all, going to be all right. She could be happy with Walter; he would help her to forget Jamie.

He lifted her and carried her over to the bed and stripped her naked before tearing off his own clothes, scattering them all over the room in his urgency. He was more heavily built than she had thought, his chest and groin matted with crisp dark curls.

'Walter, let me gather up the clothes –'

'Leave them!' he ordered, then plunged down on top of her, burrowing and snatching, bruising soft tender skin and the flesh beneath, paying no heed to her gasps of pain.

It was then that Islay realised that in her new husband's eyes marriage was a taking by the man and a submitting by the woman. As far as he was concerned there was no question of sharing love. He didn't need or ask for her love

– only her body.

And he had every right to take that whenever and in whatever manner he chose.

Because to Walter Shaw and men like him that was what marriage meant.

Chapter Thirty-Two

Pride in his new marital state made Walter a possessive husband. He liked to know just where Islay was at each moment of the day, when he was at his loom and unable to be with her.

He scowled if any of the other weavers talked and joked with her. Soon she began to start her work in the weaving shop early so that she was free to leave before the other men arrived.

It was better that way, for then she didn't have to face Walter's resentment and his accusations that she had been altogether too friendly with this man or that, once his day's work was over and they were together again.

The words 'My wife –' which he liked to use whenever possible, began, in Islay's ears, to take on a leaden ring.

She saw little of Jamie during the first weeks of her marriage. He rarely came to the weaving shop, and if he had to it was usually in the afternoons, when the place was cleaned and the pirns delivered and Islay out of the way upstairs, working at her spinning wheel.

To her relief Richard Knox had the good sense and the courtesy to stay away now that she wore another man's ring on her finger.

A month after the wedding she was hanging out washing in the back yard when she happened to turn and catch a glimpse of red hair glowing within the pend's gloom. Her heart jumped, but she resolutely turned back to her task, determined not to indicate by a look or a word that she had seen him. It was possible – indeed, probable – that he hadn't seen her, after all.

After a moment footsteps sounded on the cobblestones then Jamie said, from just beside her, 'Good day to you, Islay.'

She turned, looking no higher than the top button of his waistcoat. 'Good day, Mister Todd.'

'Are you well?'

'Aye, sir.' She ducked her head in nervous acknowledgment, and went back to her work.

'Good. You look well,' said Jamie formally. 'Marriage agrees with you.'

Her fingers fumbled on the clothes-rope. A wooden peg fell from her grasp. She stooped swiftly to pick it up just as he did the same. For a brief moment in the fabric of time their fingers touched, and simultaneously withdrew from the contact as though they had each touched a burning coal.

'Is Walter treating you well?' Jamie asked, his voice suddenly losing its formality and becoming low and urgent.

'He's a good husband.' No sense in speaking about the pain of a body regularly violated because the man who took it had no knowledge of any other way to couple with a woman. Indeed, for all Islay knew that was the only way between men and women. It might be that she herself was in some way set apart from the rest of her sex. It might be that the thrill of desire she had known when Walter's hands first rested on her naked breasts, the desire she felt at that moment, close to Jamie Todd, wasn't normal in a woman.

And so she only repeated, as the two of them rose to their full heights again, 'He's a very good husband.'

'I'm pleased to hear it, for if he made you unhappy he'd have me to answer to,' said Jamie. Then he bowed and turned away, and strode back through the pend and out into the street beyond.

She stood motionless, her hands filled with wet clothes and pegs, looking after him; then she saw Walter's face swimming palely behind the glass panes of the weaving shop, and went back to her work.

*

'What was Mister Todd saying to you?' he wanted to know when they were at their evening meal.

'Nothing much. He asked if we were settling down well together.'

'And you told him that everything was fine.'

'Of course. What else is there to say?'

'He's a good man, Jamie Todd,' Walter said. 'I've a lot to thank him for. I've got work, when many a good weaver in Paisley has idle hands and an empty belly. I've got a fine wee house –'

His hand reached out across the table and captured Islay's. His face, as he surveyed her, was alight with pride and his own form of affection' – and I've got you, Islay. Aye, there's a lot the two of us have to thank Jamie Todd for.'

*

His smiles changed to scowls when Mary MacLeod invited the newly-wed couple to a gathering in her home.

'What does the likes of us want to visit gentry in a grand house in Oakshawhill for?'

'Mistress MacLeod's not gentry, Walter – well, not real gentry.' Islay, who had been raised in a society where a man was judged by his own worth, not by his possessions, and where the clan chief and the poorest of his clansmen were judged to be on equal footing, found the Lowland obsession with class confusing. 'She's a kindly soul. And Margaret and Gavin'll be there. They're good friends of mine.'

'Well they're not friends of mine. They'd never have thought of inviting me to their fine houses if I wasnae married to you.'

'Och, Walter! They're all decent folk, with no airs and graces to them at all. Margaret Knox is a weaver's daughter, raised in a cottage herself.'

'That's as may be. Now she's a surgeon's wife, with servants and carriages and the Lord knows what else. I'm in no mind to go,' he said peevishly.

'But I can't go on my own.'

'I'd not let you. You'll stay home, with me.'

Dismayed, she put aside her knitting wires and went over to kneel by his chair. 'Walter, I want to go. We've been nowhere since the day we married, except to visit your mother. Can you not bring yourself to go, even just this once?'

Disarmed, he stroked her hair. 'Does it mean as much as that to you?'

'I want you to meet the folk that have been so good to me in the past.'

'Aye – well –' he said reluctantly. 'Mebbe we'll go – but if I don't care for them, it'll be the last time.'

'Oh, thank you, Walter!' She began to get up, but he held her where she was with one hand on her shoulder. The other hand, the one that had been stroking her hair, loosed it so that it fell softly about her face, like night-rain. Her hair, long and rich and glossy, fascinated Walter.

He gathered as much of it as he could in his fist and used it to draw her head back so that he could bend to kiss her lips and then her throat. His hand left her shoulder and travelled to her breast, and he slid from his chair and joined her on the floor, pushing her down until she lay beneath him.

*

She prayed, as they went along the High Street and through the pend that led to Oakshawhill, that he would enjoy himself, for she didn't want to have to give up her good friends. Then, as they neared Mary MacLeod's gate, the prayer slipped from her mind and she began to wonder if Jamie would be there tonight.

Margaret and Gavin were coming along the opposite way, from their own house. They waited by the gate for the Shaws and greeted Walter warmly. So did Mary, when she met them at the door.

'Most of the folk are here. Come along, lassies, and put your cloaks in my bed-chamber.'

Gavin, now fully recovered from his illness and with nothing to show for it except a gash of puckered, damaged skin that stretched from one corner of his mouth, cutting diagonally across his cheek to the lobe of his ear, put a friendly hand on Walter's arm.

'We'll go on into the parlour and get ourselves something to drink. I know where it's kept.'

'You always did, you rascal,' said Mary indulgently, and swept Margaret and Islay upstairs and into a large comfortable room.

'I'm right vexed with Jamie,' she confided as they went.

'He downright refused to come, and nothing I could say would move him. There's still a coolness between him and Duncan and Robert over this business of Richard. And Jamie felt that if they were going to be here he'd be better to stay away. That's not deterred Richard, of course. The bold man's down there in my parlour, chattering away to the Montgomerys, and not caring a hoot about the cold looks he's getting from them.'

Margaret put her cloak aside and went to the full-length mirror to see that her hair was neat. 'It's as well that I've won my battle with Gavin, or we'd not be here ourselves. He'll still not have Richard in our house, but at least he's willing to be civil to the man if we should chance to meet him elsewhere.'

'Men! You're looking bonny, Islay —' Mary circled her young guest, admiring the way her gown, the one she had worn on her wedding day, fell in graceful lines to the floor. Margaret turned from the mirror.

'You suit that colour. I've got a gown that might well do you, in much the same shade. D'you have time to come to the house tomorrow afternoon to have a look at it?'

'You've already given me too much —'

'Oh, tuts, lassie! The gown's just going to go to the moths if you don't take it, for it's no use at all to me. I've not been able to get into it since Daniel's birth. I don't know what's happened at all.'

'You're just getting older, Margaret,' her aunt said briskly, and earned herself a baleful glare. She disregarded it and went on sunnily, 'Now — shall we go down and join the others?'

*

Walter was ill at ease; Islay realised that as soon as she entered the room and saw him, glass in hand, standing stiffly to attention as Gavin Knox chatted amiably to him.

She went to him at once, sliding a hand into his to comfort him. His fingers closed on hers like a drowning man grasping at a plank of wood and some of the tension went out of his body.

But there were too many people in the room for it to be

possible for husband and wife to stay together all the time. Inevitably, as always happened at Paisley gatherings, the women gravitated to one side of the parlour while the men gravitated to the other.

The women chattered about recipes and babies and clothes and housework. The men talked on what, to them, were weightier matters. Weaving and politics and prices, the war in the Americas, which had attracted a number of unemployed young weavers to join the flag, and the proposals for a proper water supply for Paisley, a project that was dear to Gavin's and Thomas's hearts.

Glancing across at Walter now and again Islay saw that her husband, who had matured so swiftly in her eyes since their wedding day, seemed to have shrunk back into callow boyhood, talking only when a question was put directly to him, pulling nervously at the buttons on his good jacket – if he wasn't careful, she thought anxiously, he would twist them right off and embarrass himself even further – and drinking too quickly and too much.

Later, when refreshments were served, the two sexes began to mingle again, but before he could reach the safety of Islay's side Walter was swept off by Mary MacLeod, who bore down on him determined to do her duty as hostess and make him feel welcome.

Islay, on her own for a moment, was quickly joined by Richard Knox, his green gold-flecked eyes travelling over her with the confident skill of the connoisseur.

'Marriage agrees with you, my dear Islay,' he said, unconsciously using Jamie Todd's words. 'But not, alas with me. I regret that I can no longer call on you and enjoy the pretty picture you make working industriously at your wheel. Now I must content myself with recalling it from my imagination instead. If I was your husband, my dear, I think I should hire the best portrait painter in the land to capture you on canvas. Helen of Troy – or the Queen of Sheba might be a title better suited to your dark beauty – spinning her web to catch men's hearts.'

'I'm happy to say that my husband has more to do with his money, and so I'll be spared the ordeal, sir.'

'Ah yes – you threw yourself away on a young weaver,'

said Richard, turning to cast a disdainful eye on Walter. 'A lusty enough lad, I suppose. Does he pleasure you, Islay?'

She felt colour rise to her face. 'I don't know what you mean, Mister Knox.'

'Oh, you do.' Richard leaned close to breathe the words into her ear. 'You do, my dark beauty. If it should ever be that he no longer holds your interest, remember that I would be more than happy to offer my assistance.'

He turned away, leaving her furious and embarrassed. So this was part of marriage, was it? This assumption by other men that once a woman had lost her maidenhood she might be willing to spread her favours further than the marriage bed?

She wanted, at that moment, to scoop Walter from beneath the friendly hand Mary MacLeod had laid on his arm and depart for home. But he had been watching her, she knew. He had seen Richard talking to her. If she suddenly announced that she wanted to leave he would know that somehow Richard had offended her. And there was no knowing what Walter's pride might lead him to then.

She took a deep breath, pinned a smile on her face, and crossed the room to Margaret and Gavin.

Chapter Thirty-Three

As Islay had suspected, Walter didn't enjoy the evening at all. They were the first guests to leave, and they walked back to Wellmeadow in silence.

When at last they were in their own house he took her to bed immediately, and made frenzied love to her.

'You're mine, Islay,' he said into the darkness when at last he had rolled away from her and they lay side by side. 'You're mine – and from now on we don't need any fine folks in big houses!'

On the following afternoon Islay went to Oakshawhill, where she tried on the gown that Margaret had spoken of.

It was made of pale blue cotton, a simple but elegant dress cut on lines that made the most of Islay's full young breasts and small waist.

'It's even a little wide for you,' Margaret said enviously. 'You'll have to take it in here – and here.'

'That's easily done.' Islay stood before the looking-glass, turning first to one side then to the other to admire the sweep of the skirt. 'It's a bonny gown.'

'And I'm glad to see it worn again, for it was always one of my own favourites. I think you've lost some weight since your marriage day, Islay.' She began to help Islay out of the gown. 'Did Walter enjoy himself last night?'

'Aye, he –' Islay started to say, then stopped herself. She didn't have to lie to Margaret. 'No, if the truth be told. He felt like a – a fish out of water, and it vexed him.'

'I thought the poor lad was finding it all a burden.' Margaret took the blue gown to the bed and began to fold it while Islay pulled on her own brown dress. 'Men don't care for gatherings as much as women do. Gavin was the same in the early days of our marriage. But he soon got to know all the folk, and then he began to enjoy himself. So will Walter,

I'm certain. Why don't the two of you come along to our house one evening next week? Once he feels comfortable with us, we'll slip him into society without him even noticing –'

'No, Margaret. It's well meant, I know, and it's kind of you, but we'd best not.'

'But you're surely not going to come to gatherings alone and leave him at home?'

Strands of Islay's hair had been loosed from their place while she was trying on the gown. She released all of it, shook it down about her face, then began to twist it back into its knot with deft movements.

'I'm his wife now – I'll stay at home with him.'

'Oh,' said Margaret, then, 'Islay, are you happy?'

Sometimes it was necessary to lie, even to a close friend like Margaret Knox. 'Of course I am. Walter's a good husband.'

The knot was firmly in place again. She let her hands drop to her sides, turned to face Margaret, suddenly hungry for information, or perhaps reassurance that, unsatisfactory as her marriage was, it was like everyone else's. Even that would help in a way – although for the life of her Islay couldn't imagine a man like Gavin Knox using his wife as Walter used her.

'But it takes a bit of getting used to – marriage. Learning what a man's needs are. Learning –' she stumbled, trying to chose her words carefully. ' – learning not to mind if he –'

'Not to mind what?'

Islay had gone too far to draw back, although she felt her face flame as she asked, the words tumbling over each other in their haste to get out, 'Margaret, is it a sin for a woman to need – to want –' She put an impatient hand up to her mouth, then pulled it away to say, ' – to want to love as much as a man does?'

Margaret, too, was crimson. Islay had never thought it possible for Margaret Knox to blush so.

But the older woman's voice was clear and strong as she said, 'Of course it's not a sin! It's only natural, surely. We're flesh and blood the same as any man.'

'Oh –' Islay clasped her hands tightly together.

'Does Walter not – not understand that?'

'Oh yes. It was just that I wondered, that's all.' Islay swooped to the bed and caught up the folded gown. 'I must go.'

'Stay and take tea with me. The bairns haven't seen you for a while. And it's long enough since you and me had a proper talk.'

'I must go. Walter'll finish work soon, and he likes me to be at home, waiting for him.'

Islay almost fled out of the house and along the road, her mind a bubbling cauldron of thoughts. She wasn't sinful, or wicked, or out of the normal, and that knowledge was a great relief.

But on the other hand she had found out, once and for all, that there was indeed more to marriage than the relationship she and Walter shared. There was mutual caring and wanting and, perhaps, mutual satisfaction. But not for Islay Shaw.

Not for the first time in the past month Islay seemed to hear the faint clang of a prison door slamming shut in her mind.

*

That night when the children had gone to bed and Margaret and Gavin were alone in the parlour she said tentatively, 'Gavin, it's natural for women to enjoy bedding with a man, is it not?'

He looked at her in astonishment, then burst out laughing. 'After all the years we've been married, you ask me that?'

'Gavin!' Exasperated, she swiped at his head, and he parried the blow, seizing her wrist and drawing her down to sit on the arm of his chair. 'I'm asking your opinion as a medical man!'

'It's as well you told me that, for I've little experience of the matter as an ordinary man,' he said, a glimmer of mischief still sparkling in the depths of his eyes. Then he added, 'Though as an ordinary man I've no fault to find with my own experiences, ma'am.'

From where she sat it was possible – and pleasant – to rest

her cheek on the top of his head. His fingers caressed the inside of her wrist, and he lifted her hand to his lips and kissed the palm.

Gavin was in a very relaxed, contented mood. The two of them had just spent most of the evening playing with their children; at last the barriers Daniel had built between himself and his father were noticeably crumbling.

With a feeling of guilt Margaret recognised that the little boy's fear of his father wasn't due only to the day Gavin had cut his arm with a knife. It had been fostered and fed by the child's instinctive reaction to the hostility he had sensed from that day on between his parents.

Margaret blamed herself bitterly for that, and always would, even though her precious, beloved family had weathered the storm and found happiness again.

'As to your question,' Gavin was saying now, 'it's perfectly natural for a woman to benefit from loving as much as a man. Though I'll admit that often enough men insist on claiming all the benefit for themselves and treating their womenfolk as objects for their own pleasure. But why should you want to know my opinion on a matter like that?'

Margaret slid from the arm of the chair onto his knee, so that she could look into his face. 'Islay was here this afternoon.'

'I see. Margaret,' he said carefully after a moment, 'there's nothing you can do for Islay, you know that. Nobody can – or should – come between husband and wife.'

'I know, I know. But I just wish I could help her. If Jamie hadn't been so thick-headed Islay wouldn't be wed to Walter Shaw now!'

'She might be. Jamie didn't force them to wed. Walter's been hungering after Islay for some time, from what I heard. She even went out walking with him.'

'I wish I could –'

Gavin laid a finger on her lips. 'Hush now, Margaret. We've said enough on the subject, and it's closed.'

Then he recaptured her hand and kissed her palm once more, his lips setting up a thrill that ran along her arm to her heart.

'As for me – I'm content to just thank God that I have

what I have,' said Gavin, 'and leave it at that.'

*

At that very moment Walter was asking suspiciously, 'Where did you get that?'

Islay lifted her head and saw him standing before her, one finger stabbing at the gown she was stitching. 'From Margaret Knox. It doesn't fit her any more, so she thought it might do for me.'

He was scowling. 'I don't like to see my wife in rich folks' cast-offs.'

'It's not a cast-off; it's a perfectly good gown that's too tight for her now. It was kind of her to offer it to me.'

'Kind? You Highlanders,' said Walter with scorn, 'don't have the brains of hens!'

'Walter!'

'It sickened me last night, seeing them fussing over you as though you were a pet dog. And you taking it all without offence!'

'They're my friends –'

'Your friends? From now on,' he said, his voice thick, 'your friends are the folk I want to mingle with, not gentry! Not men like Richard Knox with his silk clothes and his fine horse and his purse full of money! What was he saying to you last night?'

She moistened her lips. 'He was only congratulating me on our marriage.'

Walter threw his head back and brayed with mirthless laughter. 'Was he, indeed? Telling you what a fool you had made of yourself, wedding a poor weaver, more like. Telling you that you'd have done better with the likes of him!'

He was near enough to the truth to frighten her. But she gripped the wooden arms of her chair and glared up at him. 'Don't be daft! A man like Richard Knox would never dream of marrying me!'

'No, but he'd be willing enough to take you to his bed and pay you well for your favours!'

Sheer anger brought her out of her chair so quickly that he backed a step or two. 'That's a wicked, evil thing to say, and I'm shamed that my own husband should speak such words to me, Walter Shaw!'

She stooped to pick up the gown. He caught at it, and for a moment they tussled ridiculously over it, glaring like two children disputing a game.

With a rending sound the gown tore. Islay cried out in dismay and let go to save it from further damage. With a sweep of the arm Walter threw it away from him and it landed on the hot range. As the acrid smell of burning cloth filled the kitchen he wheeled about and marched to the door, slamming it so hard behind him that she thought it was going to splinter at the hinges.

By the time she snatched the gown from the range it was too late. One sleeve had fallen against the bars of the glowing fire, and was striped with black singe-marks. The struggle had not only half-parted the skirt from the bodice; it had ripped some of the cloth as well. There was little that could be done now.

Islay sat down, the gown in her arms, and wept. But after a while she stopped. Tears couldn't save the bonny dress, or turn the clock back.

She dried her eyes and got on with her work, waiting for the sound of Walter's footsteps on the stairs.

When they finally came, the steps on the wooden staircase were slow and uncertain.

When the door opened and he came in she saw at once that he had been consoling himself in a howff.

He held onto the door-frame for a moment, squinting blearily at her as she sat by the fire in a pool of light from the lamp she had put on a shelf nearby. 'You should be in bed.'

'I was waiting for you, to make sure you were all right.'

He came in, letting the door swing to behind him, and took off his coat, dropping it on the floor. 'I'm f – fine,' he said in a slurred voice. 'I've spent the evening in the sort of house that suits me, with the s – sort of folk that suit me.'

He sat down in his usual chair with a thud and tried to take his shoes off. Islay closed the door and latched it against the night. Then she picked up his coat and hung it in its proper place before going to kneel before Walter to help him off with his shoes.

She felt his hand patting her head. 'You're a good wee w – wife, Islay. I shouldn't have sh – shouted at you, lass.'

'Come on – come to bed.' She stood up, took his hand, helped him to his feet. All at once his arms were about her, holding her so close that she could almost feel her ribs creaking in protest.

'It's just that – I wish I could give you all these things they have, Islay,' said Walter into her ear, tears in his voice. 'I wish I could give you a fine house, and bonny gowns, and – and a carriage –'

She managed to free herself and stood back, taking his hands in hers. 'I know, Walter. But I'm content enough with the things we have.'

'I'm not – not when I see what they have,' he said, suddenly resentful. 'Why should the likes of Ri –' his tongue and lips shied at the name, and tried again, 'Ri – ch'd High and Mighty Knox swagger about the town with his fine clothes and his purse full of silver when de – decent hard-working men like me have to make do with plain cloth and a few pence?'

He was working himself into another rage. Talking soothingly, she managed to lead him across the room to the wall-bed. He collapsed onto it, then reached up and touched her face.

'I'm going to look after you, Islay,' he said blearily, then rolled over onto his face and fell asleep, spread-eagled over the bed, still fully dressed.

Chapter Thirty-Four

A few weeks later Islay knew beyond any doubt that she was expecting Walter's child.

He received the news with surly resignation. 'It's the way of things, I suppose,' he said, and cast a look about the neat kitchen. 'At last we've got more room for our bairns than my mother ever had.'

Islay wasn't certain of her own reaction. Although she felt ill every morning she looked forward with happy anticipation to bearing a child of her own making. But Walter's reference to his mother, and the thought it conjured up of Mistress Shaw's tired thin bitter face and her noisy crowded kitchen, filled from wall to wall with the squalling, fighting, peevish brood she had borne, was depressing. Walter seemed to assume that that was now to be Islay's fate, too. It was a frightening prospect.

As time went by and she was forced to let out the seams of her clothes to accommodate her increasing waistline Walter became more and more sullen. As the eldest of his family, he had been the main bread-winner before his marriage. He still contributed money to his mother's house, and Islay watched and listened with dismay as he became more and more obsessed with the threat of poverty now that they had started their family.

'Och, we'll manage fine,' she tried to re-assure him day after day. 'We've got a nice wee house, and you're in employment. Now that the new cotton cloth's doing well there's no likelihood of you losing your place.'

'Aye, it's doing well – but little that means to the weavers who do the work,' he growled. 'Jamie Todd and that fine Mister Knox of yours are lining their pockets – but not a penny piece more do I get out of it.'

'You're paid good wages – enough to help your mother

and keep yourself and me and a bairn, with what I make from my spinning –'

'You'll not be able to go on doing that, though.'

'Walter, I'm bearing a child, not falling sick with the pox! I'll not be away from my wheel for long. And then there's the wee bit of money I make seeing to Margaret Knox's looms –'

He shifted restlessly in his chair and looked at her from beneath lowered brows. 'As to that, I think it's high time you put a stop to it.'

'Put a stop to it? But a moment since, you were fretting about not bringing in enough money!'

'I've no taste for living off my wife's earnings.'

'You know fine that in Paisley plenty of the women help to bring in the silver! There's nothing wrong with it. It's not as if the work's hard. All I have to do is visit the loom shops every day and see that there's enough yarn and that the finished ribbons are collected.'

'I don't like you working for the likes of Margaret Knox. You're my wife, not her servant!'

She realised, too late, that she should never have persuaded him to attend the gathering in Mary MacLeod's house. The sight of the prosperous Knox and Todd and Montgomery families had filled him with bitterness and resentment. There was nothing to be gained by reminding him that all these folk had worked hard for what they now had; Walter looked at them and saw only that they were wealthier than he was. And he despised them for it.

His resentment centred itself mainly on Richard Knox. Islay rarely saw the man herself, other than an occasional glimpse of him riding his fine chestnut horse along the street, tall and elegant in the saddle, with his dour manservant in close attendance astride his grey mount. But she knew whenever he had paid a visit to the loom shop downstairs, for on those evenings Walter was especially surly. Sometimes he would go out to a howff, coming back the worse for drink, muttering about Richard Knox and his high and mighty ways.

He returned from one of his evenings out later than usual, running up the outer stairs and erupting into the kitchen so fiercely that the door crashed back against the wall and the candle Islay had lit so that she could go on with her sewing guttered in the great draught of wind that accompanied Walter into the house.

She jumped to her feet, spilling the material she was working on to the floor. 'Walter, what's –'

'Hold your tongue, woman!' He slammed the door shut and leaned against it for a moment, his shoulders heaving as he dragged air into his lungs. When at last he turned, her hands flew to her mouth. His face, beneath an untidy thatch of wind-swept hair, was grey-white, apart from a splash of crimson all down one side, from temple to chin.

'You're hurt!'

He put his fingers to his cheek and brought them away sticky with congealing blood as Islay ran to fetch a rag and some water.

'Sit down and let me look at it. What happened to you?'

He let her lead him to a chair at the table. 'I was – making my way home when someone sprang at me out of the shadows.'

'Who was it?'

'How should I know? The brute felled me to the ground before I could turn round.'

His clothes were certainly muddy. It had been a wet late September day and there were plenty of puddles around that night. But somehow his story didn't ring true.

'But why would anyone try to attack you, Walter?'

'There's plenty of vagabonds and thieves about the streets. Who knows why they do what they do?'

'Surely they could see that you'd not be likely to have enough silver on you to make it worth whi –' She stopped, biting back a cry of pain as Walter's hand suddenly shot out and gripped her wrist, his fingers digging painfully into the soft tissue of her inner arm. The bowl of water tipped, splashing some of its contents on the table, then teetered before righting itself.

'Someone sprang out at me from the shadows and felled me to the ground – and that's all there is to it!' Walter said from between clenched teeth. 'D'you hear what I say, woman?

Then he released her arm and sat back, lifting his face for her ministration. 'Now – hold your tongue when I tell you to, and see to the wound.'

A dozen more questions hovered on Islay's lips, but she didn't dare ask them. A dozen chill fears tugged at the fringes of her mind, but she didn't dare admit them any further. She concentrated instead on gently cleansing his face and mopping at the fresh blood that still welled slowly from a nasty cut on his cheekbone. The flesh around it was already swelling and purpling. It looked as though Walter had indeed been hit by a stick; if the blow had landed a little higher, on his temple, he would have been knocked unconscious.

'Fetch the ale!'

'If I take this pad away from the cut it'll start bleeding ag –'

'I'll hold it! Just fetch the ale when you're told!'

She did, and poured it clumsily in her agitation, slopping some onto the table to join the water that had already been spilled there. She brought fresh cloths and mopped up the mess, then sat down by the fireplace again and picked up her sewing, not daring to look at Walter in case she sent him into another bout of anger.

He sat on at the table for some time, drinking steadily until the ale jug was emptied. Now and then, when the wind outside gusted and set something rattling, he jumped and looked sharply at the door.

Once he asked in a whisper, 'Can you hear someone coming up the stairs?'

'It's only the sound of the wind. Who'd come here at this hour of the night?'

'Go out and look,' he insisted fretfully.

Outside, she closed the door behind her and stood for a moment on the wooden landing. The wind caught at her skirts and pulled them tightly against her calves and thighs. The moon was hidden by low scudding clouds and the night was dark around and above and below her.

After a moment she went back inside to find Walter on his feet, still clasping the padded cloth to his face, watching the door warily. As she came in his free hand tightened on the back of a chair, for all the world as though he would have picked it up and used it as a weapon if necessary.

'Well?'

'There's nobody out there.'

He relaxed a little. 'How does it look now?'

She went to him and eased the cloth from his face. 'It's stopped bleeding, but it looks awful sore.'

'It'll do. Come to bed, Islay.'

That night he made no attempt to touch her, but lay still and wakeful by her side. Islay, too, stayed awake for a long time before falling asleep. She roused once, and knew at once that Walter was still awake, although when she whispered his name into the darkness he didn't answer. She slipped back into drowsy oblivion, and woke again to see a muted light dancing on the kitchen ceiling.

It went out even as she blinked sleepily at it, and the room was dark once more. Beside her Walter finally slept, breathing heavily. As Islay raised herself on one elbow the dim light danced once again on the ceiling and she realised that the noises she heard outside weren't caused by the wind, but by feet scraping against the wooden stairs outside.

With mounting alarm she realised that the light on the ceiling came from a lantern shining through the window. A man's voice muttered something as she slid out of bed, her heart hammering in her chest.

'Walter!'

He grunted, muttered something, but didn't waken, even when she seized his shoulder. But at the first thunderous blow on the door from a determined fist he shot up and out of the bed, twisting away from Islay's fingers, an oath ripping from him as his feet found the floor.

There was a steady rain of blows on the door now, and a man's voice bellowing, 'You in there – open this door in the King's name!'

'The militia!' All the fears that Islay had refused to face earlier flooded back. 'Walter –'

He pushed her away when she went to him, and cursed as he stumbled over a chair in the darkness. 'Don't open the door!'

'I must!' If she didn't, the soldiers would knock it down.

She found her way across the room and lifted the latch. The first man to burst in pushed her firmly aside and lifted his lantern to illuminate the room.

Walter, ashen-faced apart from the livid bruise, seized a sturdy chair by the back and swung it over his head as more men poured in. They were all clad in the smart uniforms and blue feathered bonnets of the Fusiliers quartered in the town to assist the Council to maintain law and order.

They were more than a match for Walter. Before he could as much as lash out with the chair it had been whisked from his hands and he was pinioned between two men.

Islay, cowering against the wall where she had been pushed, sick with fright, convinced that she was trapped in a nightmare and unable to will herself to waken, heard the sergeant say, 'Walter Shaw, I've been commanded to arrest you.'

'No!'

At the sound of her voice the man turned to Islay. His eyes took on a certain sympathy as they travelled over her frightened face. 'I'm sorry, lassie, but we must take your man to the cells.'

'I've done nothing!'

The officer's face was suddenly wiped clean of compassion as he turned back to Walter. 'You tried to rob an honest gentleman of this town.'

'I've not been out of this house all night! Ask my wife – she'll tell you!'

'D'ye tell me that?' The sergeant's fingers caught at Walter's chin and jerked his face savagely to one side so that the cut, bruised cheek was clearly seen. 'And is it your wee wife that did this to you, then?' Then he added, as the other men laughed. 'No sense in telling us any of your lies, Walter Shaw, for Mister Knox saw your face and told us where we might find you.'

'Richard Knox?'

'Aye, lassie, Richard Knox. Bring him along,' he ordered, and Walter, struggling every inch of the way, was dragged out of the house. Islay caught up her cloak and his jacket and made to follow him, but the sergeant's arm barred the way.

'No sense in you coming too, lass, for you'll not be allowed to see your man again until the morning.'

'Will you see that he gets this – and these –?' She darted about the room, gathering up Walter's clothes, and deposited them in the man's arms.

'Aye, I'll give them to him.'

'Will he –' Her voice failed her, and she had to try again. 'Will he be all right?'

'He tried to rob Mister Knox. You know yourself what the penalty might well be,' he said, and withdrew, closing the door quietly behind him.

The chair that Walter had used in his attempt to crush the soldiers' heads in was lying on its side. Islay set it on its legs again and sank down onto it, clutching her cloak tightly in her arms. She began to shiver, and soon she was shaking like a leaf in a gale, unable to stop.

She knew well enough what the penalty for such a crime was, if the court was satisfied that Walter was guilty. It was death by hanging.

Chapter Thirty-Five

'The fool! The stupid, addle-pated fool!' Jamie Todd raged, striding up and down the length of his mother's kitchen, unable to rest in his anger.

His red hair stood on end, his eyes blazed blue fire, and his hands fisted and unfisted themselves by his sides continually, as though itching to hold Walter Shaw's irresponsible neck in their grasp.

His mother, Kirsty, and step-father, Billy, watched him pace ceaselessly to and fro, but said nothing. They well knew that when Jamie was in one of his tempers he was best left to work himself out of it again.

He marched from door to window, swung about with a practised economy of movement reminiscent of his days as a soldier, and went on, 'And what's more, he's left me with an idle loom and nobody to finish the web in time!'

'Jamie Todd, you'll feel the back of my hand on your lug in just one minute!' Margaret Knox, the fourth person in the room, had no reservations about interrupting Jamie, rage or no rage. 'To the devil with your loom, man – what about poor Walter, lying in the Tolbooth at this very minute in fear of his life? And what about Islay, carrying his child and not knowing what's to become of her man?'

Jamie had the grace to look a trifle embarrassed. His pace slowed. 'I went to see Islay as soon as I heard,' he said defensively. 'But she wasn't in, and I'd no way of finding out where she was.'

'She spends nearly all her time now with Walter's mother – when she's not visiting the lad himself. Poor Mistress Shaw's near out of her mind with grief over what's to become of him, they say.'

'And Islay? How is she?'

'Doing bravely, as you'd expect of the lassie. The dear

Lord knows she's had enough worry in her life as it is without this coming along.'

Jamie's fists clenched again. 'What possessed the damned fool to try to rob Richard Knox?'

'We don't know that he did. According to him, he was set upon himself that night, in another part of the town entirely.'

'I'd not say it outside these four walls, but I don't believe him,' said Walter's employer, then returned to his own train of thought. 'But why did he do it? I pay him fair wages, I gave him a house to live in —'

'Some folk just naturally want more than they have,' Billy's deep, slow voice said, and Margaret nodded.

'You're right. But it'll do no good to Islay or Walter if we sit and argue over why he did it. The thing to do now is to get him freed.'

Jamie stared. 'You've little chance of that. He'll be fortunate if he escapes the gallows.'

'He didn't take a penny piece of Richard's money,' Margaret pointed out.

'Only because he was too ham-fisted to do the job properly,' Jamie said sourly.

'That's as mebbe. The thing is — Walter jumped out of the dark when Richard and his manservant were riding home, and tried to snatch at Richard's saddle-bag. But Richard struck him down with his whip and Walter ran off. So Walter didnae actually lay his hands on the money. It's only Richard's word against his — though that's small comfort to Walter, for folk are reluctant to disbelieve a well-set-up man like Richard.'

'The Sheriff Officer's a fair man,' Billy pointed out. 'He'll give both sides a hearing, and not be swayed by Richard Knox's wealth the way some might.'

'If Richard could be persuaded to change his mind about charging him, things would go easier for the laddie,' Kirsty suggested. 'Jamie, you know the man — you could talk to him, could you not?'

'He's my business partner, Mother! And it was one of my weavers who tried to rob him. How can I ask him to forgive the man and get him freed and sent home?'

'I doubt if you'd manage to make him change his mind in any case. I've already spoken to Richard, and he's set his heart on seeing Walter punished.'

Kirsty looked at Margaret with wide eyes. 'You're surely not saying the man wants to see Walter thrown into the jail – or even hanged – when he did no more than to try to snatch at the money?'

Margaret's teeth nibbled at her lower lip, then she nodded. 'He does. There's a side to Richard that none of us has seen before – except Gavin, and I found it hard to believe him when he first spoke to me of it a good while back. Mebbe it's because he spent all these years over the water, in countries where they practise cruelties we've never even heard of. As he sees it, Walter deserves to die for even thinking of laying a finger on Richard Knox, or anything belonging to Richard Knox.'

There was a stunned silence in the kitchen. Even Jamie had stopped his pacing, and was staring at Margaret.

'Sending another human soul to his death, just for the sake of hurt pride?' Kirsty said softly. 'It's cruel!'

'It is that.' Jamie shook his head. 'I'd not have thought it of him.'

'I tell you this – I'm shamed of Richard. I told him so to his face, but I might as well have poured water over a duck for all the notice he took of me. He's not a man to be over-troubled by his conscience,' Margaret said bleakly.

'Mebbe Gavin's the one who could make his brother listen to reason,' Billy suggested.

'He says he couldn't, and he'll not beg the man for any favours. So – I'm calling on all the influential folk I know in the town, to try to get some support for Walter when the sorry business comes to trial.' Margaret rose and picked up her cloak.

As she was going out of the door she turned and said, her eyes on Jamie. 'Islay's the one I'm heartsick for. If you ask me, she should never have married Walter in the first place.'

*

'My Walter should never have married you in the first

place!' Isa Shaw was saying to her daughter-in-law at that moment in her over-crowded tenement room.

Islay, preparing a meal for the hungry, noisy family, said nothing. The woman had said the same thing over and over again since the moment she heard about her son's arrest. She desperately needed to blame someone else for Walter's wrong-doing, and his wife was the natural culprit.

'I told my poor laddie from the beginning – Highlanders are a queer lot. We never mixed with them, and we shouldn't start,' the querulous voice went on. 'But he'd not heed me. He was set on taking you to wife – and what has he to show for it? Rotting in the Tolbooth, mebbe even –'

The words ended in a dry sob. Islay, who knew better than to try to comfort the woman, dipped a spoon into the simmering broth, blew on it to cool it, and put it to her lips. It was ready. She set out bowls on the table and, with an effort, lifted the heavy pot from the range and carried it to them. Nobody offered to help her; Walter's brothers and sisters crowded round their mother and watched her every movement with mistrustful eyes.

'You and your well-to-do friends, flaunting their wealth in my poor laddie's face, making him feel that he wasn't good enough –'

As Islay ladled the broth out she wondered with tired irony what the Lowlanders thought Highlanders did that made them different from other folk? She had heard of all the daft stories spread during the Jacobite disturbances about Highlanders eating babies and indulging in other barbaric practices.

Her own father had fought on Prince Charles Stuart's side, and she could think of nobody less likely to harm a baby – or anyone else – in any way than that silent, gentle man who had died of his sufferings before his natural lifespan was over.

'There's scarce enough food in this house for the bairns and me as it is, without feeding you as well.'

Mistress Shaw's voice broke into her thoughts. She and her children were beginning to gather round the table now that the broth was ready for them.

'I don't want any. I'm just going.' Islay took her cloak

from the nail on the street door. Her back ached, her head
ached, and she hadn't slept since Walter had been taken by
the militia two days earlier.

'I suppose you'll have to come and bide here, you and the
bairn both. The Lord only knows,' said Mistress Shaw, fresh
tears falling into her bowl, 'how I'm going to feed two more
mouths – and with no more silver from Walter to help me.'

'I'll not be a burden to you,' Islay said quietly.

Unfortunately the words, meant to reassure the woman,
only set her off on her journey of recrimination again. 'Not
be a burden? Not be a burden?' she screeched. 'It was you
put my boy in jail in the first place, you Highland besom –!'

*

It was a relief to escape from them all, away from the
crowded room where the air was thick and stale and sour
with hopeless bitterness.

As she tramped along to the Tolbooth in the hope of
being allowed to see Walter for a few minutes Islay swore to
herself that no matter what happened she would not go to
live with Mistress Shaw.

She would sooner birth her child in a ditch, and beg for its
bread through the towns and villages.

*

The Tolbooth stood at the corner of Waingaitend, near the
Cross. Its steeple housed six floors. The jailer's room was on
the ground floor, with the criminal cells, where Walter was
being held, above it. Then came the debtors' quarters, the
women prisoners' rooms, and finally the steeple area with
the clock, the tiny bell-ringers' room, and the bell itself.

The main building housed the sheriff court rooms where
cases were heard each Tuesday, a guardhouse, and a howff
where the jailer was entitled to add to his income by serving
porter and ale to the debtors and their visitors.

An open landing outside the court held the stocks and a
whipping post, which were rarely used. In Paisley, people
sentenced to be flogged for their crimes were usually taken
through the town at the back of a cart and whipped at
various stopping-points.

Walter was sharing a small cell with two other men. When the jailer admitted Islay the two strangers, squatting in the grimy straw and taking turns to throw a dice, looked up and ran their eyes avidly over her face and body.

Walter had been huddled in a corner, knees drawn up to his chin, staring into space. He scurried to the door, putting his hands through the bars and clutching at Islay feverishly. The other men looked at each other, shrugged, and went back to their gambling.

'You must get me out of here!'

Strangely, his brief imprisonment had made him look both older and younger. His face was grey and haggard, his hair lank, his eyes sunken. And yet there was something heart-breakingly childish and vulnerable about the bright panic in his eyes, the tremble to his mouth and chin, the terrified way his hands kept hold of her.

'I'm doing all I can – we all are. Mistress Knox and her husband, and –'

'Your fine friends trying to help me?' A sneer temporarily overcame the tremor. 'It's only for your sake!'

'What does it matter whose sake it's for, as long as they help us? Is your head all right, Walter?'

Margaret had persuaded her brother Thomas to visit the prison and tend to Walter's head. Islay, who had been afraid of what might happen to the wound if it was allowed to fester, was relieved to see that the bandage about her husband's head was reasonably clean and dry, with no trace of blood or seepage.

'It's well enough.'

'I've just come from your mother's house –'

But he didn't want to hear about his mother, or the rest of his family. The fear was back, his fingers tightening on her arms, and hurting her. 'Islay, don't leave me here. Get me out!'

'Mister Knox is determined to see you before the court.'

'You must speak to him, then!'

'How can I speak to him? What can I say?'

'Anything – just make him change his mind!'

'Margaret's already tried it, and he wouldn't listen to her.'

'You're younger – and prettier,' said Walter rapidly, in an

undertone. 'He likes you, Islay, you know that. You could persuade him. You could offer him – offer him anything he wants, Islay. Anything!'

Reading the meaning in his eyes, she suddenly felt sick. 'Walter –'

'Anything!' he insisted, his face alight with hope. 'You could make him change his mind. You'd know how to go about it, Islay –'

Chapter Thirty-Six

The words rang through her head all night as she tossed sleeplessly. She couldn't do as Walter asked, and yet she must do everything she could to save him.

The next morning after she had cleaned out the loomshop as usual she bathed carefully in a basin of water and brushed her hair until it gleamed. Then she put on her best day dress and walked to St Mirin's Wynd, to Richard Knox's lodgings.

Her heart was in her mouth, and she walked up and down, past the door several times before plucking up enough courage to go in and enquire for him.

He was still at home and had just finished breaking his fast when his manservant showed Islay into his comfortable parlour. The smell of food at this time of the morning set her stomach churning, but she forced the nausea back as Richard kissed her hand and ushered her to a seat.

He looked handsome and prosperous in a spotlessly white shirt with flounces at neck and wrist, buff-coloured breeches, knee-length brown leather boots, and a beautifully embroidered satin waistcoat in blues and reds and greens. Despite the care she had taken to dress for her visit Islay felt colourless and shabby beside him.

Richard nodded to his servant and the man gathered up the dishes from the table and seemed to slide from the room, closing the door noiselessly behind him.

'My dear Islay – a pleasant surprise, though surely it's scarcely proper in Paisley for a beautiful young woman to visit a bachelor in his quarters at this time of day.'

'I must speak with you, Mister Knox.'

His smile didn't waver, his eyes were as intent as ever, and yet in an instant a hardness seemed to overlay his features, as though someone had slid a piece of glass before them.

'If it's about that foolish lad you married, Islay, I must tell you that you're wasting your time and mine.'

'Please –'

He waved a hand to stop her, then turned to take a bottle-green jacket from the back of a chair. 'My dear, you're very pretty, and I've no quarrel with you. Indeed, if only you would permit me to shower you with silks and jewels and all the things that beauty like yours deserves I would do so with the greatest of pleasure. Perhaps – one day – but not now. Not until the matter between your husband and myself is settled to my satisfaction.'

'Mister Knox, can you feel no pity for Walter? You have so much, and he has so little –'

'Nevertheless, he should have been content with what he had,' Richard said, a steely edge to his voice. 'And he must learn his lesson. You're wasting your time, Islay. On such a worthless object, too. To tell you the truth, my dear, I wonder that you ever brought yourself to marry the man.'

The door opened on the last sentence.

The newcomer stepped forward as Islay rose from her chair and turned – to find herself being surveyed by a pair of startled blue eyes.

'What are you doing here?' Jamie Todd demanded to know.

'She's on an errand of mercy, in the name of her scoundrel of a husband. Henry –' Richard Knox said, and the manservant, who had ushered Jamie in and was still standing by the door, stepped forward to take the jacket from his master's hands and help him on with it.

'As to your business, Todd –?'

'As it happens, I'm on the same errand of mercy myself.'

'What? Another visitor come to plead Walter Shaw's case? I never knew that he had so many friends – or that there were so many gullible folk in the one town. Besides, Jamie Todd, you're my partner. I thought to find you, at least, on my side.'

'The man worked for me.' Jamie shot a sidelong glance at Islay, then said levelly, 'The man works for me.'

The correction, and the way he moved to stand by her side, comforted her. She wanted to lay her hand on his arm, to assure herself that he was really there, but she didn't dare.

'If indeed he was the man who tried to attack and rob you, then –'

'I can assure you –' There was steel beneath Richard Knox's silken tones, a flash of anger in his eyes. 'He was the man.'

' – then he made a fool of himself,' Jamie went on. 'He acted hastily and clumsily, but he's been injured and punished enough, surely. Tell the Sheriff that you've changed your mind, Knox, and let the poor wretch go free.'

The silk in Richard's voice was shredding now, the hard cold steel more apparent. 'He tried to rob me, and he must pay for his impertinence. As for you, Jamie, let me give you some sound advice. It would be foolish to make an enemy of the man who's given you the opportunity to make a very good living for yourself.'

'As to that, you need me and my weavers as much as I need you and your abilities.'

The two men faced each other angrily, then Richard shrugged and smoothed the lapels of his jacket.

Behind him, his manservant stood quietly to attention, his face as closed and cold as his master's. He looked, Islay thought, like a man capable of doing anything his employer might wish of him, without giving it a thought.

'You're right,' Richard said at last, and held out one hand to the side, palm up. His servant instantly put a silver-handled cane into it.

Richard transferred the cane to his other hand, held out his hand again, and received his tricorne hat.

'You're right, Jamie, but neither of us truly needs Walter Shaw, do we? I'm sorry, my dear –' he acknowledged Islay's presence with a slight, faultlessly elegant bow. ' – that I can't grant you your wish on this occasion. But please believe me when I say that I'm convinced that life holds more riches for you than your present husband could ever give to you. You'd be well advised to rid yourself of him – if I don't manage to do it for you. May I escort you down to the street?'

'I'm on my way to Wellmeadow. I'll escort Islay,' Jamie said icily, and put a hand beneath her elbow.

If it hadn't been for that firm grip she would never have managed to stumble down the stairs and out into the street again. The building was beginning to revolve around her ears, and Jamie had to half-carry her outside, where he propped her against the house wall and commanded, 'Breathe deeply.'

She did so, until Paisley stopped circling about her and settled down again.

Jamie regarded her anxiously. 'Can you walk, or shall I fetch a cart for you?'

'I can walk.' She pushed herself groggily away from the wall, and he took her arm in a strong grip again.

'I'll take you to my mother's house. She'll look after you.'

'No, I can –'

'Yes,' said Jamie, in a voice that forbade further argument. She realised as they set out that she didn't want to argue anyway, she just wanted, desperately, to be looked after.

'I don't know what possessed you to call on that man,' he said angrily from above her head.

She stopped and faced him, swaying. 'I must do all I can to help Walter.'

'You must care about him very much,' he said tonelessly.

'The choice isn't mine. He's my husband. It's my duty to save him.'

Their eyes locked, and it was Jamie who looked away first, taking her arm again and urging her forward.

'From what I've just seen and heard I'd say that only God can do that,' she heard him say as they went on. 'And even He might not be a match for Richard Knox.'

Neither of them spoke again until they arrived in his mother's kitchen. Then Kirsty Carmichael took charge, gathering Islay into her arms, settling her by the fireside, removing her cloak and bonnet and rubbing at her cold hands. Billy, moving stiffly, brought some hot tea and coaxed their visitor to sip at it. His lined gentle face was alight with sympathy.

'You'll stay with us until this sorry business is over – you will,' Kirsty insisted as Islay began to protest. 'There's a wee room, the one my daughter had. It'll do fine for you.'

'But my work – and my house –'

'Jamie'll see that everything's taken care of,' his mother said firmly. 'You should never have been left alone in the first place. I thought Isa Shaw would have – but there, she's a poor handless creature herself.'

Jamie hovered by the door for a moment until his mother said, 'Well, laddie, what are you standing there for? Go about your work, and leave Islay to me.'

Then he went, leaving Islay to Kirsty's ministrations.

Chapter Thirty-Seven

Walter Shaw's trial was held in October, soon after his arrest.

Richard's thirst for revenge led him to press for a charge of attempted murder as well as robbery, an accusation that was much more serious. But he failed, for Walter hadn't dealt one blow, and nobody knew whether or not he might have, given the opportunity.

He had been the only man injured in the struggle, and he hadn't succeeded in stealing one penny piece.

Much was made of this during the trial in the Sheriff Court. When all was said and done Walter was a Paisley man and Richard an incomer. Popular though Richard was the Paisley folk didn't like to be dictated to by a stranger, especially when it came to their jealously-prized rights as a Royal Burgh with a Royal charter that had been granted by King James IV almost three hundred years earlier.

The trial aroused a great deal of interest, and the court-room was packed with onlookers. They were evenly divided, Islay felt as she looked at the noisy public benches, between folk who genuinely wanted to see the young weaver absolved from blame and restored to freedom, and folk who secretly yearned for the excitement and spectacle of a public hanging. Executions were rare in Paisley, and greatly enjoyed on the few occasions when they took place.

A gusty murmur of sympathy swept through the court-room when Walter was led in, pale and somewhat shrunk in on himself, shambling between two jailers. The scar on his face was fading, but could still be seen as a purple weal.

'If Richard hadn't been so greedy for revenge he'd have tried to delay the trial until the wound healed,' Margaret Knox murmured by her side. 'It's still too clearly seen to aid Richard's case.'

Isa Shaw sat on the other side of the court from Islay, surrounded by her children and a clutch of neighbours. Every now and again she shot a malevolent look at her daughter-in-law, who was escorted by Mistress Margaret Knox and Mistress Mary MacLeod, both well-to-do townspeople.

Islay looked away from the woman and caught Walter's eye. She tried to smile, but he just stared pleadingly at her, dumbly begging her to do something – anything – to save him. She had never before felt so helpless.

Margaret's hand touched hers. 'You've gone as white as a sheet. D'you want to go outside for some fresh air?' her friend whispered.

Islay shook her head, and began to concentrate on what was going on before her as the trial began.

At first it looked as though nothing could save Walter. Richard Knox told the court confidently how a man he clearly recognised as Walter Shaw jumped out of the darkness one night as he and his manservant rode towards the stables.

Walter had caught at the saddle-bags slung before Richard – where, as everyone knew, the day's takings were – and had been beaten back by Richard's whip.

The horses, said Richard, had been terrified by the suddenness of the attack. They had to be calmed, and in the confusion Walter had managed to escape.

'You recognised the man who leapt out at you, Mister Knox?' asked the Sheriff.

'I saw him often enough when I visited the loomshop where he worked. And I met him on one occasion when we were both guests at Mistress MacLeod's house.'

As the manservant followed his master to the witness stand, and repeated Richard's story almost word for word, Walter clutched at the railing before him for support, his eyes fixed on Islay as though he was convinced that she was the only one who could save him.

'And you, my good fellow, have you accompanied your master into the weaving shop where the accused works?' asked the Sheriff.

The servant shuffled his feet uneasily and glanced at

Richard before saying, 'No, sir.'

'If you hadn't set eyes on him before, how did you know that your attacker was the man called Walter Shaw?'

A ripple ran through the crowded hall. From where she sat on Margaret's other side Islay could hear Mary MacLeod whisper to her niece, 'I shall invite the Sheriff to dine, and the shrewd man shall have my best French brandy!'

Again the manservant shuffled uncertainly, then said, 'Mister Knox told me who he was. But I saw enough of him to know that that's the scoundrel there,' he added hurriedly, pointing at Walter. Isa Shaw gave a squawk of mingled rage and despair, and was hushed by her friends.

One or two men came forward to testify that Walter had been in a howff with them, but they were fairly disreputable-looking, and it seemed clear to Islay that in the eyes of the Sheriff their evidence didn't count for much.

Then Thomas Montgomery rose and went forward. 'If it please the court, I have something to say.'

The Sheriff gave a brief nod. 'We're listening, Mister Montgomery.'

The young physician's testimony was brief and to the point. He, too, knew Walter Shaw and his wife, and knew that until the night of the attempted robbery there had not been the slightest stain on Walter's good name. He pointed out that he had treated the defendant for a fairly serious head wound while he was in prison, and that the two men who had been attacked had not been hurt in any way. He asked for the Sheriff's leniency to be shown towards the young man in the dock.

There was a stir as Thomas sat down and both Gavin Knox and Jamie Todd stood up abruptly at the same time to take his place. The Sheriff looked from one to the other, then motioned Gavin forward first. Islay glanced briefly at Richard and saw him staring from one man to the other, his face set and white with anger.

Margaret's fingers tightened on Islay's hand as her husband described Walter and herself as good friends of the family and gave his own testimony as to the weaver's good character. Then Jamie strode into the body of the court and spoke up for the accused man, describing him as a conscientious worker who had never before caused any trouble.

'And never will again, if the court can find it in its heart to be lenient on this occasion,' he said sturdily, half-speaking to the Sheriff, half-speaking to the rest of the courtroom. His blue eyes met and held Islay's as he concluded firmly and clearly, 'I'm prepared to take responsibility for his future behaviour, sir, if you grant him his freedom.'

'Indeed –' the Sheriff's voice was dry. 'I find it strange, Mister Todd, that you and Mister Knox should speak in defence of the accused, when one of you is in partnership with Mr Richard Knox and the other his own blood kin.'

Gavin came to his feet again. 'That's as may be, sir, but it seems to me that at times justice must come before blood bonds. And no doubt Mister Todd will say the same for business.'

Jamie's red head ducked in agreement.

'Your concern for justice does you both credit, gentlemen.' The Sheriff consulted the papers before him. 'The serious nature of the case – and robbery is a most serious business –' he added sharply, glaring at Walter. ' – is somewhat mitigated by the fact that no actual robbery took place, and nobody was hurt other than the man accused of the crime. In view of that, I am prepared to be more lenient than might otherwise have been the case.'

Richard Knox made the mistake of interrupting, jumping to his feet to ask furiously, 'Is this what passes for the law in Paisley, sir? That felon –' a finger stabbed mercilessly through the air in Walter's direction, ' – tried to rob and murder me and my manservant! Is this town so lackadaisical in its morals that honest men can't be safe in its streets?'

A low, ugly growl rose from the public benches. The Sheriff's thin face suddenly became a collection of sharp cold edges as he crashed his fist on the table before him.

'Mister Knox, you forget yourself, sir! Not a penny piece was taken from you. You were not hurt. You lost nothing but a little pride, you received no injury but a blow to your own self-esteem.'

'I demand that this man be punished severely!'

'Oh, Richard, Richard!' Mary MacLeod rebuked under

her breath. 'You've damned yourself now, my mannie!'

'You may demand all you like, Mister Knox. This is my court, under my jurisdiction.' The Sheriff said, then sat back, his cold gaze travelling over the faces before him.

Then he said, 'In view of the facts heard in this court, and in view of the pleas put forward by three of our own most eminent townspeople –' His glance brushed Richard Knox's livid, set face and moved on, ' – including Mister Todd's solemn undertaking that Walter Shaw shall never again have to be brought before me or any other court on any mischief whatsoever, I find that the case has not been proven to my complete satisfaction. The prisoner is therefore free to go; although –' Now the sharp, cold face was turned in Walter's direction, 'I warn you, my man, that if you should ever appear before this court or any other, your punishment will be harsh indeed.'

Richard Knox stood up so suddenly that his chair fell over. He swung round on his heel and strode out of the courtroom, his manservant trotting after him.

Mistress Isa Shaw dissolved into hysterics. The jailers assisted Walter from the dock, and left him to stand alone, dazed and uncomprehending.

Islay went to him; when she was a few yards away he suddenly woke from his trance and ran towards her, clutching her in his arms, burying his face in her neck.

Over his shoulder Islay saw Jamie Todd standing alone, watching the two of them. His face was impassive.

Chapter Thirty-Eight

After he gained his freedom Walter was quiet and subdued, leaving the house only to go down to the weaving shop each day.

In the evenings he was content to stay close to Islay, watching her as she worked at her sewing or plied her knitting wires, occasionally reaching out to touch her hand as though convincing himself that she was really there, and he was really home.

Richard Knox didn't come near the weaving shop, much to Walter's relief. Once he realised that the man wasn't going to appear he began to relax, and even went off to spend an hour in the howff with his friends one evening.

When he returned he was cheerful and confident, even inclined to boast a little about what had happened to him.

'He deserved to be robbed, that Richard Knox,' he said as he undressed for bed. 'He'd not miss a bag or two of silver – not him. And as for a knock on the head – it'd do no harm to let some light into his thick skull.'

'Walter, for God's sake!' Islay, already in bed, sat bolt upright and clutched the sheet to her in a panic. 'Stop that talk before someone hears you!'

He laughed. 'There's nobody to hear me except you.'

'You didn't talk like that in the howff, did you?'

'What d'you take me for – a fool?'

She didn't believe him. 'You heard what the Sheriff said – if you appear in court again it'll go hard with you.'

Walter blew out the lamp and slid into bed, his hands reaching out for her greedily. 'The wise thing, my lass,' he said into her ear, his breath hot and rapid against her neck, 'is not to be caught.'

Islay worried all the next day. It would only take a few careless words in the crowded howff, a pair of listening ears, a man willing to report the foolish boasts in return for a coin or two. And then the militia might be back for Walter. He had been released on a 'not proven' verdict. That meant that he could be arrested and tried again.

Part of his saving had been his obstinate refusal to admit to anyone, even himself, that he had indeed tried to rob Richard Knox. But fuddled with drink, in the midst of his friends, Walter could easily talk himself into a prison cell or a hangman's noose, she thought. Richard Knox would be only too happy to act on any further evidence he might receive.

When she tried to persuade Walter to stay at home in the evenings for a while longer, he refused.

'Promise me, then, that you'll not talk about – about what happened. Not a word.'

'Ach – women! Aye skiting at a man!' he grumbled, and went out.

The evening passed and the street outside fell silent, and still there was no sound of Walter's footsteps on the stairs. At last Islay laid her knitting aside and put on her cloak.

The street was dark, dotted here and there with lamplit windows. Hardly anyone was out now. She walked almost to Town Head, where Margaret's father's cottage and weaving shop stood. She would have liked to go on to High Street to ask for Jamie's help; but he had done enough for her. She couldn't go running to him every time she was worried.

She retraced her steps, walking now into the teeth of the chill night wind. The house was still empty when she went back to it. She drew her chair close to the range and huddled over the warmth, waiting.

A full hour went by before feet trod on the wooden stairs outside. Islay's head lifted sharply. It wasn't Walter's step – this was a heavier man, and one unused to negotiating these steps in the dark.

She ran to the door and threw it open. Then her knees buckled and she had to catch the side of the door-frame for support when the caller arrived on the top step and moved into the pool of light spilling from the room behind her.

It was the militia sergeant who had arrested Walter.

'My husband –' Islay's voice was weak with fear.

The man looked down on her, and this time his face was warm with sympathy.

'I'm sorry, lass.' He put his arm about her and almost carried her into the house. Then he put her into her chair and sat opposite her while he told her that Walter's body had just been found in a dark empty lane near the howff.

He had been killed by a knife wound in the back.

*

On the night before Walter's funeral Gavin Knox made his way to his brother's lodgings.

Richard was alone in his parlour, reclining comfortably in a chair by the fire, a half-filled glass in his hand. He didn't rise as Gavin was shown into the room, but indicated a chair on the other side of the fireplace.

'Here's a surprise – I never thought to see you calling on me. Henry, take Mister Knox's coat. You'll have a glass of rum with me, Gavin.'

Gavin shrugged his coat more firmly over his broad shoulders as he stepped away from the manservant's outstretched hands. 'I don't care for rum.'

'You have barbaric tastes,' Richard said easily. 'Whisky, then? Claret?'

'Nothing. I only want to offer you a word of advice. A private word of advice.' Gavin glanced significantly at the manservant and took up a stance in the middle of the rich thick carpet, booted feet firmly planted apart.

'Henry –' Richard flicked a hand at the man, who retired noiselessly. 'Now, brother, what sort of advice could you offer to me?' His tone implied clearly that he doubted that it could be of any value.

'Just this – if you care anything for your skin, you'll leave Paisley tomorrow. Tonight, if you can manage it.'

Richard raised a lazy eyebrow. 'Indeed? And why should I have cause to fear for my skin?'

'Because Walter Shaw's been done to death.'

'Walter Shaw,' said Richard, sitting bolt upright, his voice suddenly low and soft with hatred, 'should never have set himself up against me. That travesty of a court and that poor excuse for a Sheriff should never have let the wretch go.'

'Walter's case was found not proven by law!'

'He was guilty! And nobody,' said Richard Knox, 'lifts a hand against me or mine and escapes punishment. If this was Jamaica he would have been flogged and then executed for what he did to me, I can promise you that!'

Then the anger was wiped from his face and he relaxed again, smiling up at Gavin. 'Besides, anyone could have killed your friend – the town's rife with thieves and beggars.'

A muscle jumped in Gavin's jawline. 'Nobody could have mistaken him for a man of means and killed him for his wealth. When he was found the few pence he carried were still in his pocket, undisturbed. He had a few friends, but no enemies. You found a scoundrel willing to do your bidding for a price, and you killed Walter Shaw as surely as if your own hand had put the knife into his back.'

'Prove it.'

'I don't need to prove it, and neither do the folk who'll take revenge on you. I know it, they know it – all Paisley knows it.'

There was a short silence. Richard drained his glass, then said, 'If, as you say, the miserable creature had few friends, I've nothing to fear.'

'You still can't understand, can you?' Gavin asked contemptuously. 'You're so used to gaining what you want by using your own means, Richard. First with charm, and then with money and influence. You've forgotten what it's like to live in a tight-knit community like Paisley. Those folk look after their own, no matter who it may be. Walter was a weaver, and the weavers are the most powerful group of men in the town – and for many miles outside it too. He was born and bred in Paisley – and you can take my word for it that his murderers will be punished.'

Richard opened his mouth to speak, but it was Gavin's turn to command silence with a movement of the hand. 'Perhaps not by law,' he went on, 'For there's no proof. But I tell you this – the man who wielded the knife, the man who gave the order, and the man –' his eyes flickered to the door that had closed behind the manservant minutes earlier, ' –

who acted as go-between: they'll all be found and dealt with. Unless they have the good sense to leave. I expect the knife-man's already far away. Take my advice, Richard. Move to new pastures.'

'If I do, what happens then to your wife's business, built up with my money and my help? What happens to Jamie Todd's loom shops, dependent on my assistance?'

The muscle jumped again as Gavin fought to control his temper. 'Jamie must find his own feet. I'm quite certain that Duncan and Robert Montgomery'll come to his assistance, as he'd go to theirs if he was needed. They'll not let old grievances come between them once you're out of the way. As for Margaret –'

He slipped a hand into his thick coat and brought out a small bulky pouch. He tossed it down onto the table by his brother's side. It gave out the muffled ring of coinage. 'She's already decided that stay or go, she'll have no more to do with you. Here's the money you put into buying the inkle looms and renting the shop – and your fair share of the profits besides.'

Richard picked up the bag and opened it. Gavin watched as the money was counted and carefully stacked on the table.

'So it's goodbye, brother?'

'Aye, if you're wise. If you decide to stay I'll not lift a hand to aid you, and neither will any of the others.'

'Your candour does you credit,' Richard said dryly, and held out his hand.

Gavin looked at it, then turned on his heel and walked out, letting the door lie open behind him.

*

On the day of the funeral the rain poured endlessly from a grey cold sky. Standing at the graveside, watching Walter's coffin being lowered into the earth, Islay found it impossible to grasp the idea of widowhood.

While he was in prison she had forced herself to come to terms with the knowledge that she was almost certainly going to bear and raise their child alone – for ever if he was hanged; for a long time if the sentence was one of a term of imprisonment.

But once he was released everything had changed. Life was set to go as before – Walter and herself, their child, and no doubt, many other children after that.

The suddenness of his final going was more than she could take in at the moment.

They were all present at the grave – Margaret and Gavin, Margaret's parents and brothers, Mary MacLeod, and Jamie, who stood by her side in the dripping, chilly graveyard. and, of course, Walter's mother and her brood of sons and daughters.

At one point during the sermon Islay looked up and met her mother-in-law's eyes across the open grave. The accusation in the older woman's gaze made her shrink back slightly against Jamie's shoulder.

No matter what happened, she wouldn't – she couldn't – become further involved with the woman.

When it was done she refused all the invitations that showered on her.

'I'd as soon go home,' she said to Kirsty, to Margaret, to Meg Montgomery and Mary MacLeod.

'I'll walk back with her,' Jamie said, and steered her away from the grave with a firm hand.

'What are you going to do now?' he asked as they went back through the rain-washed streets.

'There's little I can do but go on with my life as before. Unless –' sudden fear gripped her, ' – you want the house for another of your weavers –?'

His hand tightened spasmodically on her elbow and his voice was gruff when he said, 'What d'you take me for? You can stay in it for as long as you need it. As for Walter's mother, I've already arranged to give work to one of her other children to make up the money he paid into the house each week.'

They reached the weaving shop and went through the pend. Icy rain soaked Islay's clothes, probing to her very soul with numbingly chill fingers.

In the back yard she said firmly, 'I'll be fine on my lone now.'

'You're certain?'

'I'm certain.' All she wanted was to be alone, and to sleep for ever and ever.

She began to climb the stairs, holding the railing, dragging herself from stair to stair. Her body had become very heavy. The landing seemed to be far above, almost too far to reach.

Doggedly, she went on. Then her foot slipped on a worn, rain-greased step and a sharp stab of pain shot through her ankle as it twisted.

She fell clumsily, rolling and bouncing and sliding down the steps, landing in the yard with a jarring crash. The pain spread until it was everywhere.

Jamie's face, white with alarm, loomed over her. She heard him say, 'Sweet Jesus!' felt him lift her in his arms.

The last thing she heard before the pain drowned her entirely was his voice, urgently calling for help.

Chapter Thirty-Nine

Seventeen hundred and seventy-seven was three months old before Thomas and Gavin pronounced Islay well enough to leave Margaret Knox's house and return to Wellmeadow.

She had begun to despair, during the long cold winter, of ever feeling young and healthy again.

The strain of Walter's trial, then the shock of his sudden, violent death, immediately followed by her miscarriage and a bad bout of pneumonia, seemed to have turned her into a frail old woman, fit to do nothing but sit listlessly in Margaret's parlour.

It was only as the snow melted and the daffodils blazoned their gold trumpets in the gardens and the trees began to show umistakeable signs of soft green growth that her strength began to return; first of all in a trickle so slight that she scarcely noticed it, then in a steady flow that tingled through her muscles and tissue and bones and blood.

It was then, and only then, that she began to want to get back to her own house. For weeks and months she hadn't cared whether Jamie gave it to someone else or reclaimed it as a store. But one day she found herself wondering if it had a neglected look, and the next she began to hunger to see it.

By the time Thomas agreed to let her go home she was almost beside herself with impatience. Margaret and Gavin had been kindness itself, and their home a haven of comfort. But it wasn't where she belonged.

On the day she was to go back she stood in her little bedroom in the Knox house, surveyed herself in the mirror.

'I've aged.'

'You've matured,' Margaret said from behind her. 'And little wonder, for you've had to grow up quickly, Islay.'

The face that looked out of the mirror was thinner than

before, and sadly lacking in colour and animation. The eyes, huge and dark, dominated it. There was a new, firmer set to the mouth, though the hair was as rich and thick as ever.

She had lost weight; her body was elegantly slender now.

'I'm glad you decided to stop wearing mourning,' Margaret said. Islay's hands, white and smooth through months of idleness, fluttered like night-moths in the mirror, touching the dark red gown she wore, and the crisp white lace-edged fichu over her shoulders.

'There's little sense in wearing black for a year, to my mind. I'll mourn inside for Walter and the bairn all my life, no matter what colours I might flaunt on my body. He was so young to die, Walter. And my poor wee bairn never even had the chance to draw breath.'

'There are a lot of years ahead of you, Islay,' her friend said. 'You'll meet another man, and have other bairns.'

The face in the mirror was suddenly closed, the eyes hooded. 'No,' Islay said, as much to her reflection as to Margaret. 'No, I'll not meet any other man. At least, none I'll take for a husband.'

She should never have married Walter. If she hadn't he might be alive today, and wed to someone more suited to him. As for herself, she had learned from her fatal mistake. If she couldn't marry with Jamie Todd she would take no other man. And there was little chance of her ever becoming Jamie's wife.

An hour later, with a tremor of excited happiness, she walked through the pend and up the steps – treading carefully in memory of the terrible day of her fall – and opened the door of her home.

It was just as she had left it, dust-free and with the brass and crockery and iron range twinkling and shining at her. Someone had set a fire in the range, and the kettle was coming to the boil. Someone had brought in provisions and laid them on the table so that she could put them away herself, in the proper places.

She put her bag down, and advanced into the room, tears wet on her cheeks as the house met her and closed about her, holding her safe, welcoming her back.

'So you're home again?' Jamie said from the doorway.

She spun round, rubbing an impatient hand over her face to remove the signs of weakness. 'Aye, I'm home. Who did all this?'

'The womenfolk – my mother and Meg and Mary. You're certain you're well enough to leave Margaret's house?'

'I'm as well as I'll ever be. What I need now is to get back to work.'

'Your wheel's waiting for you.' He nodded to the corner, and she saw that there was a bag of flax by the wheel, and a box of empty pirns. 'As to the loom shop –'

'I'll start on it tomorrow morning, if that's all right with you.'

He shrugged, a slow lifting of his broad shoulders. 'Aye, that's fine.'

She studied him as he hesitated in the doorway. He too looked strained. Margaret had told her that after Richard Knox's sudden disappearance from Paisley Duncan and Robert Montgomery had welcomed Jamie back to their number, and now the High Street looms were weaving linen again. But the Wellmeadow machines were still on what was left of the cotton yarn, and Jamie was determinedly searching for a market for them.

'He's restless again,' Margaret said. 'Somehow he can't seem to get back to the life he knew before. I doubt Richard's left his mark on us all.'

She herself, with Gavin's reluctant blessing, had pressed forward with the ribbon-weaving business, finding a manufacturer willing to take the ribbons, and arranging to buy cotton yarn from an English supplier.

'You can bring your pirns downstairs when they're filled.'

Jamie's voice broke into Islay's thoughts, and she coloured, realising that she had been staring at him. It was a habit she had got into during her illness – fixing her eyes on something or someone and drifting away into a trance. She must put a stop to it. 'I'll take them along to High Street myself when I go.'

'Are you working downstairs, then?'

'Aye.' He shifted from one foot to the other, then said awkwardly, 'I'm working the loom Walter used to have. I'm trying out a new cloth.'

'For Mister Montgomery?'

'No,' said Jamie, 'for myself.' And he went back downstairs and left her alone.

When she had hung her cloak neatly in its usual place she sat down at her wheel and took up a handful of flax, drawing out the beginnings of the thread between thumb and forefinger. Then she lifted an empty pirn from the box and rolled the thread around it before slipping the pirn into place.

She put her foot firmly on the treadle and set the wheel in motion, helping it with one hand. The wheel picked up speed, the pirn began to rotate, gathering the twisting yarn thread.

Islay's foot settled to the familiar soothing beat of the treadle, and she knew with a great, healing rush of happiness that she was home again.

*

The new cloth Jamie was working on occupied all his time over that summer. Often Islay's ears caught the faint beat of a single loom in the evenings, long after the other weavers had gone. Now and then, unable to sleep, she stood at the back window, and saw a golden rectangle of light splashed across the cobbles; light from the lamp he was working by.

She heard from Margaret that his attempts seemed to be doomed to failure. But Jamie refused to give up.

One night when she was preparing to go to bed, footsteps clattered up the wooden stairs and someone thundered on the door.

Islay's heart began to race. Memories of the night Walter had been arrested, and the night the sergeant had come to tell her of his death, blazed into her mind.

'Islay! Islay, are you there?'

'Jamie?' The paralysis that had gripped her muscles eased; she found the energy to cross the room, her fingers fumbling with the buttons of the blouse she had been unfastening, and lift the door-latch.

Jamie Todd stood outside, his face almost split in two by a great beaming grin.

'Islay, come and see this!'

'See what –' She didn't have time to finish the word. He caught her by the hand and whisked her out into the cool air, down the stairs and through the pend and into the weaving shop, her loosened, newly-brushed hair streaming behind her in the night air like black smoke.

They came to a breathless stop by the loom Walter had worked.

'There!' Jamie indicated the web on the loom, then lifted the lamp that sat close by and brought it nearer so that Islay could examine the cloth.

'It's –' her hand went out to touch the fine soft stuff, much finer than any material she had seen on those looms before. 'It's bonny! What yarn did you use?'

'Cotton!' The word burst from him triumphantly. 'Fine cotton – the last of the stuff Richard Knox supplied!'

'I've never seen such a cloth woven from cotton yarn before.'

His hand came to rest by hers, feeling the cloth with an expert's touch. 'And neither has anyone else in this town. It's as like muslin as you could find. D'you see what this means? I've done it, Islay – I've shown them all!'

'Oh, Jamie!' She was radiant with happiness for him. When he set the lamp down and began to dance around the looms, his red head flaming in the shadows hovering beyond the light's glow, she clapped a rhythm for him, laughing as she watched.

Finally he ran out of breath and staggered, almost falling against a loom. Islay put a steadying hand to his wrist.

'God save us, lassie, you're freezing cold!'

'It's little wonder. This place isn't warm, and you didn't even give me time to put a cloak on before you pulled me down here.'

'Och, I didn't think –'

She smiled up at him, still caught up in his happiness. 'It doesn't matter.'

'I must fetch Duncan – and Robert –'

'They'll be abed and asleep by this time!'

'So they will.' His face fell at the prospect of having to wait until morning to spread his news, then as she shivered he said, 'On you go – back upstairs with you.'

'Jamie, have you had your supper yet?'

'No. I wanted to get a good length of cloth on the machine before I stopped.'

'Come upstairs and I'll make something for you.' When he started to shake his head she said firmly, 'It's no bother – and anyway, your mother'll be away to her bed too, by this time. There'll be no food for you at home.'

He hesitated, then nodded.

Five minutes later the loom shop light had been extinguished and the two of them were in the warmth of the kitchen, with the door closed against the night and Islay busying herself at the range.

Jamie ate everything she put before him, and half emptied the ale jug, insisting that Islay had a drink as well, to 'wet the new cloth'. Then he dropped into the chair that had been Walter's and talked and talked while Islay sat opposite and listened.

The words meant nothing to her, for she knew little of weaving. It was enough to act as his audience, to see the joy in his face, hear the enthusiasm in his voice.

Time passed, and the rest of the town slept around them. But Islay and Jamie sat on in the lamplit room; for them, time had ceased to exist at all.

He finally interrupted himself with a yawn. 'God's truth, I've talked half the night away. I must go, and let you get to your bed. And tomorrow first thing I'll be out and about to spread the news that a new cloth's come to Paisley.'

'What about a market?'

'As to that, I think I'd be best to go down to England myself at once, to find a buyer. And I must find a manufactory willing to sell me more of the cotton yarn. Richard kept his business close, and I've no idea where he got the yarn he brought in.'

He rose, and took her hands in his. 'You're very patient, to listen to all this talk about cloth and yarn when you must be wearying for your bed.'

'I'm just proud to be the first to hear your news.'

'I wanted you to know,' he said simply. Then his grin died as his eyes rested on her uplifted face, framed in shining black hair. 'Somehow it was right that you should be the first to know,' said Jamie almost wonderingly, and released her hands so that he could cup her face gently between his big palms.

She stood beneath his touch, afraid to move or to say anything in case she broke the spell that curled about the two of them and took them into its fragile golden grasp.

At last, moving with agonising slowness, Jamie bent and brushed her mouth with his.

'You're so beautiful, Islay. The sight of you could wrench a man's heart from his body –' he said.

Then suddenly she was locked in his embrace, and his mouth was hard and hungry on hers, and there was no longer any need for her to worry.

'Islay?' he whispered against her throat when at last the kiss was ended. She ran her fingers through his hair; it was rich and thick beneath her hands as she had always imagined it to be.

'Stay with me, Jamie,' she murmured in reply, and he lifted her easily into his arms and carried her to the bed before moving to put the light out.

Then he came back to her, and Islay learned that being loved by the right man could indeed be a sweet and tender thing, a giving and taking, a wanting and sharing, an ecstasy beyond anything her imagination had ever dreamed of.

*

When she awoke early next morning Jamie had already gone from her side, stealing away while she slept. She stretched her naked limbs luxuriously across the width of the bed and smiled at the ceiling.

At last she had truly become a woman, blessed with a woman's understanding and knowledge.

She turned her face towards the window and smiled again, nursing her newfound secret.

*

The next day the Wellmeadow loom shop was filled with interested, excited weavers, and there was little chance of Islay seeing Jamie.

She was content to go about her work, listening to the

tramp of feet in the pend below and the buzz of deep male voices in the loom shop, while in the house above she sat spinning her yarn, dreaming her dreams, waiting for him to come to her.

But he didn't come, not even at night when the weaving shop was closed.

The next day one of the weavers told her that Jamie had gone off to England with a sample of the new cloth.

Gradually, Islay's feeling of wellbeing and contentment began to fray and tear and fall apart. She began to realise that the pain of being denied Paradise completely was as nothing to the agony of being allowed a glimpse inside the gates, then being turned away.

A full ten days dragged by before Jamie Todd returned from England and called on Islay, and offered her marriage.

And was turned down.

Chapter Forty

'But why?' Jamie demanded, stamping up and down Islay's kitchen like a bad-tempered captain on his quarter-deck. 'In God's name why?'

'Because I'll not be obligated to you or any man.'

'Obligated? I'm talking about marriage – about offering you my name and my protection, woman! Not about obligations!'

'I can manage fine on my own,' Islay said stonily, staring down at the hands clasped tightly in her lap.

'Mebbe so, but you must see that you'd be the better for a husband. Damn it, Islay, I don't blame you for being vexed at the way I never came near you after – after –'

'I wasnae vexed.'

'The truth of the matter is,' said Jamie miserably, 'I felt black ashamed of what I'd done. I couldnae look you in the face.'

'There was no need to think that. You didn't take me against my will.'

'Aye, but even so – Islay, we must get wed now, d'you not see that?'

'I see no reason why.'

Jamie ran a hand through his fiery hair, then said, 'I must go back to Lancashire tomorrow, to see about getting a good supply of that yarn. I'll be gone for a good few weeks, but mebbe that's just as well, for it'll give you a chance to consider. I'll call on you as soon as I get back –'

'I'll not give you a different answer.'

'You're determined, then? You'll not accept my offer?'

'No, Jamie.'

There was a short silence, then, 'Confound all women!' said Jamie, and slammed out of the house.

Islay closed the wildly swinging door behind him and sat

down at the kitchen table, folding her hands on its well-scrubbed surface.

After a moment the tears began to splash onto her interlocked fingers, one after the other, slowly at first, then falling faster and faster.

*

Jamie Todd returned to Paisley two weeks later, earlier than he had expected. When he walked into his mother's kitchen, glowing with good health and good humour, full of the news of his successful foray among the English manufactories, Margaret Knox was there, paying a visit to Kirsty.

'Jamie, you'll walk part of the way home with me?' she asked when she was about to leave, and he nodded willingly.

'Don't stay away too long, now. Your meal's almost ready,' Kirsty instructed as the two of them left the house.

'Five minutes only, for I'm starved,' Jamie promised.

Margaret laid a hand on his arm as they reached the bottom of the stairs. 'Come into the back yard for a minute, Jamie. Once we're seen on the street one man after another'll be stopping us to ask how you fared in England, and I want to talk to you in peace.'

He raised an eyebrow, but followed her through the back door of the passage.

It was a golden, mellow early October day. The bushes were festooned with Kirsty's washing, drying in the sun. The apple tree was still heavy with fruit waiting to be picked and the bees that lived in the skeps at the foot of the garden busily gathered nectar from the flowers that edged the long narrow path.

Margaret walked almost to the end of the garden, then turned to look up at Jamie. 'Now then,' she demanded briskly, 'what was it you said to Islay before you went away?'

His jaw dropped. He coloured to the roots of his hair, then said belligerently, 'So – she went running off to confide in you, did she? Then I hope you got more sense out of her than I did!'

'She did nothing of the sort! Islay's not the lassie to confide in anyone, more's the pity. But she's been out of sorts ever since you left the town, and it's easy to tell by the look that comes into her eye whenever your name's mentioned that you're the cause of the trouble. So what did you say to her?'

'Damn it, Margaret, I only offered her marriage.'

It was Margaret's turn to stare. 'You did that? And what was her answer?'

'She refused me. And now,' said Jamie, thoroughly bewildered, 'I've got you flyting on at me. What have I done – just tell me that?'

'Just a minute,' Margaret ordered. 'I can't make head nor tail of this business. Why should Islay refuse you when she's been heartsick for you since before she wed with Walter?'

'Heartsick? Her? Your imagination's running away with you. She cares not a jot for me – and I care nothing for her!'

'In that case why did you ask her to be your wife?'

His feet shuffled uncomfortably on the beaten earth path between the kale-beds. He moved away a step or two and began to fiddle with a red-currant bush.

Margaret waited, and finally he said, low-voiced, not looking at her. 'I – I lay with the lassie.'

'Did you, now? Against her own will, was it?'

'No, but even so – it was wrong of me. But when I went back to her and offered to right the wrong by marrying her – she near bit my nose off!'

'You great daft lummock!' Light was beginning to dawn on Margaret. 'Of course she'd refuse an offer like that!'

'Why? I'd be a good husband, a dutiful husband –'

'Och, Jamie! That's not enough for the likes of Islay! What woman would want a man who only offers her his hand out of guilt? Did you not think to tell the lassie you loved her?'

'Love?' Jamie crimsoned again. 'Margaret, for any favour!'

'Aye, Jamie Todd, love! It's a condition of the heart and the head that means a lot to women – though little enough to some men, it seems,' Margaret said scathingly. 'Islay sets great store by it, and I don't blame her. The lassie's already made one loveless marriage, and think of the heartbreak that caused her. She's not about to take on another man just because he feels obliged to offer her marriage.'

'Mind your own business, Margaret Knox!' Jamie said explosively and began to march towards the back door.

'Where are you going?'

'To eat my meal!'

'Jamie –' She caught up with him in the passageway, tugging on his good brown coat with little regard for the material or the stitching. 'Islay's leaving Paisley.'

'What?' He stopped short, one foot already on the stairs leading to the house. 'When?'

'Soon.'

'Where's she going?'

'I've no notion – and neither has she. But she's made up her mind – and once she hears you're home she'll no doubt go all the sooner. For any favour, man!' Margaret caught hold of his lapels and shook him again. 'Can you not see that if you let her go you'll neither of you ever be happy again?'

There was anguish in his face. 'Margaret, I'm thirty-four years old. I'm too old for Islay – I knew from the start that it was foolish of me to let myself care for her!'

'Tush, what does age have to do with it? D'you think Islay cares a whit for the years between the two of you? Not her! And your own father was near forty when he met and married with Kirsty, and fathered you! Did you never think on that?'

He stared down at her, wide-eyed. 'No, I never did,' he said slowly.

'Then think on it now, before it's too late!'

The delicious aroma of meat cooked to perfection drifted down from the house above as the kitchen door opened. Kirsty's voice skirled down the stairs.

'Jamie, are you there?'

He hesitated, glanced towards the sound of his mother's voice, then said tersely to Margaret, 'Tell her I have to see Islay first. And I don't know which of the two of us faces the harder task, Margaret Knox – you or me.'

Then he was plunging along the passageway, into the street, and away.

'I think,' murmured Margaret dryly, 'that it'll be me.'

And she gathered up her skirts and began to climb the stairs to face Kirsty's wrath.

Chapter Forty-One

The big wooden tub had been dragged out and filled with warm water. The bedclothes were carried downstairs and put into it then Islay, hot and tired from her exertions, kilted her skirts and climbed in to tread the blankets.

She was splashing busily when well-shod feet rattled hurriedly through the pend and Jamie almost exploded into the yard, his hair blazing round his face.

He caught the railing, began to bound up the stairs three at a time, then saw the tub and the small figure in it, and came skidding back down again.

At the sight of him Islay had lost her grip on her skirts. They dropped into the water, and were hastily gathered up again as Jamie came to a standstill before the tub and glared at her accusingly. Because she was standing high on the blankets their eyes were on a level.

'Jamie – you're back early, surely?'

'You're going away!'

'Who told you?'

'Margaret.'

'She'd no right to say anything. She knew I didn't want anyone to know.'

'Aye, but she's devious, is Margaret Knox. You should have got her to swear on the good Book,' he said tersely, then repeated, 'You're going away!'

'Aye, I am.'

'Where?'

She tilted her chin. 'I've not decided yet. There are other towns in Scotland besides Paisley – I'll find somewhere.'

'But why?'

'Because it's best that I go.'

'I'll be the judge of that.'

She stamped her foot, sending up a spout of warm dirty

soapy water. It splashed his good fawn breeches, and he moved back a hasty step. 'You? I'm not beholden to you!'

'You are! I let you stay in my house. I gave you work.'

'And I'm grateful, Mister Todd! What's wrong – did I not say it often enough?'

'If you were grateful you'd have agreed to marry me when I made the offer!'

His voice had begun to get louder. Windows opened here and there and interested, neatly-capped heads appeared.

'The offer – aye, that's just what it was. Like an offer to buy the apple after you'd bitten into it!'

'By God,' said Jamie, startled. 'You've got a straight way of putting things, Islay.'

'I'm a Highlander. We don't know any better.'

'And I'm a Lowlander. Mebbe I don't know any better than to be clumsy and – and – oh confound it, Islay,' said Jamie, 'I thought you'd have known, that night, how I felt about you. But in the cold light of the next morning I was – angry and shamed of myself.'

'I've already told you, I was as much to blame as you.'

'I was shamed to face you again,' he went on, paying no attention. 'I thought –' Then he took a deep breath, and said, 'The truth of the matter is, Islay, I want you for my wife. I – I love you, lass.'

She stood in the cooling water and stared at him. Her face was flushed, her hair had come half undone from its knot and hung in strands to the shoulders of her plain workdress. A wisp fell against her cheek and she reached up without conscious thought to pin it up again.

'Leave it,' said Jamie huskily. 'You look beautiful as you are.'

The hand fell back to her skirt, but still she couldn't find any words for him.

'Did you hear what I said?' he asked, driven to distraction by her silence. 'I love you, Islay Shaw. If you must know, I've been out of my mind with love and wanting since I first set eyes on you.'

Then he said impatiently, 'Och – Islay!' and strode forward to scoop her out of the tub and into his arms. His good coat and breeches were soaked in an instant as she struggled against him.

'Jamie, I'm all wet – you'll ruin your clothes!'

'I don't care,' said Jamie, and kissed her. 'Islay, will you be my wife?'

'But –'

'Will you?'

'Yes,' she said, then tried to fend off another kiss, and failed.

A shrill voice corkscrewed through the warm air from one of the over-looking windows. 'Jamie Todd – what are you up to with that lassie?'

He swung round in a circle, still holding Islay close, and laughed to see the heads now filling almost every window. Burdened though he was, he managed to sketch a clumsy bow in the direction of the notorious gossip who had called out to him.

'I'm making an honest woman of her, Mistress Gibson!' he called back, and there was a skirl of laughter and exclamations from the other women.

'Jamie!'

'Wheesht, Islay, I know fine what I'm doing,' he said, and kissed her again before making for the stairs. 'Maggie Gibson's the best known gossip in this part of the town. That old wag-tongue'll have the whole of Paisley told within an hour. And once that happens you'll not be able to change your mind and turn me down again.'

'I'll never do that – never!'

Islay put her arms about his neck as he carried her up the stairs and into the house, her dark head close to his red curls.

Later, she thought happily, she would tell him the news. She had known, even on the morning after their night together, that such loving must bear fruit. And she had been right.

Later, she would tell him that she was already carrying his child.

But not just yet.

Later.